JUST ONE KISS

"How you have tormented me all these years with your beautiful, rosy lips waiting to be kissed. You are the brute, Harriet, not I. I should have kissed you long ago. I should have dragged you to our marriage bed, willing or not."

"How ungentlemanly!" she cried, struggling against him a little more and at the same time trying desperately for certain images not to arise in her mind of Connought's bed and how wonderful he was to kiss.

"Well, I do not give a fig for what is gentlemanly or not this morning!" he retorted, smiling in his most maddening fashion. "I shan't let you go until I have had my kiss—for if you must know, I made a wager with Laurence and Charles that I could kiss you before noon, and here it is but a little past nine. You see how it is. The gods have smiled on me."

Books by Valerie King

A Daring Wager
A Rogue's Masquerade
Reluctant Bride
The Fanciful Heiress
The Willful Widow
Love Match
Cupid's Touch
A Lady's Gambit
Captivated Hearts
My Lady Vixen
The Elusive Bride
Merry, Merry Mischief
Vanquished
Bewitching Hearts
A Summer Courtship
Vignette
A Poet's Kiss
A Poet's Touch
A Country Flirtation
My Lady Mischief
A Christmas Masquerade
A London Flirtation
A Brighton Flirtation
My Lord Highwayman
My Lady Valiant
A Rogue's Deception
A Rogue's Embrace
A Rogue's Wager

Published by Kensington Publishing Corp.

A ROGUE'S WAGER

Valerie King

ZEBRA BOOKS
Kensington Publishing Corp.
http://www.kensingtonbooks.com

ZEBRA BOOKS are published by

Kensington Publishing Corp.
850 Third Avenue
New York, NY 10022

All Kensington titles, imprints and distributed lines are available at special quantity discounts for bulk purchases for sales promotion, premiums, fund-raising, educational or institutional use.

Special book excerpts or customized printings can also be created to fit specific needs. For details, write or phone the office of the Kensington Special Sales Manager: Kensington Publishing Corp., 850 Third Avenue, New York, NY 10022. Attn. Special Sales Department. Phone: 1-800-221-2647.

Zebra and the Z logo Reg. U.S. Pat. & TM Off.

First printing: March 2003
10 9 8 7 6 5 4 3 2 1

Printed in the United States of America

To Fred and Dorothy Beer.
England was wonderful.
Thank you.

One

Kent, England
1817

Harriet Godwyne stood at the edge of her uncle's cherry orchard, her attention caught by the distant thundering of horses' hooves. She watched with some interest—and not a little concern—as a rider emerged from around a nearby hillock, bent over the neck of his white steed and racing in her direction. He was just to the south of the orchard, which eased down to the lane near the border of her uncle's property. She wondered what cause the man, clearly a gentleman, had to be galloping so hard. Was there perhaps a fire in the vicinity of Shalham Park?

As the identity of the rider burst upon her unprepared mind, a strangling fear of the most ridiculous kind seized her. She knew, without the smallest proof, precisely what the gentleman's intentions were and that she herself was the object of his headlong flight.

She retraced her steps and began scurrying back into the orchard, walking faster and faster, finally picking up her skirts and running full bore. She did not understand this particular impulse, except that the man was the Earl of Connought and she did not want to meet him here, in an orchard, so completely unprotected.

When the galloping ceased, she glanced over her shoulder and watched in horror as Connought leaped from his horse, gathered his reins in a swift movement, and tied the leather straps to a nearby blackthorn bush. She knew precisely what he meant to do and for that reason did not hesitate to run a little faster in the direction of her uncle's house. Unfortunately, a stream, a wood, and two acres of carefully hedged and walled gardens separated her from safety.

Onward she ran, harder still when she heard Connought call to her.

"Harriet . . ." The wind carried her name. "Harriet Godwyne . . . why do you run from me? Oh, Harriet . . ." She heard the teasing quality of his voice and the laughter which followed and knew she was in the most desperate of straits.

How beastly Connought could be at times, though she had little doubt that his current wicked conduct was due to the fact that last night, at Jane Eaves's house, she had been a trifle in her cups and had said things which she ought not. She had called him an odious rogue, hiccuped, then fallen into a fit of laughter, which apparently had caused him to believe that she was attempting to get up a flirtation with him. As soon as she had seen her error, in particular that a wicked light had taken possession of his eye, she had strolled away from him. Well, perhaps stroll was coming it too strong, for she had tripped a trifle once or twice and supported herself in crossing Lady Eaves's drawing room by holding onto the backs of several chairs, one after another. She had made her escape along with her cousins, Margaret, Elizabeth, and Mary Weaver, who had joined her quickly in seeing her back to Shalham Park.

Now here she was, running from Connought in the cherry orchard, with little chance of escape.

Just before she left the far edge of the orchard, his hand caught her elbow and she came to a flying stop.

"Why must you be a brute, Connought?" she cried, as he whirled her around to face him. His hat had fallen to the ground, and in the warmth of the July day, his dark brown hair stuck to his forehead in short spikes.

"Not a brute, surely," he retorted, his smile crooked. "A rogue, as you have said times out of mind. Even last night you accused me of it. I remember it most particularly! And you had smiled so very prettily, hiccuped, and laughed! I was charmed and felt certain it was an invitation of some sort. So here I am."

"I was in my altitudes, as you very well know, having imbibed a great deal more champagne than was at all good for me. Oh, do let me go! Must you always play the rogue?"

"Of course," he countered readily.

"You are the most abominable creature! But why must you surrender to your roguish nature? And why, pray tell, have you pursued me when you know very well that my answers to any of your questions will never change? Why will you not release me?—which you should do at once!"

"Too many questions!" he retorted, gathering her more fully to him.

As she planted her hands against his chest and looked into his laughing countenance, her breath caught in her throat. She thought he was never more handsome than when he smiled and laughed. If only things had been different. If only he had not kissed Margaret all those years ago. "What do you propose this morning, my lord? You may as well begin your arguments, as you are wont to do, so that I, in turn, may begin refuting them!"

"I have no intention of doing so, my dear Harriet. Of what use was arguing ever to me? I never succeeded in my object, therefore today I mean to do better by merely kissing you—without your permission! Something I begin to think I should have done seven long years ago."

"You may not kiss me!" she returned severely. "I do not give you leave to kiss me! Do not even think of doing so!"

He glanced about in a wholly facetious manner. "But where are your knights to protect you, *m'lady?* I see no one in the orchard except that rather obnoxious magpie, which is watching us quite curiously. What do you suppose he is thinking at the moment?"

She glanced at the bird that cocked its head first this way then that, as though trying to make them both out. "He thinks you have gone completely mad, of course. Oh, I do not give a fig for that bird! How you infuriate me!"

"And how you have tormented me all these years with your beautiful, rosy lips waiting to be kissed. You are the brute, Harriet, not I. I should have kissed you long ago. I should have dragged you to our marriage bed, willing or not."

"How ungentlemanly!" she cried, struggling against him a little more and at the same time trying desperately for certain images not to arise in her mind of Connought's bed and how wonderful he was to kiss.

"Well, I do not give a fig for what is gentlemanly or not this morning!" he retorted, smiling in his most maddening fashion. "I shan't let you go until I have had my kiss—for if you must know, I made a wager with Laurence and Charles that I could kiss you before noon, and here it is but a little past nine. You see how it is. The gods have smiled on me."

She stopped struggling. "But . . . but however did you find me?" she asked, bemused.

"Margaret was most helpful. She seemed to have not

the smallest qualm in telling me you were walking in the cherry orchard."

"Oh," she growled, "but my cousin will have a great deal to answer for!" She squirmed in his arms anew. "I tell you now, however, you shall not have that kiss. I care not the smallest whit whether or not you engaged in a wager with a dozen of your friends. I will not . . ." She got no further. His lips were suddenly on hers.

She froze, as a small animal in a trap. He was kissing her. He had violated every gentlemanly code and pressed his lips to hers. She was outraged, and yet she could not move. She was furious and yet . . . and yet he was kissing her ever so tenderly. She should push him away, strike at him, call him every name imaginable, except that . . . except that, oh dear! She had forgotten what it was like to be kissed by Connought. His lips were the sweetest search upon hers, tender and beguiling. The soft movement of his lips over hers led her on a journey away from all her grievances and toward a place that was all light and wonder. How could a kiss transform her so magically, and that so suddenly? A mere kiss!

"Harriet," he murmured.

"I had forgot," she whispered in response.

He kissed her more fully still, snaking his arms more tightly about her. He had been her first love, perhaps even her only love, for in the ensuing years not one gentleman had commanded her heart as Connought had. All the love she had ever felt for him rose up anew, so many precious sentiments lost in the intervening years, but now remembered and swirling through her heart and her mind until she no longer knew where she was.

"I hope you will always remember me," he responded.

He drifted his lips over hers until the smallest sob that was not a sob escaped her throat. "How could I ever forget you?"

"Harriet, tell me there is a chance," he whispered, drawing back slightly to gaze into her eyes.

However, just as swiftly as these precious memories had arisen, less pleasant ones followed in a torrent of remembered pain and treachery, of learning of Connought's betrayal, that he had kissed her cousin Margaret not more than twelve hours after he had knelt on one knee before her, professing his eternal love and begging for her hand in marriage. He had kissed Margaret, and he had boasted of his conquest—or so it had seemed to her, for they all had known of it—Jane, Laurence, Charles, even Lord Frith.

Connought was a man to whom she could never entrust her heart. A sudden, raging fury overcame her and she battled him with flailing limbs. He did not hold her for long, particularly since he had begun to laugh.

"And you pretend your indifference," he cried, mocking her. "I vow, Harriet, there was nothing disinterested in the way you returned my kisses just now. Indeed, the way you looked—"

"Indifferent?" she cried. "Disinterested? No, I am not in the least either of these things! One must be completely detached to profess to indifference, and I am far from that, for I despise you heartily! You have the character of a worm, and in all these years you have not changed even the smallest little bit!"

"Not changed?" he cried. "No, I suppose I have not, for I have never believed kissing your cousin was a capital offense. Nor have I changed in essentials. I am still the man with whom you tumbled quite violently in love!"

"There is, I suppose, where we differ, for I have always seen that kiss as a profound betrayal of not just myself but of Margaret as well."

"Margaret? Why?"

"What if I told you she had been in love with you at the time and has cried herself to sleep every night since because of that kiss? What would you say to that?" Of course there was no truth to it in the least, but she wondered if he had ever considered the consequences had there been.

"I would not believe you," he responded, but his expression sobered quite suddenly. "Do you mean to tell me Margaret is in love with me?"

She was silent apace. "Would that make a difference in how you viewed your conduct?"

"Had I thought I was risking her heart as well that night . . ." he murmured, but his gaze had shifted away from her.

Harriet stared at him in disbelief for a long moment. She could not credit he could be so unfeeling. Why would Margaret's sentiments have been more significant than her own? She did not understand Connought, not one whit, and all the hurt she experienced seven years ago returned to her anew.

His gaze snapped back to her. "Only tell me, Harriet, is she in love with me? I would wager my entire fortune she never was."

She tossed her head. "Of course she was not in love with you. She always knew you for what you were. Indeed, she warned me away from you time and again, and I only wish that I had been so wise as to have heeded her early on! I did learn my lesson, however, while you seem incapable of doing so. You trifled with my cousin while injuring me, yet you still seem perfectly unable to own to how wretchedly you used either of us."

"There you are out! I do comprehend quite fully the scope of my thoughtless conduct, and I have apologized more than once. However, I will not do so again today. I am sick to death of your prosy accusations, particularly in light of the fact that I did acknowledge my wrongdoing but you were unable to forgive me. Such a cold heart, Harriet!"

"I had rather have a cold heart," she said, "than not to know the meaning of honor!"

His color receded ominously and his jaw worked strongly. "Were you a man, I should call you out for that!"

"Were I a man, I should have accepted the challenge!"

He picked up his hat, brushed off a few scattered leaves and bits of grass, then slapped it hard on his head. "Good day, *Miss Godwyne!*" He whirled around and headed in the direction of his white horse.

"I despise you!" she flung at his back, but he merely lifted a hand and waved without turning around even to look at her.

Harriet watched him go and, like a child who is frustrated, she stomped the ground with one foot. She hated him! She hated that he could raise her hackles with but a handful of words. She hated him because he had kissed Margaret. But mostly, she hated him because with but a soft kiss on her lips, she was reminded of just how easy it would be to tumble in love with him all over again!

Connought made his way swiftly back to his horse. This most recent wager, entered into in a spirit of daring and fun, had ended more badly than he could have imagined. Initially, he had delighted in pursuing Harriet through the orchard and kissing her, exacting a certain retribution for her deuced stubbornness over the years. The kiss itself had been both surprising and heavenly, for she had given him a kiss in return, soft and yielding.

The pleasure of taking his revenge, however, had not lasted much beyond her first accusing words about his errant nature. She had, over the past several years, let him know time and again just what her opinion of him was. And yet he did not feel she was justified in thinking so very ill of him. Yes, he had kissed Margaret, but that had been a mistake, an error of his youth for which he had paid dearly in the ensuing years. The worst of it was, he was bound to an oath of secrecy concerning the reason why he had stolen a kiss from her cousin, and the price for revelation was far higher than he could ever pay without betraying the Connought lineage, past and future.

And yet something within him rebelled at the notion that Harriet Godwyne had decided he was unworthy of her hand in marriage because of that kiss. Even had it been in his power to reveal the circumstances which led up to the kiss, he doubted he would ever tell her—certainly not now, at least. In his opinion, her stubbornness, her inability to forgive him for this indiscretion, was a much greater flaw than his own weakness, which had led to kissing Margaret in the first place.

So it was that when he mounted his horse, he felt enraged all over again that Harriet was as mulish as ever on a subject that had grown hackneyed beyond belief.

Two

Having come from the direction of the stables, Connought entered the portals of Kingsland, his ancestral home, in high dudgeon. Even the knowledge that he had won his wager and would very soon be able to triumph over Laurence and Charles did not soothe his temper in the least. He marched down the hall leading to the billiard room, where he had left his friends an hour past, and heard the clack of the solid balls long before he reached the chamber. Even after galloping the entire distance from the cherry orchard to his stables, he still found himself in a towering passion.

When he crossed the threshold, Laurence rose up from his shot to lift an inquiring brow and Charles settled his cue upright on the carpet, his gaze fixed as well on Connought's face. Both men stared at him for a long moment, then each tossed a ten-pound note on the table in his direction.

"I have not even told you whether I succeeded!" he cried, their joint assumption aggravating his already lacerated temper.

Laurence leaned well over the edge of the table and began lining up his shot again. "After you had gone," he said, glancing up at him at an odd angle, "we agreed that should you return appearing stunned or indifferent, we would know you had failed in your exploits. On the other hand, should you arrive possessing either a countenance of exceeding joy or venomous wrath, we should know at once that you most certainly had kissed our dear Harriet. If you wish to comprehend our deductions, you have but to peer into a looking glass, for there can be no two opinions about your present state."

"Even a simpleton could see you are in the boughs," Charles added.

Connought threw himself into a chair near the door and looked from one friend to the other. Charles brought him his winnings, which he folded carefully and secreted into the small pocket of his waistcoat. He wondered how it had happened that either of the gentlemen before him had come to know him so well.

Of course, they had all been at Cambridge together, quite inseparable, plotting and executing every manner of devilment. Laurence had been rusticated three times during the course of his education, while Charles had escaped unscathed quite miraculously. That had given him a reputation as something of a conjurer, for he had been involved in as many larks as Laurence. As for himself, he had been sent down only once, for having brought three goats into his rooms while completely foxed. He had awakened to find his room smelling rather like his home farm and a very expensive set of evening clothes partially devoured by the otherwise contented beasts.

Charles's consistent escape from punishment was generally set down to his looks, for he had the appearance of an angel, with light brown curly hair groomed in the loose arrangement known as *a la Cherubim.* He had large hazel eyes, enjoyed teasing his dearest friends, and was loyal to a fault. Laurence Douglas, on the other hand, was of a different style altogether, from his shockingly red, wavy hair, which he wore cropped quite short, to his white, faintly freckled skin and his intense blue eyes. He was not only game for any lark, but generally instigated a good many of them, which frequently saw him in the basket. His heart, however, was as big as the sky. No better friend existed than Laurence Douglas—or Charles, for that matter.

"Harriet has always been able to make me as mad as hops. If ever a young woman needed to be taught a lesson or two, that lady is Harriet Godwyne."

Charles addressed Laurence. "He is still in love with her."

"Damme, don't I know it!" Laurence called back, his gaze fixed to the glossy balls waiting on the green baize.

Laurence slung his cue. The balls clacked again. Charles groaned and Laurence danced a jig in a circle. "You owe me another five!" he cried with glee. "Another round?"

"Yes!" Charles retorted. "I intend to win all my money back, only you certainly have had the devil's own luck this morning."

"Enough of that nonsense," Connought said, rising to his feet. "Only tell me, Charles, what the deuce do you mean by saying that I am in love with her? And you, Laurence. Why did you agree with him so readily?"

Both gentlemen turned to regard him steadfastly.

"Cannot you see that I am furious with her? And I wish you would stop staring at me like a pair of deuced gapeseeds!"

"You may abuse either of us all you like," Laurence said, shaking his head at him. "But the truth is that you are still in love with her, and I believe you always will be."

"Stuff and nonsense!" he cried. He knew he was protesting far too much to be believed, but there was nothing for it. He was still too wretchedly piqued by her words to him to be capable of examining the exact state of his heart. Dash it all, how dare she accuse him of not knowing the meaning of honor?

The truth was, he had never known quite what to do about Harriet. Did he still love her? He recalled the kiss he had so recently taken from her and realized that he could not have felt so exhilarated merely by holding her in his arms without still being a little in love with her.

"She ought to have married Frith and borne him six or seven insipid brats by now. He always wanted her. Even that night . . ." He could not finish the thought. Frith was one of the reasons he had ruined his own betrothal almost before it had begun. Even now, he could not credit he had been so foolish as to have kissed Margaret, and all because Frith had tricked him into the wager!

"Yes, his intentions have always been perfectly clear," Charles agreed, moving around the table and lining up a new shot.

"I only wonder she has not tied the connubial knot with him," Laurence said, his arm wrapped about his cue, his gaze tracking Charles's every move. "He is never far from her side even after all these years, and she seems to have formed something of an attachment to him. Rumor has it he's offered for her at least three times, probably more."

"Undoubtedly more!" Connought cried. "Once a year for the past seven years, if I don't miss my mark. What a gudgeon!"

"He is that," Charles agreed. With a swift jolt of his wrist, he sent one of the balls rolling into a corner pocket. "Hah!"

"Lucky shot!" Laurence cried in a true competitive spirit.

"Though normally I would take exception to such a provoking remark," Charles said, running his hand loosely through his brown, curly locks, "not today. Any shot I've made this morning has been by pure chance. Too much of Sir Edgar's brandy last night. My head still feels as though it's stuffed with sheep's wool."

"Someone should warn Harriet," Connought said.

"About what?" both gentlemen intoned, once more staring at him.

"About Frith, of course."

Laurence nodded in agreement, but Charles lifted a facetious brow. "I thought you said she should marry Frith and give him a passel of mealymouthed brats."

Connought glanced at him, his temper rising sharply once more. "Oh, go to the devil!"

Charles merely laughed, then gave Laurence's cue stick a slight nudge just as he made his shot.

"What the deuce! Good God, Charles, how old are you anyway?"

Charles merely laughed.

Connought sighed heavily and moved to the windows overlooking the southern vista of his estate. There were few things lovelier, he thought, than the steep rise of the weald hills on the opposite side of the valley. He had been master here for a very long time, his father having paid his debt to nature many years past—nine, in fact. His mother, though still living and enjoying a renewed bloom of health in recent years, had married again and was the wife of a genteel man in possession of an easy competence. Presently, she resided quite happily in Bath's Royal Crescent, a mere Mrs. Willes.

His three brothers served in the army, while his two elder sisters were married, ensconced in country houses, and raising a large brood of children each, Marianne with eight and Charlotte with seven and hopeful of another successful confinement in October.

Thinking of his sisters brought Harriet to mind again. Of late, whenever he thought of her, he often bemoaned her single state. He had spoken truly when he had said that she ought to be married, for she had always seemed to him to be well suited to domestic happiness, were she to marry the proper man. Frith was not that man, of that he was certain, having become acquainted with his true character seven years ago. Yes, Harriet ought to be warned about Baron Frith, but not by him. She would no more believe him than she would a passing Gypsy. He wondered if she had even the smallest notion that beyond Frith's gentlemanlike demeanor, he was cunning, dishonorable and rarely sought out a friendship with anything other than motives of self-interest. What would she say, for instance, were she to learn that Frith had been the true author of that damnable kiss he had shared with Margaret?

However, he could hardly expose Frith's true character to Harriet without revealing the nature of the wager that had set so many follies in motion that fateful day. He shuddered inwardly as he recalled the events which led up to the undoing of their engagement.

The entire hapless event had occurred at Ruckings Hall, Laurence's ancestral home, where a three-day party had been in progress. The day he had proposed to Harriet was the finest of his life, for he had tumbled in love with her quite deeply and she with him. Long after the ladies had retired to bed, he had remained in an utterly exhilarated state, for he was to marry the woman he loved before the end of the following month. Nothing, he thought, could possibly disturb his happiness.

Mr. Douglas had always kept a most excellent buttery, in which were stored fine wines, champagne, and a formidable brandy. His forthcoming nuptials had been toasted by the men perhaps as many as twenty times, and to each offer of congratulations, he tossed off another glass of brandy. Lord Frith, in particular, had been excessive in his compliments and toasts while, as came to be understood in the ensuing days, keeping his own head quite clear.

Somehow or other, he had been led to the billiard room, not to play at billiards but rather to toss the dice at hazard for an hour of rollicking good fun with Charles, Laurence, and Frith. He had never laughed so hard in his life, and still the brandy flowed. Who would blame him for drinking, especially when Harriet was held up as a model of womanly perfection time and time again?

Somehow or other—to this day he was not certain how it had come about—Frith had challenged him to a bet involving as the stakes a portion of the Kingsland estate against Frith's horse, a fine black thoroughbred Connought had coveted for over a year. All that Connought had to do to win the wager was to steal a kiss from Margaret, Harriet's cousin, before midnight on the following day. One kiss and Connought would own Lightning Velvet! The brandy had spoken for him and he had agreed to the traitorous wager. He had signed his name to it, for Frith had insisted the terms be set down on paper.

And so it was on the following morning, while nursing a very sick head and attempting to drink a cup of weak tea, he had been brought the barely remembered wager in the form of the signed document.

He had read the agreement in horror, the terms of which demanded the utmost secrecy. No one, outside of his two bosom bows and Frith, was ever to know of the wager, or Connought would be required to forfeit the property by default.

After fortifying himself not with more of the tea but with another glass of brandy, he immediately sought Frith out and begged to be released from the wager for Harriet's sake and because he had been completely foxed when he had agreed to the disastrous terms of the challenge. He had fully expected Frith to have a good laugh over it and, as a gentleman, allow that the brandy alone had been the means by which Connought would ever have assented to such an odious wager.

Frith, however, had been steadfast in his refusal, even insisting laughingly that Harriet would think very little of a mere kiss, particularly given Connought's general reputation.

Only in that moment did he begin to suspect Frith's misdeed. He was further convinced of it when none of his entreaties, whether presented in a good-natured manner or in an aspect of abject humility and sincerity, succeeded in moving the baron. In the end, Frith grew impatient with Connought and finally insisted that as a gentleman, and having entered into the wager as such, he ought either to concede failure and deed him the property or to proceed with the terms of the challenge and see if he might get his kiss from Miss Weaver.

After all, Frith was making no complaints at having wagered his favorite thoroughbred. In the end, there had been no other recourse open to him but to proceed.

The property in question was quite extensive and marched beside Frith's modest estate in Lincolnshire, but had belonged to the Connought family for seven generations and was used as a hunting lodge. Had he had only himself to consider, he would not have hesitated in doing what was for him the more honorable course of simply relinquishing the property. To betray Harriet at any time, but most particularly immediately following his betrothal to her, was a matter of complete abhorrence to him. However, the greater claim had been his duty to both the memory of his father and grandfather, as well as his future progeny, by keeping the entire estate intact.

Having resigned himself to what he must now do,

he had had every intention of stealing a very insignificant peck on Margaret's lips, perhaps after having teased her into it as a well-wishing for the forthcoming marriage, but keeping it as innocent as possible. He had known Margaret for a very long time since her family's property, Shalham Park, was just to the south of his own.

However, once he had cajoled Margaret into the kiss and had leaned forward to barely touch his lips to hers, she had stunned him by throwing her arms about his neck and kissing him quite thoroughly. To this day, he had never been able to comprehend why Margaret had done so, unless it had been as Harriet had said, that she had thought herself at the time in love with him.

Afterward, however, Margaret had flushed a rosy hue, trilled her laughter, and said she had thought the whole thing a great joke. Only then had either of them noticed Miss Arabella Orlestone at the far end of the garden, her mouth agape, apparently having watched the entire encounter. He had meant to beg Margaret to say nothing of what had transpired between them, but of what use would that be when Miss Orlestone would have no reason not to speak of what she had just witnessed? Indeed, it became a very terrible scandal so quickly he felt he had hardly blinked before his troubles began.

He had asked Margaret to forgive him for the kiss.

"Will you forgive me as well?" she had asked. "I . . . I am so sorry. I should not have . . ."

"Nor I," he had murmured. "The property be damned!"

"I beg your pardon?"

"Nothing!" He cried. "It hardly signifies. Dash it all! What a fool I am!"

"You do not love Harriet, then?" she asked, an odd light in her eye.

"Love Harriet?" he had responded with a brittle laugh. "Dear Margaret, I love her to the point of madness!"

"Of course you do," she had said wistfully. "And do not worry. I shall tell Harriet all that transpired, that you were requesting an innocent kiss for good luck—hopefully before Bella opens her mouth, although she is quite young and is not always as discreet as she ought to be."

He watched Margaret hurry back to the house, a feeling of dread taking strong possession of his senses. He was not so sanguine as Margaret. He had not lived in the world, enjoying the society of ladies as much as he had, without coming to understand them a trifle. "Good God!" he had murmured. "What have I done?"

With that, he turned on his heel, marched into the lane lined with poplars, and partook of a very long walk. He had much to ponder, not least of which was just how he was to explain his conduct to Harriet.

By the time he had made his way back to Ruckings, he was stunned to find that not only had Harriet quit the house, having decided to return with Margaret to Shalham Park, but that she had left behind for him a tightly written missive ending their brief betrothal.

All his subsequent attempts to win her back had failed utterly, much to Frith's obvious satisfaction. She had held to the simple belief that because he had kissed another lady within a matter of hours of having become betrothed to her, he had proven the worthless roguishness of his character. A day had not gone by since in which he did not ponder the possibility of relinquishing the hunting lodge to Frith after all so that he might explain to Harriet his true reasons for having kissed her cousin. Yet something within him remained equally as intractable as Harriet. Some part of him did not trust a woman who could not forgive when he had all but prostrated himself before her in apologizing for his stupidity.

So, here he was, seven years later, contemplating the events that had haunted him for the same length of time, without being one whit closer to a satisfactory conclusion. She ought to have married, just as he had said earlier. Then he would not have had a right to continue being consumed by thoughts of her.

Frith, on the other hand, had been a different matter entirely. Scarcely three days had passed when he had come to understand, through the keen smugness of the baron's expression upon presenting him with Lightning Velvet, that he had been in some manner duped. He was not himself a man to scheme and play at the subtleties of life. He preferred openness and directness in all his dealings.

Frith had won the day that particular July so many years ago through a carefully orchestrated plan which had worked to perfection. Take a young gentleman of honor who is deeply in love, ply him with a strong spirit, and goad him into a wager he can scarcely remember, a wager that would effectually put a blight on his lady's love for him. Perfection, indeed, save for one small rub—Harriet may have cast off her betrothed, but she did not turn around and cast herself into Frith's arms, something Connought was convinced the good baron had been fully expecting. Indeed, in seven years, with the most faithful of courtships, Frith had still been unable to win her heart.

Yes, there was at least some satisfaction in that.

He turned back to the billiard table and watched as Charles grimaced anew.

"Another round?" Laurence asked, smiling hugely.

"Of course," Charles countered readily, taking up his cue stick and polishing the tip with a piece of chalk, which he proclaimed had cost him quite an exorbitant sum. "A man by the name of Carr says it will improve my game immensely."

"Indeed?" Laurence queried. "And the purpose of it?"

Charles shrugged. "To smooth the tip, I suppose. Do you think it will do the trick?"

Laurence lifted a skeptical brow. "I suppose it couldn't hurt. You can scarcely do worse today, at all events!"

Charles laughed. "You are right, of course. Very well. Let's see how this performs." He aimed the cue and slung the next shot. The cue hit squarely and with a tidy, straight roll, the ball plopped into the corner pocket. "Well, I'll be damned!" he cried.

"Let me have a go!" Laurence cried, rounding the table briskly, his hand outstretched.

Charles, however, prevented his friend from snatching up his magic chalk. "Not on your life!" he cried. "At least not until I have won my money back!"

"Oh, very well," Laurence relented. He glanced at Connought. "Still in a brown study? You know, while you were staring out the window, a notion struck me that I think you might find intriguing. What if you were to revenge yourself on Harriet for all the dust she kicked up about your having kissed Margaret? Perhaps then you might be able to free yourself of her, of this deuced hold she has over you."

Connought shrugged. The subject was as old as time, as far as he was concerned, and tended to surface each summer when Harriet arrived at Shalham Park to spend the month of July with Margaret. For some reason, perhaps because the same players tended to resume their annual places, tensions grew high once more, just as they had done this morning.

"Revenge, eh?" he queried. "You do not think her

justified in condemning me? After all, in her eyes I had all but told her I did not truly love her."

"Good God, man, you became a monk for her! What greater proof would a woman need that your affections were deeply and truly engaged? Doing it up too brown by half! She ought to have forgiven you at least once, given you a second chance, but she did not even do that much. I believe her to have been wholly in the wrong on that score. No, I have thought about this a great deal over the past twelvemonth, and I am persuaded that you must have a measure of revenge for her stubborness and then perhaps you may be able to get on with things, take a wife, raise a passel of mealymouthed brats yourself, and perhaps even be content."

Connought smiled, then laughed outright. "This from a confirmed bachelor?"

"I should be happy to marry, were I to find just the right woman."

Both gentlemen laughed at him, since it was no secret to either of them that he had been in love with Margaret for years.

Connought watched Charles hit another shot square to the mark, but his thoughts were centered upon what Laurence had said. Was this what he needed, a little retribution for the pain she had caused him in her stubborness? Perhaps.

After a moment, he addressed Laurence. "You may be right, now that I think on it. Perhaps a trifling piece of vengeance would finally set me free of her, for I simply cannot explain why, after all this time, she can make me as mad as fire with but a lift of her brow." The balls clattered. Charles yelped his delight at having sunk another ball. "Have you a suggestion?"

Charles rounded the table and lined up a final shot. Laurence frowned at the table for a moment, then reverted his attention to the earl. "What about another wager, since we are all so fond of the sport—a wager in which your object must be to win Harriet's heart back within, oh, say, a sennight's time. Not for the purpose of wedding her, not in the least, but merely to prove the truth of what we all believe to be her sentiments where you are concerned. Then you may tell her to go the devil, once you are sure of her heart!"

"What proof of her heart do you seek?"

"That she must tell you she would accept of your hand in marriage were you to offer it."

For some reason this notion pleased him. "I see. And should I succeed, what would I win? What are you willing to relinquish to me?"

Charles settled in to make his final shot. He brought the cue back, aiming carefully.

Laurence laughed loudly. "If you were actually able to succeed, I promise you that I would ask Margaret Weaver to marry me."

The balls clattered noisily. "The devil take it!" Charles cried. "You made me miss my shot! Are you indeed serious? Would you truly ask Margaret to marry you?" He stared at Laurence in utter disbelief.

"You would offer this?" Connought asked, stunned.

Laurence drew in a deep breath, his gaze fixed unseeing to the green baize of the table. "I would," he murmured. "God knows I should have done so any time these past several years."

"I must say, I am shocked," Connought responded.

At that, Laurence shifted his gaze back to him. "Well, perhaps you ought not to be. Perhaps I offer this as my stake in the wager because I know you haven't the smallest chance in succeeding with Harriet."

Connought stared at him and shook his head. Laurence always did know how to offer a challenge. "What is it you expect me to wager should I lose?" he asked, suddenly suspicious.

Laurence levelled his cue across the table and began lining up his shot before answering. He let the cue fly and the clacking of the billiard balls resounded again through the chamber. "The devil," he muttered, for he missed a last, easy shot. Straightening up, he moved away from the table. From the corner of his eye he watched Charles reach onto the table and snatch the last ball two inches to the right. Charles loved to cheat—in a purely harmless manner, of course.

"Charles!" Laurence barked. "Put it back."

"Put what back?"

"You know very well what!"

"Good God! You cannot have seen me do it, man!"

"I did not need to *see* you do anything."

"Oh, very well," Charles grumbled.

To Connought, Laurence said, "We both ought to be married, for we both have estates to consider as eldest sons. Margaret will do well enough for me, should she accept me, and if you fail to get Harriet to agree to wed you, then I suggest that as a condition to the wager under discussion, your forfeit would be that you would then have to offer for Arabella. She would wed you in a trice, and she would do as well as any female to take up the position as the next Countess Connought."

Connought shook his head and grimaced. "This is by far the most harebrained scheme I have ever heard you propose, and you've proposed many in your day!"

"Do but listen," he said grandly. "Arabella is suitable, and you need a wife, as do I. Let the wager stand and see where fate takes you because of it—or me! You have not done so well on your own, and we might as well have a bit of fun in the prospect of choosing the ladies to whom we must be leg-shackled. Besides, if you win the wager, you will not have to marry at all."

"But what of Harriet? You have said I must offer for her."

"No, no, you misunderstand me completely. Here is the beauty of what I am suggesting. I did not say you would have to marry her, only that you must get her to say she would marry you if asked. Your reward will be to laugh in her face while at the same time to see me humble myself and beg for Margaret's hand in marriage. I should think you would agree to the wager merely to see that."

"I vow you do tempt me, quite sorely." He could not help but smile, and within his chest he experienced a quite familiar sensation of intrigue and excitement. Was there an Englishman born who did not love a good wager? And this one was promising in the extreme.

Charles lifted his head from examining the table to ascertain the peculiar dips in the baize-lined wood as he prepared for his last shot. "It cannot be done," he proclaimed. "Harriet's heart is as frigid as frost on a windowpane."

Laurence frowned slightly and feigned a rather large sigh. "I suppose you are right, Charles," he mused. "We cannot expect Connought to perform a miracle, can we?"

Connought narrowed his eyes at his two bosom bows. "You would even reduce yourselves to this?" he cried. "Trying to manipulate me in this most absurd manner?"

"Why not?" Charles returned, laughing.

Connought drew in a deep breath. A sennight only to secure Harriet's acquiescence. Could it be done? Indeed, he did not know, as stubborn as she was. However, he had never truly applied himself to the task before, and in this moment, he confessed he felt a certain exhilaration at the thought of it. He had known a roguish life many years ago, and there had been a certain art involved in the seduction of womankind, of which skills certainly he had retained a few for the purpose!

"Very well," he said aloud. "I accept the wager, and your terms. A sennight's time and Harriet's profession that she would willingly wed me. Charles, put the ball back."

Charles grunted, but when both men glared at him, he returned the ball to its proper position. Once more he chalked his cue stick.

Connought shook hands with Laurence who said, "You have until midnight, Wednesday next."

"Done!"

The balls clacked one last time and Charles sent up a loud whoop! "Damme, if this isn't magic chalk after all! You owe me ten pounds, Laurence!"

"Five!" Laurence countered. "We have been playing for five!"

"Oh, very well!"

Afterward, Connought remained with his friends, playing billiards for the next hour. Only as he lost a round to Laurence did the full weight of the wager he had just entered into settle upon him. How the devil was he to get Harriet to agree to marry him in seven days?

"I nearly forgot," Laurence said. "Guess who is come to Kent and staying at the Bell Inn?"

"I cannot imagine," he responded, not really caring very much one way or the other. With the wager set, he only wondered just how soon he could begin his assault on Harriet's heart.

"Frith," Laurence stated, smiling broadly.

Connought stared at him in disbelief. "And you knew of this, yet you let me agree to the wager anyway?" he cried.

"He was bound to show up. Besides, I know you love a challenge. It shall be quite interesting to see how easily you are able to disengage Harriet from his side!"

Connought strongly resisted the impulse to land his good friend a facer. Instead, he contented himself with beating him three times in a row at billiards.

Three

"Frith is come? And so very soon?" Harriet asked. She was still as mad as hops, but this welcome news upon entering the cool, humid conservatory of her uncle's home gentled her nerves considerably.

"Yes," Margaret responded. She sat before her easel, dabbing gray paint onto a large canvas. "He called while you were out walking, but a prior engagement for nuncheon at the Bell prevented him from staying longer than he wished to."

Jane, who was watering a lemon tree, looked up from her task. "Connought was here as well," she offered. "He asked after you, and when we mentioned you were walking in the cherry orchard, he said he might seek you out. Did you happen to see him?" Her expression was all innocence, but Harriet was not deceived.

"Yes, I suppose you could say that I *saw* him." She strolled into the chamber, pulling off her gloves and moving in the direction of Margaret's easel.

"Did you speak with him?" Margaret asked, turning around to watch her approach.

"Yes, indeed, I did *speak* with him."

Margaret donned a serious expression, which Harriet could well see was facetious in nature. "Your cheeks are quite red. Did you forget your parasol? I vow you appear to be a trifle sunburned."

"Oh, do stubble it, Margaret!" Harriet cried.

"Out of reason cross again. Yes, indeed, you most certainly must have encountered Connought." She resumed dabbing at the canvas.

Harriet viewed her cousin's latest artistic endeavor and tilted her head. "What on earth is that?" she cried. "A camel? An elephant, perchance? I vow I cannot make it out at all!"

Margaret's face twisted into a frustrated scowl. "Is that what you see?" she cried, groaning. "An elephant?" She flung her hand in a flourish above the mass of rippled grays and browns which dominated the canvas.

"Yes, I suppose," Harriet returned uncertainly.

"These are the downs!" Margaret cried in exasperation. "The majestic sweep of the downs! Have you no perception at all?"

"But . . . but you've made them all muddied in color. I thought . . . well! Never mind, then. I believe I can see now what you were attempting."

"The downs on a cloudy day, of course!" Margaret returned, peering at her own picture and sighing heavily. "I never was very good at this. I vow I do not know why I continue."

"Because it gives you pleasure," Harriet said, patting her cousin's shoulder. She glanced down at Margaret and could not help but smile. As well as being her cousin, Margaret had been her dearest friend since time out of mind. From their earliest years, they had formed a bond as strong as sisters.

They were, however, as different from one another as could be. Margaret's hair was a brilliant red, casting her own completely in the shade by comparison, for hers was a light brown and, though pretty in its own way, scarcely designed to compete with the dramatic nature of so many wild red curls. Her cousin's eyes were a delicate blue, contrasting sharply with her own dark brown. What they did share in common was a fine complexion, although even in this they differed, since the hue of Margaret's skin was almost bluish, while her own tended to a faint peach.

Where they differed the most, however, was in temper. Margaret was not always easy to know, while she knew herself to be as easy to read as a childhood primer.

"Enough of Margaret's artistic genius," Jane said, intruding into her reveries. "Only tell us what Connought said to you. He seemed most anxious to see you. Did he have something of a very particular nature to communicate?"

Harriet watched her carry what appeared to be a large, laden watering can to a pot containing a pale pink columbine. Jane was a petite young lady of two and twenty years and the eldest of four siblings. Her hair was a lustrous black, her eyes a very light blue, similar to Margaret's, and her features quite pretty. A faint smattering of freckles across her nose and cheeks, combined with her short stature, gave her a youthful, fragile appearance. She rarely saw but the happiest side to any event.

"If you must know," Harriet said, catching Jane's eye as the water began to flow from the long, curved neck of the can, "he kissed me."

This sudden announcement caused Jane to drop the can, which made a loud clattering sound on the stone floor. "Oh, but how wonderful!" she cried, righting the can immediately.

"He kissed you?" Margaret cried in some disbelief, turning to look at her again.

Harriet clasped her hands behind her back and rocked on her heels. "He came upon me in the cherry orchard and kissed me. I was never more astonished, nor more . . ." She paused, wondering just how she was to express the rage she had felt.

"Delighted?" Margaret offered.

"Aux anges?" Jane suggested.

Harriet rolled her eyes. "Furious, of course!" she countered. "Why would I feel anything else?"

Margaret and Jane exchanged a disbelieving glance.

The former responded, "Because there is no handsomer man in all of Kent than Lord Connought, as you very well know."

Jane picked up the can and poised the spout at the soil line of the columbine plant. "I only wish he would kiss me."

"What a scandalous thing to say, my dear Jane!" Harriet cried, startled.

"Nonsense," she retorted. "There isn't a lady of my acquaintance who has not said as much—or wished as much! So, tell me, was it wonderful?"

Harriet felt a blush rise on her cheeks. For a moment, she forgot her pique and recalled just how extraordinary that kiss had been. There had been a moment when time and place had been completely lost to her and she had wished, more than life itself, that she was his wife after all.

Fearful that her two dearest companions would comprehend the true nature of her feelings, she said hurriedly, "He was a veritable brute, and kissed me when I told him most vehemently not to!"

Margaret and Jane merely stared at her, their expressions so very knowing that she could not help but wonder just when it was they had both come to comprehend her so well. "We quarreled," she confessed, hoping to parry a discussion of the sentiments she strove so hard to keep in check. However, her declaration served to bring a spate of tears flooding her eyes, something for which she was completely unprepared.

Margaret rose from her place at her easel and immediately embraced her, while Jane once more clattered the watering can on the stone floor. She hurried to Harriet's side and embraced her as well.

"I said such wretched things," she confessed. "You can have no notion!"

Margaret drew back and handed her a kerchief. "I think we might, if but a little."

There was such a warm, affectionate light in her eye that Harriet could not help but chuckle. "I do have a temper," she admitted, dabbing at her eyes and cheeks. "And unfortunately, Connought can so easily send me into the boughs. Although I believe today was not without enormous provocation."

"Because he kissed you?" Jane asked softly.

Harriet shook her head. "No, it is much worse than you know. He made a wager with Laurence and Charles that he could kiss me before noon!"

The ladies gasped as one, quite justified in their shock.

"Horrid, horrid men!" Margaret exclaimed. "Have they no sense of propriety?"

"None at all!" Harriet returned heatedly. "They are blockheads, to a man!"

This sent Jane into a peal of laughter. "I have always enjoyed that particular expression. I vow everytime I hear it I see a head in the shape of a perfect square! And in this case, I think it wonderfully fitting!"

Harriet burst out laughing, for the image was quite amusing. At the same time, she found she could dispense with her kerchief. "Thank you for that, dear, dear Jane, for I was nearly ready to fall into a fit of the dismals."

Jane shook her head. "It is all so confusing. Men are strange creatures, are they not?"

"Quite strange," Harriet agreed.

"And it seems to me," she added, all the while returning to her watering can and retrieving it once more from the stone floor, "that if a lady does not make herself perfectly clear on every occasion as to what precisely she expects of a gentleman, then given the choice, a man will always conduct himself like a perfect cretin, without the smallest notion he has done so!"

"Hear, hear!" the ladies intoned.

"I do not mean to malign their sex necessarily, but I have frequently observed that only the most stalwart, forbearing, and instructive of ladies have marriages that resemble anything near to equanimity. It is most fascinating and yet lowering at the same time." She returned to water the columbine.

"Well then, dear philosopher," Margaret said, resuming her seat before her elephant downs, "Pray, what would you advise our dear Harriet in dealing with such a man as Connought?"

"That is an intriguing question, for he is, at least in my estimation, quite a superior gentleman in so many ways. He has a great deal of intelligence and would not be easily led down any particular path."

"I have no interest in leading him anywhere," Harriet said. "However, I would not be loath to give him a proper setdown."

Margaret picked up her brush once more and dipped it in the muddy gray paint. "I still think you should have wed him seven years past."

"You know very well I could not . . . not after he used both you and me so very ill."

Margaret glanced up at her. "Do you not think it odd that neither of us have wed, nor even drawn close to the altar, in these past seven years?"

"Do not forget Jane," Harriet added.

"She is but two and twenty, a full three years younger

than you and I, and must therefore still be considered of a respectable, marriageable age. We, however, appear to have grown into spinsters."

"What nonsense!" Jane cried. "Whatever the mode of the day, I do not believe a woman is truly a spinster until she has reached a very advanced age at which she is no longer able to bear children and still has had the misfortune never to marry."

"I have been corrected by our sage," Margaret said, speaking in a confiding and quite teasing voice to Harriet.

Jane grinned. "Well, you ought to thank me for saying so, since my mother, dear soul that she is, called the pair of you ape-leaders only last night."

"She did not!" Margaret exclaimed hotly. "Were she two decades younger, I vow I should pull her nose!"

All three ladies laughed heartily at the picture of anyone pulling the imperious and quite large Lady Eaves by the nose.

After a moment, Jane sighed, "I do love my mother and shall always be a dutiful daughter to her, but sometimes—well, I suppose nothing more need be said."

Harriet could not have agreed more. Jane Eaves was the dearest girl, but she possessed a bear of a parent with more hair than wit and as much style as Margaret's unfortunate painting. She glanced at Jane and cried out, "Have a care! The water is spilling over the sides!"

"Oh!" Jane exclaimed, pulling the spout back. "I was lost in thought, for the most intriguing notion has just popped into my head."

"Indeed?" Harriet queried, turning to her.

"But it is too ridiculous, too frivolous—"

"I begin to think it quite delightful, whatever it might prove to be," Margaret said, rising from her seat once more. "Tell us, Jane! What wicked idea is now whirling through that very clever brain of yours?"

"Well," she said, setting the can on the stones and moving back to her friends, "I think your speaking of having grown into spinsters set me down this particular path. I have always felt, Harriet, that you should have married Connought, and I beg you not to tell me yet again what a vile creature he was to have kissed Margaret, for I have heard that particular opinion expressed a hundred times—only do but hear me out! I also think that Margaret should marry Laurence. For all *their* brangling, they are well-suited. Besides, I should dearly love to see all the red-haired children they should produce!"

"You are grown into the most nonsensical creature!" Margaret cried, obviously affronted.

"Hush!" Jane adjured her. "For there is more, and you will like it! I am proposing a wager involving Connought and Harriet, and here is the cream: If Harriet fails at the particular scheme I have in mind, then not only will you *not* have to marry Laurence, but she will *have* to marry Connought!"

"What are you talking about? Why would I *not* have to marry Laurence? You are making no sense at all. What scheme?"

"A wager between you and Harriet, which would see one or the other of you married, or at least likely to be married, before summer's end."

"It seems to me, Jane," Harriet said severely, "that whatever notion you have in mind does not so much serve to punish Connought or either of his friends but rather one or the other of us!"

"That depends on how you view the matter!" Jane cried, approaching them both. "What greater punishment could we afford Laurence than to see him wed to Margaret?"

Harriet began to laugh and could not stop. Margaret was so horrified by the prospect of marrying Laurence

Douglas that her fine, bluish complexion had paled to a pasty chalk.

"Perhaps . . . you had best . . . sit down!" Harriet cried, between chortles.

Margaret did just that. Looking up at her black-haired friend, she said, "You are as mad as Bedlam, Jane Eaves, and I will hear no more of your ridiculous scheme, whatever it entails."

"Do but think, Margaret!" she cried. "If at the end of, let us say, a sennight, our dear Harriet has failed in her task—whatever it is we decide to lay before her—then she will be forced to wed Lord Connought."

At this, Margaret's expression grew very still and Harriet, seeing the look in her eye, found that her laughter died quickly away. "What is it?" she asked. "You appear almost ghostly."

"Jane is right," she said. "Whatever she proposes, we ought to do it! I swear we should!"

"You cannot be serious!" Harriet cried. "Jane is, just as you have said, as mad as Bedlam for even proposing anything that would involve casting our fate into the wind in so heedless a manner."

"But perhaps we should do just that! I mean, I cannot explain it, but I believe we ought to do as Jane says, whatever it is she is proposing."

Harriet turned to Jane, perplexed. "Just what are you proposing, dearest?"

"That there be a wager between you and Margaret, the terms being that should you fail in the task I am about to propose, then you must wed Connought. Should you succeed, then Margaret will have to oblige us all and marry Laurence."

Margaret shook her head. "Regardless of the particulars, Jane, do you really believe Laurence would *desire* to marry me?"

Jane nodded. "I believe he would. That is not to say I think he is in love with you, merely that I have always felt he would not be wholly averse to the notion."

"Charming!" Margaret cried sarcastically. She then frowned. "What task?"

"Harriet must acquire, by means fair or foul, three things belonging to Connought within the space of a sennight—let us say by Wednesday next at midnight."

"Which three things?" Harriet asked.

Jane thought for a moment. "His grandfather's watch—"

"I should never be able to get his watch!" Harriet cried.

Jane grinned. "Remember, fair means or foul. You can always return it to him at a later hour if you so desire once the challenge is concluded, but he mustn't know of your purpose in collecting his things or the wager would be forfeit!"

Harriet frowned a little more. She knew of Connought's attachment to his watch. He would never relinquish it, at least not readily. Yet at the very same moment, while pondering the possibility of detaching him from the watch, a certain wiggling of excitement entered her heart. She did so love a challenge! *Fair means or foul!* Well, perhaps if she was very, very clever, she might be able to acquire his watch. Her gaze snapped back to Jane. "What other articles did you have in mind?"

"His riding crop."

Nothing simpler, Harriet thought. To her knowledge, his whip had no especial value to him. "And lastly?"

"This might be the most difficult—his emerald stickpin, the one he wears to all the balls, assemblies, and fine parties."

At that, Harriet drew in a deep breath. The stickpin would be difficult, indeed, since he reserved it for full evening dress. During the coming sennight, she wondered if he would wear it even once—but then Jane had said she might employ whatever means she desired, so he did not necessarily have to be wearing it for her to acquire the emerald. She wondered absently just how difficult it would be to steal into his bedchamber at Kingsland and snatch the emerald with no one the wiser. She glanced at Margaret, whose expression was still rather solemn. "What do you make of this, cousin? Shall we accept of Jane's terms and make the wager?"

Margaret blinked twice and then nodded, as though the full weight of the wager had just settled over her. "Yes," she murmured. "I think it an excellent notion, even if at the end of it I am obliged to wed Laurence. Though I suppose there will always be the hope, for instance, that should I approach him with the notion, he would merely laugh at me and stroll away."

Harriet nodded. "Very true, but I begin to think he would be a fool to do so. You are well matched, I think, or perhaps it is as Jane has said—I, too, would like to see all your red-haired children racing about Ruckings Hall!"

"Is it settled, then?" Jane asked, her eyes glowing. "For I think it a famous wager and one which, since it has every promise of ending for either of you in matrimony, will mean I shall finally be a bridesmaid!"

Harriet laughed but nodded. Margaret as well.

"Then let us seal the agreement," Jane continued, "by joining our hands together." She held hers outstretched.

Harriet moved close and overlaid Jane's hand with her own. Margaret rose in what appeared to be a rather unsteady manner to her feet, drew a deep breath, and settled her hand atop Harriet's.

"Done!" Margaret proclaimed.

"Done!" Jane agreed.

"To Connought and Laurence. May the best man prove to be a bridegroom after all!"

Four

On Friday morning, quite early, Lord Connought stood before the mirror atop his highboy and shook his head. What the devil had he been thinking to have agreed to such a terrible wager, and with only a sennight to see the job done?

He shook his head, mystified again at his own folly. How was he to soften Harriet Godwyne's heart sufficiently to get her to confess that she would accept of his hand in marriage were he to offer for her? He soaped his face in slow circles, trying to make sense of his whole deuced relationship with her.

Whatever he might have felt for her over the years, he doubted that, regardless of her feelings, she would ever relent. He had made numerous attempts to retrieve her good opinion, but no amount of cajoling, flirting, arguing, or obsequious apologies had served to subdue her heart.

Now a new wager was on. Only just how was he to succeed this time when he had failed so miserably in the past?

Taking his razor in hand, he held the sharp blade at a familiar angle to his cheek.

The task of wooing Harriet seemed utterly impossible, particularly given the dressing down he had received yesterday from her fiery tongue. At least the picnic today at Laurence's home would afford him an opportunity to begin—only how the devil was he to begin?

"Damn and blast!" he cried.

"Yes, m'lord?" his valet called to him across the chamber.

"I have just cut my cheek!"

Harriet regarded her face in the mirror of her dressing table and realized her lips were shaped in a perfect *O*, as though she had just uttered the word of the same shape. She was still in a state of shock, for there could be no other explanation as to why she was still sitting in front of the dressing table when five minutes past her maid, Pansy, had completed the dressing of her hair.

She fiddled with a box of perfumed powder, dabbing a little on the end of her nose, on her cheeks, on her neck. Was he still in love with her? Did she truly have the ability to command him sufficiently to get a riding crop, an emerald, and a watch from him?

She thought for a moment about the kiss they had shared—was it only yesterday? She could not help but think that there had been a moment when he had seemed stunned by the kiss, almost as much as she had been. Were Margaret and Jane right? Did he still truly love her? If another question rose to her mind pertaining to the state of her own heart, she ignored it entirely. She had made her decision seven years past,and that was that.

Whatever the past, she had a wager to win, and at least the picnic today would allow her to begin her assault on Connought. Oh, dear! However was she to get even one article from him, nonetheless three?

Without warning, or even the simplest comprehension as to how it might have come about, the box of powder toppled onto her lap and a giant cloud of the fine talc puffed into the air. She flailed her arms, rose to her feet, and began coughing.

"Pansy!" she managed, summoning her maid from within the adjacent chamber where her wardrobe was kept. "I need your help at once!"

Her maid came running. "What is it, miss? Oh, miss . . ." Pansy began to laugh.

Harriet might have laughed as well at her inexplicable clumsiness had she not been sneezing by that time.

Later that afternoon, Harriet sat beside Lord Frith in his fine glossy black curricle and pair, twirling her parasol, a smile fixed on her lips. He was driving her to the picnic to be held on Mr. Douglas's estate and had been chatting about something or other for some time.

She nodded now and again, for he was speaking, but just what it was he was talking about she did not know. Her mind, nearly from the moment of the good baron settling his hat on his head and picking up his whip, had become fixed solely upon the day's most necessary object—the acquiring of Connought's watch. She knew to a certainty he would not be sporting the emerald, which was reserved for formal evenings, and she understood from Margaret that he and Charles were planning on driving over to the picnic in Charles's high perch phaeton—in which case he would not be in possession of his riding crop. Therefore, she had determined early on that she would not leave Mr. Douglas's property without the watch in her possession.

Only how to get it?

Fair means or foul!

"No, why?" she murmured, having heard Frith pose the question, 'Could you imagine my discomfiture?' She even turned to him and allowed her smile to broaden if a trifle.

She watched as Lord Frith took his eyes from the

dusty lane in front of them and glanced at her. "My dear Miss Godwyne, have you not been attending me?"

"Of . . . of course I have."

"Then what were we discussing?"

She sought about in her mind. "Your estate in Lincolnshire?" she offered hopefully.

"Yes, but what in particular about my estate in Lincolnshire?"

She sought about again and a word now and then filtered back to her. "About the management of your estate, your housekeeper?"

"What about my housekeeper?"

She searched the edges of her mind further and her spirits suddenly sank. "That she has been wishful of a mistress there for a very long time." Oh, dear.

"Uh-huh."

Harriet cringed inwardly. "My lord, were you by chance speaking of matrimony again?"

"Yes, as it happens, I was. You have dashed my hopes completely!"

"I do beg your pardon. No, I was not attending. I . . . I have something pressing on my mind today, something which I must accomplish hopefully before the sun has set, yet I know not just how to go about achieving my object."

"Then my timing has not been propitious."

She glanced at him. He was quite good looking, being tall, lean, and sporting a head of thick black hair which he wore cropped very short and swept forward *a la Brutus*. His eyes were so dark that though they were brown they appeared almost black. If he possessed a defect, it was that his face was rather narrow, as was his nose. Otherwise, he was a pleasant enough fellow in so many ways. Charming, rather sweet-tempered, he had a fine countenance and had been her suitor for a long time—years, in fact.

To her knowledge, he had offered for no one but herself. For the briefest moment, she wondered if she ought to accept his hand in marriage. Margaret had spoken truly when she had said they were both dwindling into spinsters . . . well, not dwindling, perhaps, more like tottering on the brink of spinsterhood, whatever Jane might have to say about it. She was five and twenty, well beyond the age most young ladies of the *haut ton* married, and she was of just such a competitive nature herself that she did not at all like the notion that so many others had succeeded at reaching the altar before her.

Good heavens, should she win this present wager—which she had every intention of winning—even Margaret would finally be called upon to marry!

She glanced up at Lord Frith once more. Could she marry such a man?

He laughed. "Good heavens, Miss Godwyne. In this moment, you have the appearance of a frightened rabbit. Why? Do not tell me the prospect of accepting of my hand in marriage has brought just such an expression to your face."

"I fear it has," she returned, then gasped at her horrid candor in responding as she had.

He shook his head. "Oh, dear, I believe I am in the basket now!"

"I do apologize. If it is any consolation, I was thinking not of you but of many other concerns as well."

"Do you mean I have cause to hope?" he inquired.

"You are being brave today."

He laughed anew. "Never mind. Do not answer that question. Time enough to be rejected properly. For now, let us enjoy Mrs. Douglas's picnic."

She relaxed in that moment. Lord Frith was nothing if not kind. She therefore let her mind wander anew. Only, since they were at that moment passing by the very orchard heavy with ripening cherries in which Connought had kissed her, certain memories could not help but intrude.

She felt a warmth on her cheeks that had nothing to do with the bright July sunshine. There had been a moment when the kiss had felt utterly sublime, a circumstance she could not in the least explain, since she had detached herself from Connought so completely.

Her mind traveled backward, farther and farther, until she was just eighteen and freshly arrived in Kent to visit with her cousin Margaret during another summer, the summer of 1810. She had tumbled quite violently in love with Connought, and he with her, or so she had thought. The first kiss he had ever given her had taken place on the Douglas Estate, beneath the rose arbor. She could not but catch the heavy fragrance of the rose without remembering the sweetness and tenderness of that kiss.

He had asked her if she liked kittens—such a silly question!—and then he had simply swept her up in his arms as though he could no longer contain his passion. She had felt drunk with love in that moment, completely intoxicated. She had known she would marry Connought, be his wife, raise his children.

Several heady weeks passed, mingling with a dozen more stolen, secretive kisses. She had discovered, along with him, every secretive spot on each of the neighborhood estates, places where he would take her, profess his love and adoration, and turn her head anew.

Such adventures had frightened her, even when she thought of them now. But always, once within the protection of his company, all her fears would evaporate. When he had offered for her at a weekend fete at Ruckings Hall, Laurence's home, the joy she had felt was inexpressible, as though she was fulfilling every girlish dream in that moment.

She had awakened the next day to a new life, of that she had been so certain. She would be a bride, a wife, the new mistress of Kingsland, a mother. But only a handful of hours had lapsed before young Arabella Orlestone had come to her, quite breathless, with news that she had seen Connought kissing Margaret under the very same rose arbor but minutes before!

The dark doubts which had succeeded all of her fine dreams had both stunned her in their complexity and driven a wedge of gigantic proportions between herself and Connought. She realized they had been waiting, from the beginning, at the edges of her mind for just the right moment to surface, warnings which had always been there but to which she had paid no heed because Cupid had struck her heart so deeply with his gold-tipped arrow.

Now, as she rode beside Lord Frith, she wondered about all those doubts, most of which she had never truly examined. It was enough that Connought had wounded her by kissing Margaret, proving her largest doubt, that a man of Connought's stamp, a rogue amongst men, could ever change.

"Well, at least you are not looking so frightened," Lord Frith said, drawing her sharply from her reveries. "Ah, here is Harry Eaves, sporting his new tilbury and frightening his poor sister out of her wits!" They were approaching a crossroads from the east at a spanking pace.

Harriet could not help but laugh, for she could hear Jane, who was clinging to the side of the carriage, calling out, "Good God, Harry! Draw rein or we shall collide with Lord Frith and Harriet!"

"Nonsense!" the whipster called out.

Frith, having long since left his salad days, merely pulled in his own horses sharply. Harry, just twenty, was so caught up in the excitement of the moment that he but barely checked his team sufficiently to keep the carriage from overturning as he rounded the corner. Their last sight of brother and sister, as Frith let them gather distance to keep the dust from eating up their own carriage, was of Jane taking off her bonnet and fairly pounding her brother on the head with it over and over.

Harriet began to laugh and could not stop for a very long time. Even Frith, generally a rather sober fellow, had his share of laughter as well.

After that, Harriet determined not to allow her former hapless relationship with Connought mar what otherwise appeared to be a very fine day indeed. Whatever her own troubles and concerns, a picnic was always a good thing. Who could be distressed when surrounded by good friends, excellent food, and quite delightful, sunny weather?

Five

"I understand there is a wager afoot this good day."

Much startled, Harriet looked up at Mr. Douglas and saw the warm, amused glint in his blue eyes. He had offered his arm to her, for she was a favorite of his and had been since she first met him as a schoolgirl of sixteen. Presently, he was escorting her to the morning room, from which vantage he wished to show her the activity about his beehives. Mr. Douglas was in every sense an Englishman: a gentleman, a bruising rider, yet perfectly capable of becoming enslaved to the delight and minutia of tending a garden.

"A wager, sir?" she inquired, feeling a blush rise on her cheeks. As they drew near the windows, she averted her gaze and pretended to be looking at his hives with the keenest of interest.

"You know deuced well, m'dear, that your cousin cannot keep a secret longer than the space of a breath, at least not from me."

"But that is because you have wheedling ways, my dear sir," she returned, smiling up at him.

"That much is true!" he responded, apparently pleased.

"Am I to presume then, that you know the particulars?"

"Of course," he returned. "Of *both* wagers."

"Both?" she cried, alarmed anew. "Whatever do you

mean? Would you be speaking of something ridiculous your son and his cohorts have concocted?"

"Perhaps," he drawled. He appeared very satisfied with himself in this moment.

"As usual, I can see that you mean only to torment me."

He pressed a hand to his chest. "You wound me, Miss Godwyne! Indeed, you do!"

She turned toward him, laughing. "There can be no use prevaricating, for I see the truth in your eyes! What a devil you are, Mr. Douglas! Your wife should have long since had you secured in the village stocks for a year or two to teach you not to harry young ladies of quality!"

He laughed heartily at this, just as she supposed he would. She also knew that however loose Margaret's tongue had been, Mr. Douglas would be as silent as the grave about the other wager, so long as his silence amused him.

Movement drew his attention to the left. "Is that Frith?" he cried. "I thought he was with you."

Lord Frith moved swiftly down the path leading to the long stretch of grass near the lake where the picnic was to be held. "He drove me to the front door but insisted upon seeing his own cattle settled in your stables."

Mr. Douglas grunted. "Sapskull," he murmured disparagingly beneath his breath. "As though I haven't the finest head groom in the county—save for Connought's, of course!"

Harriet knew Mr. Douglas held a very poor opinion of her most stalwart suitor, an opinion which was corroborated by the appearance of a honeybee or two, at the sight of which Lord Frith began flailing his arms and running out of harm's way. Even she could not take umbrage at the disgusted snort which erupted from Mr. Douglas's nose and mouth.

Harriet cleared her throat. "And are your bees happily

employed in making the county's finest honey this year?"

"Yes, indeed, they are!" he responded enthusiastically.

They were stationed by the windows, looking down into immaculately groomed gardens in which the domed and spiraled roofs of the hives could be seen scattered throughout. Though the situation of Mr. Douglas's land in a rather flat stretch of the Medway Valley did not lend itself to grandeur, she rather thought the cheerful, gentle sprawl of his gardens, punctuated by tall yew hedges, was far more charming and welcoming than many other local manors of better situation.

"Ah, here is Connought," he said. "He marches like a soldier. I always suspected he envied his brothers, all three of them having served at Waterloo. Cut from the same cloth, that lot."

"And all wed except him," Harriet observed.

"He is waiting for the right woman. I daresay she will be along shortly. I do believe, this summer in particular, that he has arrived at that age when a man feels the want of a wife. He may not have articulated such a thought, but I see it in him."

Harriet watched Connought move briskly down the same path that Frith had used not a minute earlier. She wondered if this much was true. Was there such a thing as a man becoming desirous of the wedded state? She could see several bees swirl about his shoulders, but he ignored them—as any sensible man would. He stopped suddenly and whirled around. Muffled through the windows, she could hear him say, "Charles! Where the devil have you been!" His object clear, he began retracing his steps.

Harriet continued to let her gaze follow him. He slapped his hat against his breeches in an attempt to dislodge some of the dust from the countryside, revealing a head of dark brown hair which he kept cropped *a la Brutus,* as was the prevailing fashion. His features were even, his blue eyes keen and intelligent, his jawline determined. His figure was something remarkable to behold, and in this he cast all the gentlemen she knew quite in the shade. He was a confirmed Corinthian, with broad shoulders and muscular thighs, strong evidence of this particular predilection. However, she rather thought that it was his height, at over six feet, which gave him so remarkable an appearance. Other men might be taller, but the combination of his height and his athleticism put her forcibly in mind of a thoroughbred.

Harriet knew Mr. Douglas was speaking, but his voice had become an odd sort of hum in her ears. So Connought was in want of a wife. What a curious sensation suddenly afflicted her chest, as though fingers had taken hold of her heart and squeezed very hard.

She drew in a deep breath, her gaze fixed on the earl. Mr. Douglas was right. He did march about as though he was commanding a regiment instead of crossing a garden to greet an old friend.

She could only smile, particularly when she recalled the kiss of yesterday morning. She had been stunningly aware of the strength of his arms surrounding her and could recall thinking that she would never feel so safe again as she did in that moment when she was locked in his embrace. An odd tingling sensation swept over her arms and chest as though she had just been immersed in warm water. Her heart, most oddly, began to ache in the sweetest way imaginable.

When Connought met Charles, together they continued moving back in the direction of the stables.

Mr. Douglas's laughter disrupted her reveries.

"What is it you find so amusing?" she asked.

"You," he responded, turning her about and offering his

arm again. "And now I wish to see you ply your bow and arrow. You have a precision of eye that quite pleases me."

"That is all very well and good, but why were you laughing?"

"My dear," he responded, "I will say only one thing. If you permit any other lady the marrying of Connought, I will forever consider you one of the silliest goosecaps of my acquaintance!"

Following Charles past the stables, Connought at last caught sight of the event which his friend had promised would provide him a vast deal of amusement. He could not help but laugh heartily at the sight of Harry Eaves leaping about in the lane in an attempt to retrieve his driving whip from an overhanging tree branch. The whip had gotten entangled on the lowest limb while Harry was passing beneath the old oak in his tilbury and trying to show Nancy Douglas what a clever nonesuch he was.

"Saw the whole thing!" Charles said between chortles. "Nearly unseated him! At least the stripling had enough sense to let go of the whip before he found his face in the dirt."

"Where is Nancy?"

"She, quite wisely, returned hastily to the house with Alison and Sophia, even though his sisters laughed themselves silly at his expense. Do you know, I think Alison grows prettier every day. One day I do believe she may even rival Jane in her beauty."

Connought turned back to the gardens with Charles. "Have you formed a *tendre* for Alison?" he queried.

"Good God, no! I have merely been noticing of late that any number of the younger neighborhood misses have begun to flower quite prettily. I vow I have not seen such a bevy of beauties in a long time, not since Harriet arrived some seven years past and bowled us all over with her looks. Faith, Connought, do you remember how we all stared the first time we saw Harriet?"

"I do, indeed!" Connought returned. He could not help but recall that first fateful day. The month had been July, just as it was now. She had been wearing a pink gown, which set off her light brown curls to great advantage. A beauty indeed. An elegant, oval face, a charming retrousse nose, the most beguiling of dark brown eyes that sparkled with intelligence, and lips that had been so kissable.

He was brought back to the present by a feminine voice drawing his attention to the house. Horatia Douglas, all blond ringlets and blue eyes, was leaning out an upper window and calling to Alison, who was hidden from view. Charles nudged him. "Do you see what I mean? Both Laurence's sisters are grown into beauties."

"So they have. Speaking of which, has Arabella arrived yet, or has she changed her plans to spend the next month with Horatia?"

"And have you developed a *tendre* for *her?*" he inquired, answering in kind.

"You know I have not. I merely wondered if a lady who might possibly become my wife in the very near future has yet made her way into Kent."

"Not as yet, but Laurence said she was due to arrive at Ruckings at any time. No doubt she will make as stunning an entrance as she can manage."

"No doubt." Arabella, for all her beauty, was a rather vain creature who enjoyed displaying her feathers as often as she might. In any other young lady, such absurd conduct would be deserving of a setdown, but Arabella had just such a playful nature as allowed her to transport her vanity lightly.

With Charles in tow, he made his way once more

through the maze of gardens and beehives of Mr. Douglas's estate, in the direction of the lake. He entered the grounds in time to see Harriet adjusting her stance, raising an archery bow to a suitable height, and drawing back an arrow. Frith was nearby, complimenting her as usual, but she was fixed entirely on the target some fifty yards away. There was purpose in her calculations and a certain determination that worked strongly within his heart. In this moment, he thought he understood something critical about her, how fixed she could become on any object of importance to her.

The arrow left the bowstring with a faint but quite sharp whistling sound. Frith of course applauded, but Harriet frowned, her disappointment obvious. Connought could not help but smile. Yes, he understood this much about her: she liked to hit her targets dead center.

As though having read his thoughts, she turned toward him, her bow gripped in her left hand. She eyed him in her measuring way and nodded slightly. He could see that she was entirely caught up in her sport.

He offered a flourish of a bow in return, smiled broadly upon her, and was rewarded with a slight roll of her eyes as she turned back to the target. The sun was behind her, and through the thin muslin of her gown he saw her fine figure outlined. Desire sharpened in him, as it always did when he viewed Harriet Godwyne for any length of time. He was reminded of holding her in his arms but yesterday, of how wonderfully she had felt trapped in the circle of his embrace and how for the longest moment he had known her to be enjoying the experience as much as he was.

Charles drew up next to him on his right. "That light shade of blue always suited Harriet. Good God, I am always stunned by her beauty!"

Connought turned to look at him, laughing. "You are

quite struck with all the ladies this afternoon, are you not?"

"Who could help but be so," he countered, shading his eyes with his hand as he continued to look at her.

"With so marked an interest in Harriet," Connought said, "I only wonder why you never courted her."

Charles shrugged. "I do not know, really, having never given the matter a great deal of thought. I suppose I was never convinced we would suit. She has a bit too much fire for me. Besides, you would have hardly forgiven my doing so, you know."

"There you are out," Connought returned. "I should have been well rid of her."

"The devil you would." When Margaret joined Harriet and Frith, he added, "Did you ever notice that Margaret's hair is almost pink in the sunshine?"

Connought viewed the red halo of her hair. "It is quite odd, is it not?"

"Of what are we speaking?" Laurence queried, joining them.

"Margaret's pink hair," the earl said.

"By Jove, it is pink!" he cried. "Well! What do you think of that!"

Connought chuckled. "Only that you will be wedding a pink-haired lady by the end of August, once the banns have been posted for the appropriate four weeks."

Laurence snorted. "Cocky this afternoon, I see. Well, I saw the way Harriet rolled her eyes at you but a moment ago. Hardly an auspicious beginning for a man who is supposed to achieve an acquiescence to marriage by Wednesday."

"Jane should never wear brown," Charles remarked. She was sporting a light brown silk walking dress trimmed in yellow lace.

"I've always liked her freckles though," Laurence

added. "Somehow they quite become her. She has a jolly expression because of them that even a dowdy gown cannot diminish."

"Lady Eaves ought not to have the dressing of her," Charles stated.

On that point, Connought agreed most sincerely. All three gentlemen turned to look at her ladyship, who was seated with Laurence's mother beneath a fringed white canopy and upon a small part of what was an extensive array of pillows, carriage rugs, and blankets. Lady Eaves was sporting a hideous poke bonnet of enormous proportions, an orange veil thrown over the top of it against the July sunshine. She tended to fat and fairly spilled from her purple gown.

"I do believe she looks like a purple-fruited eggplant," Laurence murmured.

"Good God! So she does!" Charles exclaimed.

Since Lady Eaves nodded in their direction at that moment, Connought held his smiles with some difficulty as he offered a bow in return. He quickly redirected his attention to Harriet. "I can see that Frith means to remain fixed by her side, so I will simply have to begin waging my war in spite of his presence—unless either of you lads would be willing to disengage him for me?"

Laurence and Charles exchanged a glance.

"Do you think we ought to make his task any easier by coming to his aid?" Laurence queried.

Charles smiled confidently. "He will hardly succeed in winning Harriet, of that I am certain, so I do not see why we should not assist him, if but a little. I daresay Frith would not object to a game of billiards if he thought he could *win* a few pounds."

Connought listened to this disparaging comment on his abilities and shook his head. "Doing it up rather brown, Charles!" he stated roughly, then laughed.

The gentlemen were as good as their word and immediately set upon Frith, teasing him to a game of a billiards, dangling the promise of a pound per point if he would oblige them. Though Connought could see his hesitation in abandoning his post beside Harriet, the battle was actually won when Harriet said, "Oh, do go have a game or two, Frith! I might do better without you at my elbow!"

"I say, Miss Godwyne—" he protested.

She lowered her bow and patted his shoulder. "I only meant that I find myself quite distracted, something for which no female could possibly blame me." Her smile was so sweet, incredibly so, that the wonder to Connought was that Frith actually believed her. So he did, however—or at least chose to—and was soon marching in the direction of the house.

With that, Connought was free to begin his own assault on Harriet's heart. Only how the deuce could he succeed now when she had proven so prickly in the past? There was nothing for it, however. He had a wager to win, and he had no intention of letting his doubts keep him from succeeding at his object.

Six

A few minutes later, Harriet greeted Connought upon his approach and immediately sensed that he had come to her with some design in mind, though just what she could not imagine. She recalled Mr. Douglas speaking of a wager the gentlemen held amongst themselves and had become convinced some intrigue was abroad the moment Charles and Laurence led Frith away.

For her own part, she had been plotting just how she was to acquire at least one of the requisite articles in order to fulfill her own wager with Margaret and Jane. She was therefore happy to welcome him no matter what his motives. Behind him and outside the range of his vision, both Margaret and Jane made motions by way of wishing her well, then excused themselves to sample a very fine peach ratafia about which Mrs. Douglas had been boasting not a half hour prior.

Connought's gaze followed them. "You know, Harriet, you would do well to recommend to Jane to leave off wearing brown."

"I have told her often and often, but her mother favors the gown."

"In which case, Lady Eaves would do well to place herself under the tutelage of Mrs. Weaver. Her daughters are always gowned impeccably. I do not see her, however."

"She remained at Shalham. She said she had some

business to attend to that could not be postponed. I am, however, very much in agreement with you. Lady Eaves has not the least sense of proper fashion and poor Jane wears that odious gown strictly to please her. Do you think that wrong of her?"

"Actually, I think it quite devoted."

"Jane Eaves is a very good girl," Harriet responded. "Too good at times, but then some would say I would be wise to emulate her."

He glanced at her. "I would not say as much," he said. "You are a spirited young woman and there are many, like myself, who far prefer a little pluck to so much gentle submissiveness."

Harriet frowned slightly. She could not recall the last time Connought had actually offered a compliment. What was he about? she wondered. Regardless, she could see the moment was favorable to begin her own campaign.

"You seem to be in high gig today," she offered.

"I suppose I am. But then, if you will recall, I won a wager yesterday, so I am very much disposed to being content with the world."

His reference to having kissed her on the day before ordinarily would have caused her to answer him in kind. Of the moment, however, she had larger game to bring down. "Are you *sufficiently content,* then, to engage in a contest with me?" she suggested, meeting his gaze boldly. "I know you fancy yourself an expert with bow and arrow. How would you like to test your skill against mine? The winner, of course, to have something of *her* choosing."

"So in your mind you have already won?"

"Of course." She knew Connought well. He always responded to a gauntlet thrown at his feet.

"As a representative of my sex and therefore as a point

of honor, I do not believe I could refuse, but I give you fair warning, you shan't win today. I am feeling quite lucky."

"As am I," Harriet countered quickly. "Only—what do you desire, should you win? I have a ten-pound note in my reticule, or you could take a lock of my hair, or perhaps . . ." Here she smiled. "A forfeit?"

He narrowed his gaze. "I believe you mean to shock me, Miss Godwyne!" he cried playfully. Lowering his voice, he queried, "You are referring to a kiss, yes?"

She nodded, thinking it was just like him to be so easily led by anything resembling a flirtation. "You stole one from me yesterday, as you so obnoxiously reminded me, which made me think another today would appeal to you—although I must say I do not comprehend why you should desire one after all these years. How they could have the smallest affect upon you, I shall never comprehend."

"Oh, men who know nothing of honor take their kisses where they might."

Harriet stared at him, her mouth slightly agape. She did not know what to say. Of course he was referring to their argument of yesterday, and though she immediately desired to defend her position on the matter, she thought it would hardly serve her to once more point out his flaws. She therefore remained silent, though she could feel her lips were pursed in annoyance.

"I beg you pardon, Harriet," he said. "I should not have spoken thusly. I fear I was tempting you to berate me again, and it was unkindly done, particularly when you have been so civil to me today."

"I hope I am always civil."

"Yes," he admitted, "you are. To your credit, you have never spoken harshly to me save when I deserved it, and yesterday I had most certainly earned a dressing down.

I should never have teased you and accosted you in that blackguard manner as I did. Forgive me?"

He appeared so sincere that she could only nod. "Of course."

"As for your offer of a kiss, I shall accept it, but I beg you will not be deceived on any score." He leaned forward, his breath touching her cheek as he spoke. "*Your* kisses always affect me!"

Even though he drew back quickly, Harriet felt a spate of gooseflesh travel with lightning-like speed down her neck and side. She had trouble catching her breath. She looked into his eyes and felt lost for a very long moment, unable to think of anything to say.

Fortunately, he filled the gap once more. "But what of you? Should you chance to win our contest, what do you want of me? I should happily let you have a kiss as well, if that is to your liking this afternoon."

The entire conversation had Harriet on her heels. By now, she found it exceedingly difficult to place one thought before the other. Instead, she found her gaze locked to his, the suggestion he had just made swirling through her mind. Another kiss? A very deep sigh passed her lips.

Almost she agreed to it, forgetting for a moment her own particular reasons for having suggested the contest in the first place. A sudden breeze blew over the sloped lawn, across the lake, and tugged at her light blue skirts, redirecting her thoughts once more.

She turned around, letting the cooling wind drift over her face. Perhaps if she did not look at Connought, her mind would clear and she would once more be able to converse rationally with him. On the lake, Harry Eaves was standing up in a small rowboat, causing it to rock ominously, while Nancy Douglas squealed her fears of being tossed into the water in her very fine gown of cambric overlaid with silk.

She laughed at Harry's antics and was truly grateful for the distraction, but she remembered suddenly that this was how it had been with Connought when she had met him some seven years past, the teasing, slightly naughty banter that had captured her fancy so completely. She had fallen under his spell as quickly as the cat could lick her ear. Then he had kissed Margaret, and she had come to understand that what might be a transient delight to the senses was not always worthy of lifelong devotion.

She drew in a deep breath. "Your watch," she declared, turning back to him. "I have always admired it. What do you say to staking your watch?"

"My watch?" he returned, clearly startled.

"So you do fear losing our contest," she stated, taunting him.

"Of course not," he countered. A frown puckered his brow, and he appeared to be wrestling with her demand. "Very well, then. If this is what you wish for, then my watch shall be the prize."

"Do you have it in your possession?"

He pulled it from the pocket of his waistcoat and allowed her to see it.

Harriet's heart leaped. Her breath caught in her throat and she felt tingly from head to toe. Yes, she dearly loved a contest! "Then it is settled?" she asked.

"At least the nature of the spoils," he returned, eyeing her carefully. "As for the challenge, I want something that proves our abilities. I suggest that we engage in no less than five separate contests today for the purpose of accumulating points, ten arrows each time, say, on the hour? At the end of the afternoon, after all five contests have been played out, only then will there be a true winner."

"I like your idea very much," she cried, smiling. "Particularly since I am persuaded my abilities become sharpened the longer I ply my bow and arrows in a given day."

"Very well," he said. "An afternoon of archery it shall be, my watch wagered against your lips."

Harriet gasped slightly. In the excitement of the moment, she had forgotten how very roguish he could be. At the same time, she trembled at the thought of losing the wager. Would he truly kiss her? Of course he would! There could be no two opinions on that score, and she would let him, since it would be a matter of honor.

As she set about negotiating with him as to how many points to assign to each of the three rings of the archery target, she marveled at how easily their relationship had changed once she had agreed to her wager with Margaret and Jane. Again, she pondered the nature of the mischief he was engaged in. Given how badly they had quarreled in the cherry orchard—was it only yesterday?—she was suspicious of his kindly attitude toward her. If he was truly involved in a wager himself, and one that appeared to include her, his actions in this moment could only be viewed as highly questionable, probably even reprehensible if she knew the man before her.

Points were assigned to the various rings of the targets, five points for the center, two points for the middle, and one point for the outermost ring. A penalty was then assessed to missing the target altogether—a forfeit of ten points. A harsh penalty, indeed! Once an hour, they would each take ten shots, alternating five and five, then repeating, for a total of fifty for the day—a great many shots, unquestionably! Harriet had little doubt that her back, shoulders, and fingers would ache before the day was through, since each shot would matter.

When the party as a whole learned that there was an ongoing contest in progress, although terms were said to be merely a wager of ten pounds to the winner, the picnic came to revolve around the contestants. Frith, having lost forty pounds to Laurence and Charles at the billiard table, was greatly subdued and spent his time obligingly bringing Harriet each discharged arrow, as any good puppy might, while Charles and Laurence took turns helping their friend.

Harriet could only laugh at their antics, for by the time two hours had passed and the third round of arrows was about to be aimed at their respective targets, both Charles and Laurence were in a jolly state, having imbibed a great deal too much of Mr. Douglas's home-brewed ale. Connought would be fortunate to get his arrows at all.

The third contest began with the scores being quite close. Harriet was in the lead, at sixty-eight to sixty-five. She was pulling back the bowstring for her first shot, when Connought called to her in a quiet voice. "Hold, Harriet, for just a moment."

She immediately lowered her bow, surprised at the interruption, and wondered what had caused him to stop her. Glancing at him, she could see that his gaze was caught by something past her shoulder. Just as she turned, a melodious feminine voice explained Connought's odd conduct.

"What am I missing, pray tell?" Arabella Orlestone called out. "It would appear I have arrived at a most intriguing moment. Are we having an archery match?"

Harriet turned to see Arabella standing on a slight rise which overlooked the gathering of the neighborhood families. She waved to the crowd, a broad smile on her lips. She was sporting the most magnificent of bonnets, which possessed a massive poke of cherry red silk accented by three large and well-draped white ostrich feathers. The elegant, stylish confection framed her porcelain complexion, black ringlets, and large green eyes quite to perfection. The added feature of a large bow tied beneath her right ear caused a general gasping.

Evan Douglas and Harry Eaves hurried forward to draw the diminutive beauty into the circle of onlookers, while the latter hurriedly explained the nature of the contest.

"Oh, how very exciting!" she exclaimed, clapping her hands so that her matching reticule of red silk bobbed several times in the air. She was a picture of spring loveliness, and Harriet was filled with a sudden and unexpected desire to—what had Margaret said only the day before about Lady Eaves?—a desire to pull her nose! She was irritated further when Connought begged Arabella to come forward and touch his arrow for good luck. Harriet rolled her eyes anew and turned away. Good grief! Could the pair of them be any more ridiculous than they were?

For some reason, Mr. Douglas's words of earlier came to her. *If you permit any other lady the marrying of Connought, I will forever consider you one of the silliest goosecaps of my acquaintance!*

Would Connought consider wedding Miss Orlestone? She stole a glance in their direction just as Arabella placed her gloved hand on the arrow and offered a dimpling curtsy to him at the same time. She then whirled away and took up a place beside Evan Douglas. Harriet would allow her this: however magnificent her entrance, at least she knew when to retire!

Harriet once more lifted her bow and aimed her arrow. She found, however, that her arms trembled slightly, something she was certain had everything to do with Arabella Orlestone. She fired anyway and narrowly hit the outer rim of the target, earning a single, quite undistinguished point. Her next four shots were scarcely much better, though she did manage a respectable center shot for the last of the five. Her score was seventy-nine and since Connought, whose first arrow had been graced with Arabella's magical touch, had performed far better than she, she found herself outmatched by eight points!

For the second group of five shots, she fared extremely well, ending with a score of one hundred and one to Connought's one hundred and three.

At this juncture, since both Laurence and Charles were fairly staggering about under the influence of Mr. Douglas's ale, a fine picnic dinner was served.

Seven

Spread out on a long table was a varied and delectable dinner including an excellent Yorkshire ham, slices of cold chicken, boiled leg of lamb, pickles, a slice of tongue, broccoli, cauliflower, potatoes, and several sauce boats which three footmen carried to each of the guests in a continual procession of hospitality. Consulting her own preference, Mrs. Douglas served champagne, or her much-prized peach ratafia if the ladies preferred, claret, and as much ale as the gentlemen desired. Though a remove of deserts was promised as well, she suggested that the fourth contest in turn would make an agreeable interlude between the meal just consumed and tea, which was always accompanied at Mrs.Douglas's table with an array of treats designed to satisfy the sweetest of palates.

Harriet took up her place once more, feeling that nothing so delightful as an excellent meal could add to her sense that she would in the end win this particular contest. Her beginning was uneven, however, and after five shots she had reached but one hundred sixteen when Connought took his turn to fire the first five of ten arrows. He fared little better and was leading her by only five. Another round of shots and the fourth game came to an end. She still trailed six points at one hundred thirty-four to one hundred forty, which might have cast her down a trifle had there been scarcely a person present who did not marvel at their combined accuracy. Neither had missed the target itself once in forty attempts.

"I vow after five shots," Lady Eaves cried, "I should have fainted because of the heat alone!" Indeed, even seated beneath the canopy, which had been drawn close to the contestants, her face was bright red against her purple gown.

Harriet took up a seat on a large, comfortable pillow and permitted Frith to fetch her a cup of tea and a plate of sweets. She smiled at the speed with which he performed this service, and she realized he always strove to please her in everything, yet his obvious love for her had not tempted her even once to the altar. Why? she wondered.

She thanked him for the tea and the plate of what proved to be a nicely arranged assortment of sweetmeats, macaroons, biscuits, a narrow slice of cherry pie, and a raspberry tartlet, but she found herself entirely unable to converse with him. Drawing the cup of tea to her lips, she scarcely tasted the lovely bitter brew, for her thoughts were fixed on the contest and on Connought. Ten shots remained. Would she secure the watch, or would she be required to relinquish yet another kiss to him?

She lifted her gaze from the plate, settled somewhat precariously on her knees, and watched as he flirted quite audaciously with the beautiful Miss Orlestone. How her eyes sparkled, how she tossed her black curls now freed from her bonnet, how she trilled her laughter at something or other Connought said to her. Could a lady be more pointed in her attempts to bring a gentleman up to scratch? She thought not. Someone ought to warn the beauty that her eagerness would not win the day, and yet she had to admit there was nothing in the earl's demeanor that suggested she was giving him a disgust. Indeed, Connought seemed well pleased with her—almost as much as she was with him.

She continued watching him and wondering. She could not remember having passed so pleasant a day with him in a very long time. Certainly the activity of having a contest to occupy their minds had kept them from brangling. Yes, there was that. But he also seemed so attentive and solicitous toward her, something she had not experienced from him in a long, long time, a circumstance which once more set her suspicions to work.

Regardless, she realized she had been enjoying his company prodigiously.

His coat had disappeared at the outset of the match so that the elegant breadth of his shoulders was continually on display. She thought yet again that there was no man so handsome as Connought. Why wouldn't Arabella be ready to split her face with so much smiling?

When Frith asked her if the pie was to her liking, she forced herself to finally withdraw her gaze from Connought and instead attend to her loyal swain. Though she had some difficulty in concentrating on his discourse, since her mind was still snagged by her need to win Connought's watch, she made a valiant effort to listen to his description of the horse he had apparently sold to Connought so many years ago.

"The finest stallion!" he cried, his black eyes glittering with fond remembrance. "I had meant to breed him to several of my best mares. There was no finer thoroughbred to be found at Newmarket the year I acquired Lightning Velvet. Connought had him for a time. Then he sold him to some Irish horse trader."

Harriet frowned faintly. "I do not understand, Frith. If you had so great a fondness for the horse, why did you relinquish him?" Mr. Douglas might have called Frith a sapskull for having seen his horses properly tended to at his stables, but Harriet's long acquaintance with the baron had given her an understanding of his love of his horses.

He shrugged. "A moment of madness, I suppose. Connought possessed something I wanted, so we agreed to a trade."

"Then you did not sell it to him?"

"No. Is that what Connought told you?"

Harriet shook her head. "We never discussed it. I suppose I always assumed he had purchased the horse from you. What, then, did he offer in trade for so superior a horse, I wonder?"

At that, Frith seemed a little conscious. "Let us just say that I entered into an arrangement with him that has not yet proved as beneficial to me as I had at one time hoped—an investment of sorts."

Since he appeared completely disinclined to offer details of the trade, she could hardly comprehend his meaning. He did, however, turn more fully toward her and laugh. "I am, however, quite hopeful of eventually receiving a very high return for my investment." Much to her surprise, he suddenly took her hand in his, lifted her fingers to his lips, and saluted them with a kiss.

He was so far from being a gallant gentleman that she could not help but chuckle as she released his hand. "Doing the pretty today?" she queried.

"No," he responded. "Merely *attempting* to do so, and with scarcely the success I wish for. Must you always laugh when I kiss your hand?"

"Am I in the habit of doing so?" she queried.

"Unfortunately, yes!" he returned.

She chuckled softly a little more, her gaze once more drawn to the sight of Connought flirting with Arabella. "Then I shall try to do better," she responded somewhat absently. Connought offered his arm to the petite beauty and began leading her in the direction of the archery targets once more. "I see his lordship is ready to begin again," she murmured, setting aside her plate and cup.

Frith helped her to her feet. "I believe he is," he remarked cryptically.

Harriet detected a subtler meaning and might have inquired as to what he meant by it, but at that moment Connought picked up his bow and a nearby arrow and began fitting it against the strings. Her heart once more soared with excitement at the prospect of shooting the last of the arrows, of watching Connought attempt to hold on to his lead, of trouncing him instead and winning his watch. How much she longed to do so!

The fifth and final contest drew everyone to the targets, particularly since the score was so very close. Within a few minutes, the entire party was grouped in a semicircle behind the archers.

Harriet picked up her bow and a single arrow once more. She took careful aim, but her heart had begun pounding in her chest. She knew she was far too excited to aim as accurately as she could wish for, but there was nothing for it. She released the bowstring and hit the middle ring. Two points.

She picked up another arrow, but Margaret called out. "On this last round, Harriet, why do you not alternate?"

The suggestion was cheered by the crowd of onlookers.

"An excellent notion," she cried, deferring to Connought. She hoped in doing so the pounding of her heart might decrease.

Connought strode forward, glanced at her, and winked. She thought she understood him—he wanted to win . . . and he wanted his kiss!

He lifted his bow, and with steady hands and a careful eye aimed his arrow true. Harriet knew he had hit the center mark before ever she heard the sharp twang of the bowstring. She now trailed him by nine points. She groaned inwardly. Would she win a watch this day or lose a kiss? Which did she truly prefer? But she could not think of that, not now as she lifted her bow anew.

Her ridiculous heart! If only it would settle into a proper cadence! If only she had not remembered that she had wagered a kiss! Twang! The crowd groaned. She missed the target entirely!

Connought approached her and whispered. "Is something amiss?"

She was embarrassed and frustrated. "I most stupidly," she began, whispering, "thought of the nature of our wager and the prospect of losing!"

He caught her gaze and an odd, wild light entered his eye. "I hope you do lose," he returned.

She gasped.

He picked up his bow and aimed at the target. He stamped his foot. He lowered his bow. He shook his head and laughed, and then she understood. Now, *his* heart was hammering in a manner that did not allow for excellent marksmanship.

Zip!

Another groan of the crowd followed by a great deal of laughter.

Connought, too, had missed the target entirely, and he turned and bowed to her. The relief she felt was enormous, and with such relief came a settling of her heart into a steadier rhythm.

She aimed her arrow. Thump! Five points. He matched her.

Fourth shot, five points. He matched her again. Fifth

shot, five points. Again, he equaled her score, still leading her by nine points.

On the sixth shot, Harriet once more fired perfectly. Connought lifted his bow, aimed and hit the middle ring! Two points—which gave her a gain of three.

Harriet drew in a deep breath. The lead had been closed to six, with four arrows remaining. She thought of his watch. She aimed at the center circle. Twang! Five points. The crowd cheered. He nodded to her and smiled in acknowledgment of five shots in a row at five points each. He fired again—another five points!

How long could she sustain her perfect score? She drew in another deep breath. Steady. Steady. Thump! Her eighth shot was once again perfect! Five points! *Six in a row at five!* The crowd broke into a roar of applause and cheering.

Connought aimed. Twang! The middle ring again! Harriet gasped. The lead had closed to three at one hundred fifty-six to one hundred fifty-nine. Two shots remained.

Harriet thought only a miracle could produce seven in a row at five points, but all she had to do was to think of the watch and her wager with Jane and Margaret and her heart grew as calm as a cat sleeping in the sunshine. She released the arrow. Zip! Five points. More cheering and huzzas! Even she could not credit her performance. She felt giddy.

Connought took aim. Thump! Five points. The crowd groaned. He still led by three points.

Connought turned back to look at everyone, a crooked smile on his lips. "And who will champion me against so formidable an opponent?" No one lifted a voice in his defense, not even Arabella Orlestone. He laughed heartily at this, as did the crowd.

The time for the last shot had arrived. Harriet took

aim, steadily, carefully. Once again, her heart grew very still. Zip! The crowd sent up a startled cry as she hit her eighth perfect shot in a row. She wanted to celebrate, but all Connought had to do to win the match was hit the center ring one last time. She turned toward him. She tried to breathe, but found she could not. He took exceedingly careful aim. Zip!

When the crowd broke into another cheer, her gaze flew to the target. He had hit the middle ring. The match was tied on the fiftieth shot.

Harriet swallowed. Her heart was beating so quickly she still could not quite draw breath. He drew close to her. "It would seem the game begins anew."

She nodded but whispered. "Unfortunately, my heart is racing again. I fear I shall once again miss the target entirely."

"Thinking of the kiss?" he whispered.

She thought it quite unhandsome of it to have said as much, though in truth she had not been thinking of the kiss at all. "No, as it happens, I am not! However, now that you mention it . . ." She simply looked at him and let him think what he would. She wondered.

Your kisses always affect me.

She continued to eye him, a smile on her lips.

She watched his eyes narrow. "Trying to cause me to stumble?" he queried.

"I will only say this . . . you spoke first!"

He grimaced. "So I did. Served with my own sauce."

"Uh-huh," she responded. She gestured to the arrows."Shall we, then?"

He nodded.

She slid an arrow against the bowstring. Even though her shoulders and arms ached, just as she knew they would, a wonderful confidence came over her, something she was certain she owed to Connought in this moment. She took deadly aim and, without hesitation, let the arrow fly. The crowd roared the moment she struck her ninth five in a row.

Connought bowed to her and another crooked smile passed over his lips. He took up his arrow and slid it against the bowstring. He lifted the bow, took careful aim and with a sharp twang, sent the arrow flying.

Had Harriet not seen the result for herself, she would have known it by the sudden roar of the crowd and that a moment later Margaret and Jane had fairly jumped on her and were twirling her in circles. Connought had hit the middle ring. She had won the contest! She had won the watch! She was well on her way to winning her wager!

When she had calmed down a trifle, she allowed Connought to congratulate her properly. He took her hand in his and there, couched within his palm, was the watch, concealed from view. She took it from him with a smile and, with Margaret and Jane still near, she quickly slipped it into the deep pocket of her gown.

"An excellent match, Harriet!" he said. "Perhaps next time I shall win and then receive a far better prize than the one I have given you."

He moved away a little as others crowded about her. The congratulations flowed for several minutes as everyone came forward to compliment her on her performance, particularly her succession of perfect marks at the end of the match. Harriet felt as though she was bursting with delight as she shook hands and embraced one after the other of Mrs. Douglas's guests.

After a time, the party began to disperse, some to revisit the table of refreshments, particularly the gentlemen, who noted that Mr. Douglas's butler had brought forward a fresh keg of ale, others to stroll about the perimeter of the lake. Harriet was just replacing the bow in its proper case, along with the five arrows, when Connought approached her.

"You were rather magnificent at the end of the match," he said. "No one could have beaten you."

"Except you," she returned, eyeing him carefully. "Only what possessed you to tease me about the kiss? You knew there was nothing I could do but answer in kind."

He grinned. "And that is precisely what I have always expected of you, though I must admit I forgot myself in that moment. What a halfling I was to bring forward the notion of kissing you."

"Too green by half!" Harriet cried, laughing.

"It was always thus," he said, holding her gaze forcefully. "Between you and me, that is. Kissing you—"

He got no further, for at that moment, a footman approached her with a missive in hand.

"A servant awaits a response, miss," he said politely.

Harriet was surprised and could not imagine who would find it necessary to deliver a message to her, particularly when nearly everyone from the surrounding estates was already present. She broke the seal and scanned the contents.

Connought, who had remained by her side, murmured, "What is it? You are grown nearly as pale as a ghost."

"My parents are arrived at Shalham. This note is by my mother's hand. She says my father is quite ill and has been so for some time. I must go to them . . . at once!" She addressed the servant. "Be so good as to inform Mr. Weaver's man that I shall be returning at once to Shalham."

"Very good, miss."

"I do not understand," Connought said, a frown creasing his brow. "If your father is so very ill, how has he been able to travel such a distance—for I can only presume they have come from Hertfordshire."

"Yes, that is the case. I had a letter a sennight past from my mother saying they were fixed at home for the rest of the summer. I . . . I believe you must be right, unless there was some desperation. And if that is the case—"

"Say no more," he said hurriedly. "Speculation is foolish. You must go to them at once. Allow me to drive you to Shalham that you might be at ease."

She shook her head. "It is not in the least necessary, Connought," she responded. She realized she was trembling as she glanced about the various groups of guests.

"For whom do you search?" he queried.

"Frith. I feel I ought to lay the matter before him."

"I saw him earlier go into the house, but permit me to say that I am as perfectly capable of driving you as Frith!" he cried, clearly offended.

She was slightly taken aback. "Yes, of course you are, Connought. I did not mean to offer any disrespect. However, he was so kind as to have escorted me here that I feel under some obligation to allow him to return me to my aunt's home."

She felt she had given him a reasonable answer despite the sudden anger in his eyes and fully expected him to let the matter drop. Instead, he hooked her elbow. "You would do better to allow me. Frith . . . is not all that he seems to be."

"What do you mean?" she asked, surprised.

"Only this—I have for a long time felt you ought to be warned away from that man. You do not know what he is."

"And you do?" She was piqued that he should criticize her most faithful beau.

"Yes, as it happens, I do."

"I would ask you to enlighten me, but I am persuaded you cannot. I am fully acquainted with the degree of animosity that exists between you and will say only that I have come to know him quite well over the past seven years. He is in every respect a gentleman. He would never think of brangling with a lady as you do so easily with me!"

"What?" he cried. "Is this your opinion, that somehow because we quarrel on occasion that I am not a gentleman?" He laughed harshly. "Harriet, were you always so missish? Have you so narrow a view of the world, of love? Yes, that's it, is it not? Love must be orderly and without bumps! Good God, I never knew you until this moment. My dear girl, I begin to believe you know nothing of the world."

Harriet was livid, and in her ire tears filled her eyes. "I . . . I must go to my father!" she cried. "You will excuse me."

He was immediately contrite. "Harriet, I am so sorry. I should not have addressed the matter at such a time. Pray forgive me! Of course you should go to your father."

"Yes, I most certainly should," she murmured.

"Let me fetch Frith for you."

"No, Connought. He has just emerged and is coming to me."

"Again, I apologize. My timing was truly wretched." He bowed, if a trifle stiffly, and moved away from her.

She watched him go, feeling utterly bemused by him. He had behaved so very oddly today that she simply did not know what to make of him. As he approached Arabella, however, a new sensation surfaced, something she did not want to feel in that moment—a renewed desire to pull the raven-haired beauty's small nose!

She gave herself a slight shake and began walking

swiftly to meet Frith. When he reached her, she immediately showed him her mother's missive.

"Then we must go," he stated. "Come. We shall walk directly to the stables."

A few minutes more and they were bowling down the lane in the direction of Shalham Park.

Eight

Once at Shalham, Harriet bid good-bye to Lord Frith and hurried into the house. She passed quickly through the entrance hall, tugging off her gloves in sharp jerks, afterward entering her aunt's formal drawing room. She felt rather faint, her imagination having worked quite feverishly the entire trip from Ruckings to Shalham. She had imagined no less than seven fatal diseases presently at work within the now undoubtedly shriveled body of her once powerfully framed parent.

She found her father seated in a wing chair, grimacing strongly as he shifted sideways in an apparent attempt to make himself more comfortable. She saw at once that though he had not become an emaciated corpse, his foot was heavily bandaged and supported by a prettily embroidered footstool, one of a half dozen similar footrests scattered about the long chamber.

She would have addressed him immediately, particularly since he smiled in that familiar warm manner upon seeing her, but her mother was before him.

"Harriet, my darling!" she cried, rising swiftly to her feet from a sofa of lavender silk damask and crossing the room to her. She embraced her fondly. "Do not tell me you left Mrs. Douglas's party so precipitously? We did not expect you for hours!"

From the grip of her mother's affectionate hug, she

craned her neck to see her father more clearly. "Your note, Mama, seemed most desperate. Only, how are you, Papa?" she asked, disengaging herself as politely as she could from the cradle of her mother's arms and moving to stand before her father. "Is . . . is your illness serious?"

"The gout," he complained bitterly. "That is all, dearest, the gout. I begged your mother not to compose that ridiculous missive, for I feared just this, that you would hurry here when it was not in the least necessary." He glanced past her and glared at his wife.

Harriet was bewildered and also looked at her mother. *"The gout?"* she queried. All seven diseases, from the apoplexy to the plague, disintegrated from her mind. *"A swollen toe from the gout?* Your note sounded as though he was at death's door!"

"Well, if you had heard all the moaning to which I was subjected from the time we quit Hertfordshire, you would not wonder at the manner in which I sent for you. He certainly persuaded me he was very near to sticking his spoon in the wall. How was I to know it was merely the gout? Once we arrived here, your aunt sent immediately for her favorite physician, and I must say she is most fortunate in having one of England's finest doctors but a mile from Shalham! While your father was being examined, I sent for you, since I had not yet learned the nature of his illness and I was greatly concerned. I suppose when I wrote my note, it expressed my worst fears, and for that I am sorry. By the time good Dr. Mersham informed me of just why your dear papa was afflicted with so many desperate pains, it was too late to rescind my summons that you attend us immediately." She then huffed an impatient sigh. "Of course, the treatment is simple enough. He must do as I have been begging him to do this past twelvemonth and more. He must stop drinking his bottle of wine each night!"

Harriet turned back to her father. "Papa! You drink an entire bottle of wine? By yourself?"

"Now, now, I will not have you complaining as well. What is a bottle with supper?"

"Sometimes two bottles," her mother muttered darkly.

"If you would hire a new cook," he shot back, "I would not need to wash each bite down with an entire glass of claret. That last haunch of venison was nearly splintered, it was so dry."

Harriet found herself quite speechless, nor did she understand the meaning of the situation. "You traveled all this way because of the gout? To see Dr. Mersham?"

"No!" her mother cried. "Of course not. I have long been desirous of paying my sister a visit, particularly in the summertime, because she has for the past three years boasted of having the finest flower garden in all of Kent. The gout," she added bitterly, "was merely the wretched nuisance which insisted upon accompanying me." She returned her husband's glare.

Quite bemused by so much antagonism between her parents, she asked hurriedly, "Is John come with you? Or Marianne?" The twins were just eighteen.

"No," her parents chimed.

"They were both engaged," her mother explained. "John is in Margate on holiday with his particular friend, Mr. Lymbridge, and Marianne would not leave Hertfordshire, since she is become much attached to Mr. Hawking's society. She is residing with Isabella Brabourne. You remember Isabella?"

"Yes, of course, but you surprise me when you speak of Mr. Hawking. Is he not twelve years Marianne's senior?"

"Yes, it is most promising, for as you know he has three thousand a year and a very pretty wood attached to his manor, but your father can do nothing but complain of the match."

"The fop wears a quizzing glass! It is beyond pretentious. What next? Will he take to bathing in rose water, as Brummell was used to do?"

Harriet withheld a sigh. She tried to recall more of her youth and wondered if her parents had always been this trying. She had not lived at home for several years, having her own handsome quarterly allowance and residing much of the year in London in a town house with her cousin and companion, a widow, Mrs. Farthingloe. She worried that something had arisen to have disturbed their usual marital felicity.

Mrs. Godwyne gestured to the sofa. "Pray, sit down, Harriet, and we will enjoy a comfortable cose." She took up her former seat and patted the cushion next to her by way of invitation. Harriet joined her, glancing from parent to parent as yet uncertain. "There, that is much better. So how are you enjoying Kent?"

"It is quite beautiful this time of year," she responded, still waiting for some hidden truth to surface. "The orchards are heavy with leaf and fruit."

"The Garden of England, Kent," her father offered.

"Mama," she began quietly, "is everything satisfactory at Paddlesworth?" The ancestral home of the Godwyne's bore a name that had always been of particular charm to Harriet.

"Infinitely so," her mother returned, "except, of course, that Cook—who is *not* so unworthy as your father has suggested—has her recurring sniffles, which seem to afflict her every spring and summer. She grows worse during the hay-making season."

Harriet listened and nodded. "So all is well at the manor?"

"Yes, I have said so."

Harriet was wholly bemused, for she could not in the least account for her parents' sudden arrival at Shalham.

Her father intruded, "I have need of a pillow for my back, dearest Eugenia. I hope you will oblige me."

Harriet glanced sharply at her father. There was just such a tone in his voice that would have set up the back of a saint.

Her mother ignored him quite steadfastly. "I vow my roses have never been so full or so fragrant as this year. Old Bing attributes it to the mixture of his mulch, but I think it was because of the steady rain all spring—not too much nor too little."

"A pillow, *Eugenia?*" the request resounded again.

Harriet moved to retrieve one, but her mother caught her arm and gave a small shake of her head. "Now as for the broccoli, I fear we lost most of our flowering heads to the white moth caterpillars, but . . ."

"Mrs. Godwyne, if you please!"

At that, her mother turned to her husband. "If I please, what, Mr. Godwyne?"

"A pillow for my back. I have asked you three times!"

"I did not travel all this distance to wait upon you! Why did you insist on coming when you were so unwell? You would have been wiser to have remained at home and tortured the housekeeper with your incessant demands!"

"A pillow . . . now!" he snapped.

Mrs. Godwyne narrowed her eyes, reached behind her, and flung a small pillow at her husband. It hit him in the chest.

Harriet gasped once, and then a second time when her father threw the cushion with as much force as he could manage at his wife's head. The pillow dislodged a silk flower from amongst her silvery brown curls, and it was as though her head sprouted snakes. She rose to her feet and began a tirade that stunned Harriet, for it ranged from the complete selfishness of the being before her to his intrusiveness in having journeyed with her in the first place when it was as plain even to a simpleton that she wished to travel *alone* into Kent for once in her poor, desperate life.

She was still ranting and pacing several minutes later when Harriet finally stole from the room. Once in the entrance hall, she was met by her aunt, who bore a sewing bag in one arm and a bottle of laudanum in the other.

"Oh, dear," she murmured, but not without a smile. "I see that my sister is in prime twig. I daresay the servants will have a great deal to laugh about this evening as they sit down to their supper. Do you know that I could hear Eugenia from the housekeeper's room?"

"Aunt, I am deeply distressed! Whatever is the matter with them? I have never known them to brangle so!"

Mrs. Weaver appeared quite perplexed. "No? I cannot imagine how it could have escaped your notice or perhaps . . . oh, I daresay they were more circumspect when you were still in the schoolroom. Marianne's letters are always full of their latest row."

Harriet was so stunned she could not speak. She stared in some wonder at her aunt.

Mrs. Weaver smiled and laughed. "Come, my dear! Surely you are not so missish as to actually believe your parents are any different from the rest of us."

Harriet frowned as Connought's scathing criticism returned to her. Was it possible she knew very little of the world? "I am not certain I take your meaning. For one thing, I have never heard you brangling with my uncle."

"We do so in private." She fell into a muse. "I remember one particularly sanguine evening several years ago when we had been *discussing* the proper age for Margaret to come out. I threw a very fine, and very expensive, ormolu clock at my husband's head. Very sad occasion that was!"

"Did you injure him?" she asked, much shocked.

"What? Oh, goodness no. That is to say, the bump did not recede for four days and he sported a very large sticking plaster for nigh on a fortnight—though I have always been persuaded that was strictly to torment me!—no, no. When I said it was a sad occasion I was referring to the loss of a much beloved clock. It fell to the wood floor and shattered to bits. *Very sad occasion, indeed!* And now, if you will excuse me, I believe a little laudanum will end this unfortunate spate of brawling. My brother-in-law, I fear, is in a great deal of pain, and he married the most unsympathetic woman in the world. I love my sister dearly, but I fear she has a heart of steel!"

"And they have come to visit you. If they continue to quarrel in this manner, how will you bear it?"

Her aunt regarded her for a long moment. "If you must know, Harriet, they did not come to visit me especially. As it happens, I sent for them, on your behalf. Well, I sent for your mother, and your father refused to be left behind at Paddlesworth. I suppose it could not be helped. He detests being left out of anything that has the appearance of a party."

Harriet could not have been more surprised if her aunt had thrown a cold glass of water in her face. "You sent for them on my account? But why?"

"My dear, I do not like to mention it, but you have made a terrible muddle of things, and your parents are here to help you sort things out."

Since there was a loud crashing sound from within the drawing room, Harriet was struck with the notion that her parents were the least likely persons to be of use to anyone, let alone herself, certainly not for the present. "I do not know what you mean. What muddle?"

Mrs. Weaver nodded her head knowingly. Shifting the

bottle of laudanum to the hand clutching the sewing basket, she patted her arm. "Just as I suspected. Poor child! You have not the smallest notion how things stand, have you? It has been rumored these past three weeks that Arabella Orlestone is about to become engaged to Connought. Yes, well you may stare, and now you know why your mother and father have come."

Harriet's mouth fell agape. She knew Arabella had designs on Connought, but in her opinion there had been very little in the earl's demeanor to suggest that he would soon be offering for her, particularly if he was still ranging about the countryside and accosting young ladies of quality in cherry orchards for the purpose of stealing what kisses he could. "No, I believe you to be mistaken. It is gossip, after all. Besides, even were it true, of what use can either Mama or Papa be should Lord Connought offer for Arabella?"

"As to that, I am not certain, but since you are still in love with him—no, no, it is of no use protesting to me! I have seen the pair of you together for years and if ever two people went about smelling of April and May, despite the quarreling . . . well! At any rate, I felt a push ought to be made. Arabella Orlestone is a very good girl in her way, but I do not wish to see her installed at Kingsland. She would be the most trying neighbor! As for the gossip, Laurence Douglas informed me they were as good as betrothed only yesterday."

With that, Aunt Weaver swished quite efficiently into the drawing room. "Here we are!" she called out, effectively ending the squabble.

Harriet stood very still and stared at the formal black and white tiles beneath her feet. Laurence Douglas believed Connought to be ready to offer for Arabella? She felt very odd, as though the foundation of her life was slipping away right beneath her feet. She slid her hand into her pocket and smoothed her fingers over Connought's watch. Connought and Arabella?

She felt in a state akin to panic. Retrieving her gloves from the table near the drawing room where she could hear her aunt's calm voice explaining to her father all the benefits of a very mild dose of laudanum, she turned and mounted the stairs to her bedchamber. Once within, she sat on the edge of her bed for a very long time, indeed.

Nine

On Saturday morning, Harriet awoke to the oddest sensation that she had misplaced something. She lay very quiet, staring up at the ceiling, where some very pretty frieze work formed an elegant circle.

Lifting her arm and resting the back of her hand on her forehead, she sought about in her mind for the source of the wiggling of anxiety which moved through her so steadfastly. She had Connought's watch. She certainly had not misplaced that! Her parents were under her aunt's roof and, though she wished them anywhere but at Shalham because of their wretched squabbling, her aunt's invitation made it clear they would be staying for a considerable time.

She sat up abruptly, as the reason for her anxiety revealed itself. "Connought and Arabella!" she said aloud.

The strangest drift of nausea passed through her stomach. Indeed, for the barest moment she felt quite ill. Was he truly going to propose to her? Was that why Arabella's green eyes had sparkled so brightly at the picnic yesterday? How at ease she now suddenly seemed to Harriet, as though everything was as good as settled between them.

And yet . . . and yet Connought had flirted with her during the archery contest. He had! He had told her that her kisses always affected him, and she had believed him. She squeezed her eyes shut as more of Mr. Douglas's words came to her: *I do believe, this summer in particular, that he has arrived at that age when a man feels the want of a wife.*

What if it were true? Was it possible after so many years Connought was now inclined to marry and would actually consider wedding so insipid and vain a female as Arabella Orlestone?

She crossed her arms over her chest and scowled. If he did, she thought ungenerously, then he deserved her! He knew Arabella's temper—she would plague Connought to death before the end of the first year of marriage. She ought to have taken some delight, some comfort in knowing he was about to receive the punishment he so richly deserved for his having used her so ill, yet she could not.

Instead, she recalled with too fine a degree of clarity for comfort his diatribe of the day before. *Is this your opinion, that somehow because we quarrel I am not a gentleman? Were you always so missish? Have you so narrow a view of the world, of love, of life?*

She jumped from her bed and began pacing the floor. She felt as though she was walking on hot coals. She was *not* missish and she did *not* have a narrow view of the world. Yet even her aunt had hinted at something very similar. She refused, however to believe she could be so very wrong about these things. Love and marriage were meant to be joyous, honorable estates, engaged in with purity and forthrightness. Connought had betrayed her by kissing Margaret. How could he then say she was being missish? Rather, he should have honored her for her principles.

She stopped in her pacing and chanced to look at what she now realized was a quite rumpled bed, which appeared as though the counterpane had been kicked about at will for most of the night. Clearly she had been troubled even in her sleep to have made such a mountain of her bed linens. As she examined in the most dispassionate manner possible all the events of the last seven years that had kept her separated from Connought, she could still find no fault with her decision to end their betrothal, only a terrible dislike of Arabella Orlestone.

She rang for her maid and decided that her ruminations on what she felt was a quite ridiculous subject were a fruitless occupation. She turned instead to contemplate something of a much happier scope—the archery contest of yesterday, which ended just as it ought to have ended, with her being in possession of Connought's watch. In this, she had no regrets, no frustrations, no ripplings of anxiety. In this, she was perfectly content.

She smiled, drew a deep breath, and decided that whatever her aunt or Connought might think about life, love, and marriage, these were not her concerns today. Today, her only desire was to do something that would give her the strongest pleasure and could even be accomplished at breakfast. With her thoughts directed toward a much happier quarter, she hummed while her maid dressed her hair and assisted her in donning a sprightly yellow-flowered walking dress of a very fine calico.

Descending the stairs with the earl's watch bouncing in the most delightful manner against her leg, she went in search of Margaret and most fortuitously found her at breakfast in the morning room. She was herself famished and thought the encounter wholly serendipitous.

The chamber was a cheerful place, its pale pink walls and colorful chintz curtains encouraging even the dullest spirits not to despair. In the center of the room was a round, highly polished table at which

Margaret sat reading a small calfskin volume, a cup of tea settled before her.

She lifted her gaze from her book and showed Harriet the title, which proved to be a copy of Fordyce's sermons. Margaret shook her head. "Who can read this without wishing to crawl into a grave?" she complained, tossing the book aside.

Harriet chuckled. "Is there no one else abroad yet?" she inquired, moving forward.

"Mama has taken soup to an ailing neighbor, and my brother and sisters have already completed their breakfast. As for your parents, I believe your father requested a tray in his room and your mother is still abed."

"And Uncle Weaver?" When she reached the table, she picked up the leather-bound book.

Margaret grinned. "He, of course, is locked within the confines of his study."

"Of course." Mr. Weaver was of a bookish nature and spent most of every day closeted in his favorite chamber and reading a great variety of works. Turning the book over in her hand, she frowned slightly. "Where did you get this? Is it your father's?" she asked.

Margaret grimaced. "He would never have given the book to me to read, believing as he does that the female mind is incapable of rational thought."

"Oh, dear! Do not tell me Lady Eaves gave this to you yesterday?"

Margaret nodded. "Apparently, she believes I am in some need of improvement, my spirits being far too elevated to be at all seemly!"

Harriet shook her head. "Though I do not like to speak ill of anyone, she can be the most trying creature."

"Poor Jane."

"Indeed, poor Jane. And that purple gown!"

Margaret lowered her voice. "Laurence said she looked like an eggplant—the purplish variety, of course!"

Harriet averted her face and bit her lip, for the entire conversation was not at all proper. However, a chuckle escaped her when for a moment she met Margaret's dancing eyes. Afterward, she made her way quite speedily to the sideboard, upon which was settled a wondrous variety of dishes.

Having chosen toast, eggs, and thinly sliced ham, Harriet was about to return to the table when the pounding of running footsteps was heard in the hall beyond. She froze purposefully in her steps. She had little doubt what was to follow, having years ago endured the antics of siblings seven years her junior, and was not in the least surprised when her cousin, Edward, just twelve, his eyes shining with triumph, raced into the chamber, a bonnet dangling precariously at the end of one of its ribbons from his tormenting fist.

"Do not tell Constance I have been here!" he adjured his eldest sister in hushed accents.

"Not a word!" Margaret assured him as Edward passed into the garden, closing the door quietly behind him.

Harriet, hearing more footsteps not far distant, still did not move, for the drama surely was not over yet. Constance, but two years older than Edward, her face red with fury, burst into the chamber.

"Where has that beast of a brother gone with my best bonnet?" she demanded of Margaret.

Margaret, having taken a sip of tea, settled it on the saucer, and pointed toward the door. "Into the garden, not ten seconds past!"

Constance darted toward the door and Harriet, in order to keep her plate from becoming a casualty of the sibling war, whirled around in a circle away from her cousin's hasty and determined movements.

Once Constance had disappeared through the door and she could be heard shouting at her brother, Harriet turned toward Margaret. "But you told Edward you would not say a word!" she said, grinning. "Rather ignoble of you, I think."

"Edward should have been given a brother with whom to exchange a proper amount of torments. As it is, even I have been so sadly afflicted by his pranks that I have no reason to keep my word to such a cretin. Boys! What monsters they all are, and to think we grow up only to tumble in love with some gentleman, glowing with a little Town Bronze, who undoubtedly spent much of his childhood in just the same manner of mischief!"

"It is a wonder," Harriet agreed, settling her plate on the table and taking up her seat. "John was not very much different. But he is eighteen now and hardly interested in torturing Marianne, and I have not lived at home for years!"

"How do they fare?"

"John is preparing to enter Cambridge next term and is presently enjoying all the pleasures of Margate. As for Marianne, she chose to remain behind in Hertfordshire to continue receiving the attentions of Jack Hawkhurst."

"Do we know Mr. Hawkhurst?" she asked.

"Only a very little. Mama rather fancies his home wood but Papa thinks his quizzing glass quite foppish."

Margaret shrugged. "But it is Marianne who will have to live with him. I am certain she does not give a fig for his home wood and as for a quizzing glass, all the younger gentlemen wear them these days."

"Sounds like a match, then," Harriet smiled.

"We shall certainly know soon enough. Your sister writes quite often to Mama."

"She has always been excessively devoted to Aunt Weaver, and who would not be? Your mother is a saint."

"Very nearly," Margaret agreed with a sigh. "She never raises her voice, except on occasion to Papa when he has remained cloistered in his study for too many days in a row."

Harriet's thoughts were drawn instantly to her aunt's story of the broken ormolu clock. Repressing a sigh, she turned her attention to her breakfast.

After she had made an excellent meal and discussed at length with Margaret a particularly fetching bonnet she had seen at the milliner's shop in Kenningford, she remembered the watch hidden in her pocket. A fine piece of devilment occurred to her.

"What is that sound?" she asked, pretending to hear something.

Margaret glanced toward the door to the gardens. She shook her head. "I hear nothing unusual. One of the stable boys calling to . . . ah, yes, the scullery maid. I believe he is violently in love with her."

"No, not that sound. Another one, rather like church bells."

"I still hear nothing."

"You are much mistaken, Margaret," she said, rising to her feet and sliding her hand in her pocket. Moving to stand directly behind her cousin, she continued, "I hear the bells quite distinctly, *wedding bells,* as it happens! Your wedding bells, surely!" She dangled the elegant piece of plunder beneath her nose, almost to the table.

Margaret's hand sliced through the air as she jerked the watch from Harriet's hand. "You won the watch from him! Yet you said nothing last night! How very sly of you!"

"Not so sly as you might think. Actually, because

of my father's gout and my mother's exacerbated temper, I forgot all about it until I had long since retired to bed."

Margaret stared at the fairly simple silver timepiece and shook her head. "So, you won the watch," she repeated. "I never thought he would relinquish it."

Harriet took up her seat once more. "Nor I," she admitted, frowning slightly. "Which only makes me wonder why he did."

"Who can say?" Margaret murmured, shrugging slightly. "But though I do not like to mention the matter since you are so completely transported by your success of yesterday, I feel it my duty to point out to you that you have but five days remaining—today, Sunday, Monday, Tuesday, and Wednesday until midnight—to secure Connought's riding crop, let alone his emerald."

Harriet blinked at her. Somehow in laying out the days as she had, Margaret had forced her to see just how little time she truly had left in which to complete the terms of the wager. She realized how foolish she had been to have agreed to such difficult terms when so much was at stake. Of the moment, she felt quite foolish and not a little frightened.

Margaret handed her the watch with a rather imperious lift of her brow. "Now whose wedding bells are you hearing?"

Harriet snatched up the watch and once more tucked it away in the deep pocket of her gown. "I will not permit you to spoil my sense of triumph in the least. I won Connought's watch in a very difficult contest, of which I am exceedingly proud."

"Yes, yes, that is all very well and good, but I do believe your right eye is twitching!"

A servant appeared in the doorway.

"What is it, Sheldwick?" Margaret queried.

"A note, miss, from Lord Connought. His lordship's man awaits a response, if you please."

"Thank you," she murmured, extending her hand. The servant approached the table.

Connought. Harriet could not escape him even for a single morning.

Margaret took the missive, broke the seal and scanned the contents swiftly. "An invitation to nuncheon at the Bell!" she cried. "Jane has been included, as well. Although, I wonder . . . do you think we should accept?"

Harriet saw the teasing light in her eye. "What a vixen you can be. Oh, but do wait! I believe I hear those bells again—and not for me!"

"I beg you will stubble it, Harriet! You were lucky yesterday, that is all!" She rose to her feet and addressed the servant. "I shall send a note in response. See that Connought's man partakes of a little refreshment. I shan't be above fifteen minutes."

"Very good, miss."

Harriet watched her cousin quit the chamber, and her former thrill at having succeeded in already getting Connought's watch was intensified by the prospect of being able this very afternoon to attempt to acquire one of the two remaining articles. She thought it even likely he would be using his riding crop, for the gentlemen often rode into Kenningford rather than tool their gigs or curricles.

Her thoughts turned to the manner in which she needed to set about teasing Connought into giving her either the crop or the emerald. She thought it likely that were she too bold in her efforts, the earl might become suspicious and grow wary of her stratagems. Then she would be in the basket, indeed! No, she must be clever and quite discreet if she hoped to win the wager.

She could only wish yet again that she had been wiser

at the outset and not permitted Margaret to hold her to a mere sennight for the wager. A fortnight would have been a great deal better. However, what was done was done, and for now she must turn all her thoughts to the Bell and whether or not a different, more provocative gown would better suit her purposes.

Ten

A bend in the High Street of the village of Kenningford revealed a great many beauties as a lovely sweep of fifteenth century, timber-framed cottages and shops came into view. The day was idyllic, and with the promise of traipsing through any number of mercantiles in an ever-present hunt for treasures that delighted the feminine eye, Harriet hooked arms with her two dearest friends. "I shall forget for the moment that a most difficult chore awaits me and shall instead be content with seeing if the milliner has sold the bonnet I have been admiring. If not, I begin to think I shall purchase it today!"

"I begin to comprehend your design!" Margaret cried.

"Indeed?" Harriet returned innocently.

"Yes, for I now recall that the bonnet is a lovely shade of cornflower blue and until this very moment I could not account for your having changed your yellow gown for this white muslin and a spencer of blue-flowered calico."

Harriet could only laugh. "Connought once told me he favored me in blue. I thought it best to make every effort since, as you so kindly reminded me at breakfast, I have but five days left to fulfill my part in the wager."

"Oh, dear!" Jane cried. "Is it really only five days? Whatever shall you do!"

Harriet grimaced. "Do you mean to frighten me as well?"

With that, Jane laughed.

After spending an hour so agreeably engaged, Harriet now sported the lovely blue bonnet as all three ladies made their way up the High Street to the Bell Inn.

Harriet's pulse quickened as she mounted the stairs to the private parlor on the first floor. How willing, she wondered, would Connought be to relinquish his riding crop? As she entered the parlor, however, she saw at once that the gentlemen had not yet arrived. Awaiting her was one of the earl's footmen who bowed and immediately made Connought's apologies.

"Are you saying they are not to come?" Jane inquired impetuously.

"I beg yer pardon, ma'am," the servant said, turning to Jane, who was in the process of removing her bonnet, "but his lordship will be here and wished me to tell you that the fault is Mr. Badlesmere's, since at the last moment, his horse threw a shoe and there was nothing for it but that the gentlemen must return to Kingsland." He paused, then added, "And I was to offer you lemonade, or ratafia if you prefer, while you await their arrival."

Harriet released a sigh she had not known she was holding. She had been so ready to begin her campaign to get his riding crop that to be presented with the necessity of waiting a little longer somehow served to take the wind from her sails. She removed first her spencer, since the day had proved quite warm, and then her bonnet, the latter a disappointment in itself, for she had been so certain that in wearing it she would have caught the earl's eye and hopefully gained an advantage over him.

Settling the bonnet on a table by the door, she added her request for a glass of lemonade.

Once the servant quit the room, both Jane and Margaret turned toward her, laughing.

"I wish you might have seen your face!" Margaret cried.

"Yes," Jane agreed. "I have never seen an expression fall so quickly before."

"I beg you will stop laughing at me! It was just that I had been so prepared to do battle. Can you imagine my frustration in finding that the opposing general had not yet arrived on the field?"

"Five days," Margaret drawled provokingly.

"Oh, hush!" was all Harriet could think to say to her.

Connought slapped his riding crop on his gelding's haunches and had the delight of feeling the excellent beast lengthen his stride. Hedgerows with blackthorn in full leaf, the white blossoms having long since given way to sloe berries, lined both sides of the avenue.

"Make haste!" he cried. "Or the ladies will quit the inn completely exasperated!" The pungent smell of the dry dirt lanes was fully reminiscent of youthful days spent in mischief. Sheep in a nearby field darted away from the sounds of their hooves.

He leaned forward, slapping his crop against his horse's flank and settling more deeply into the steady gallop. Whatever the day might hold, whatever his own progress might be this afternoon in winning Harriet's heart anew, this moment would always belong to him, of feeling the warm sun on his shoulders and the rush of air beating against his face.

Behind him, he knew his friends were pushing their

mounts as well, for the lane thundered with the sound of pounding hooves.

He laughed aloud. Life was good.

A half hour later, Harriet took to pacing the long chamber. She had long since finished her first glass of lemonade and poured herself a second, and still the gentlemen had not yet arrived. She wondered just how long she and her friends should wait for them. As she walked, she worked to quiet her nerves with the feel of the watch bouncing against her leg and reminding her that she was not without the power to succeed in her ridiculous campaign. Would Connought give up his riding crop easily today? What would she have to do in order to persuade him to relinquish another article to her? She could only hope that regardless of what happened, he would not become too curious about her sudden interest in possessing his things or, worse still, interpret her actions in a romantic sense.

The sound of riders approaching drew her to the window. "They are come at last," she called back to her friends. Margaret and Jane joined her, and all three ladies watched the gentlemen dismount their sweating horses. Stableboys raced from the innyard beyond to take charge of the well-lathered beasts.

Margaret pushed back a length of muslin. "Why do all men appear most lively after they have been riding? They are never this content, for instance, when engaged in a country dance."

"That may be due to your dancing!" Jane countered teasingly.

Margaret shrugged and smiled rather sheepishly. "You may well have the right of it. I have no skill in a ballroom."

Harriet chuckled at this exchange, but her gaze was fixed to the men below. The gentlemen did seem at their best in such moments as these, their features alive with the exertion of having ridden into the village with great dash and flare. Connought wore a coat of Russian flame, a sturdy brown woven waistcoat, buckskin breeches, and glossy top boots. His hat he slapped against his leg and along the sleeves of his coat in an attempt to remove some of the dust from his clothing.

He chanced to look up and, upon seeing her, doffed his hat and made a grand, flourishing bow that was utterly ridiculous.

She could not help but smile, and in smiling her heart seemed to pause and then burst into its next beat. She could never gaze upon Connought, particularly when he was smiling, without feeling a little overpowered. Always when she but looked upon him, she felt the strongest tug of attraction, a sensation she doubted a thousand ill-fated kisses would ever diminish.

When the gentlemen passed through the doorway below, she turned away from the windows. She discovered that her heart was racing, a circumstance which caused her to place a hand at her bosom.

"Harriet," Margaret called to her. "The color on your cheeks is quite high. Are you well?" Since these words were accompanied by a tormenting smile, Harriet ignored her, particularly since the gentlemen were now heard on the stairs.

Connought marched into the parlor well before his friends, having fairly ran up the stairs. After the excellent gallop, all of his senses were heightened as he entered the ancient, timber-framed room, which had seen several centuries of use. The smells from the kitchen below and the redolence of a fine, home-brewed ale acted like cannon shot to his appetites. The wonder of the simplest of pleasures flowed over him in a brisk wave—ale, food, and the company of women he admired. Did life hold any greater enjoyment than this?

"Since we knew you would be riding hard to keep your engagement with us," Harriet began, "we provided you with a little ale." She gestured to the sideboard, upon which sat a tray bearing three full tankards.

Connought, being closest, grabbed the first and nearly tossed it, laughing, to Laurence, who in turn settled it with a hard thump on the table in front of Charles, who had seated himself beside Margaret. When each of his friends had a tankard in hand, he lifted his own and proposed a toast. "Will you ladies take up your glasses of lemonade?" When they followed suit, he continued, "To fine nuncheons in July at excellent inns, to gallops on a dry country lane, and to the company of lovely ladies."

"Hear, hear," the gentlemen intoned.

He watched Harriet smile as she in turn exchanged amused glances with Margaret and Jane.

Over the rim of his mug, he eyed Harriet, wondering just how the deuce he was to make her fall in love with him before Wednesday at midnight. Faith, but she was beautiful today. She stood near the window gowned in a summery walking dress of white muslin embroidered with small blue rose buds about the bodice, a trim which drew his eye to the swell of her bosom. She was undoubtedly a handsome woman in every possible respect.

A stray sunbeam struck her light brown hair, reflecting a glittering of golden highlights. When she found him staring at her , she smiled anew, which for some unaccountable reason had the effect of squeezing his heart. The devil take it, he thought! Would he ever be free of his love for this chit?

Only she was no longer a young miss just emerged from the schoolroom. She was a woman who carried herself with all the assurance of one who had experienced seven years in London, a woman who knew her own mind. Although, in truth, Harriet Godwyne had always known her own mind. That was the rub. She had rejected him seven years past because of a wager and now, while caught in the grip of new wager to win her heart, he risked being rejected again.

He took a long pull on the tankard, and afterward resisted the urge to smack his lips. *Courage, lads!* Which of his military brothers was used to say that at the beginning of a campaign? All of them, no doubt. Well, there was only one thing to be done. He must begin his assault now or never.

As a stream of servants entered the chamber bearing a generous nuncheon repast, he crossed the room to her and watched as a speculative gleam entered her eye.

"You seem quite pleased with yourself," she began, her smile broadening.

"Not with myself," he countered readily, "but with this beautiful day!" He gestured in a sweep toward the windows and the blue, sunny skies beyond.

She turned and let her gaze drift over the rooftops of the shops opposite and a rise of weald beyond. "Exquisite," she murmured.

"Indeed," he responded, but he was looking at her. He could never look at Harriet in such close proximity without remembering what it had been like to kiss her not just recently, but for the very first time.

He had courted her assiduously, as had a dozen others, for besides being a diamond of the first stare, she was also a considerable heiress. However, he had not been long in her company without sensing that her affections inclined toward him, in part evidenced by the sparkle of her brown eyes whenever she would look at him and in part because her suitors quit the field, one after another, within but a fortnight of his having become acquainted with her. To his knowledge, she had never spoken a word to hint any of them away. Rather, she had never been shy in making her choice known in her conduct. He had understood himself to be first in her eyes almost from the start.

He had taken the lead immediately and had guided her on a riotous and joyous courtship that had culminated one night in taking a stroll into the rose garden at Ruckings Hall, where he had simply gathered her up in his arms and kissed her.

She had been an utter delight to embrace, as though she was a piece of heaven come to earth. There had never been the smallest hesitation in her as she slung her arms in response about his neck and gave him kiss for kiss in what was an embrace as full of inexperience as it was of passion. Harriet had been an innocent and he a man too full of himself to comprehend the gift he had been about to lose.

The absurd wager with Frith had followed that very night. The next day, he had kissed Margaret in order to keep his land. That same day, he had lost Harriet.

Here she was, however, standing before him, still unwed, still quite as beautiful as when she had been in the first blush of youth. Yet here he was, caught up in another wager. Could he make her love him with but five days remaining? What arts must he employ?

He took a step forward, drawing close to her, and whispered against her ear, "Do you ever wonder what might have been?"

He heard a faint gasp pass her lips. She took a small step backward so that she was nearly touching the window. She looked up at him, her brown eyes seeming in that moment as ancient as the inn sign now creaking in a sudden gust of wind. The windows rattled.

"Of course I do," she whispered, pain flashing through her eyes.

"Forgive me, Harriet," he said hurriedly. "I did not mean to grieve you with such words. For some reason, as I watched you just now, I was reminded of our season of courting and how much I delighted in you."

He expected her to beg him to cease speaking of such things. Instead, her expression became arrested, almost speculative. He could not know her thoughts, so he continued. "What do you think we would say to one another if this was the first day we met?"

He watched a shy smile touch her lips as she averted her gaze. He wondered if she would dare answer such a question. He was a little surprised when she responded swiftly with, "I would imagine I would find it difficult to say anything to you, at least at first, but I would watch your every movement all the while hoping you did not notice my interest."

"Is that how it was?" he asked, almost on a whisper.

She lifted large brown eyes to him. "I recall that when I first met you, Connought, I felt as though I was thirsty but could not drink enough to slake my thirst." A blush climbed her cheeks, and he found himself so completely charmed that he wished more than anything they were alone instead of with four of their mutual friends. He glanced back at them, wondering if he could steal even a little kiss from Harriet, but though the others were seated at the table and talking together in an animated fashion, he had little doubt such a scandalous act would fail to escape their notice.

He turned back to Harriet. "That is how you felt all those years ago?" he asked quietly.

"Of course," she responded, lifting her eyes to him once more.

"But you never told me."

"Did you expect me to admit as much on a first acquaintance? And that to the finest matrimonial prize of the season? A lady would be nothing short of a simpleton to reveal such feelings to so highly eligible a gentleman."

"And later?" he asked. "You never spoke of it when our courting became serious."

At that she grinned. "I was too busily employed having my thirst satisfied. Oh, how many kisses you took from me—and we were not even engaged!"

"Shocking, I know," he murmured.

She frowned suddenly. "What of you? If this were our first meeting, what do you think you would say to me?"

He chuckled. "I would tell you how much I love your hair. Did you know that it sparkles in the sunlight?" He tugged a ringlet near her left ear.

"I see," she said, nodding. "So you would begin by flirting with me?"

"Is that how it seems when I speak of your hair?"

"Yes," she responded succinctly.

"Would you dislike it very much were I to continue flirting?"

A smile played at the corner of her mouth. "No," she responded, her smile once more broadening. Her eyes were suddenly full of laughter, and in that moment he realized that was one of the things he loved most about her, that when she laughed, her eyes danced with equal merriment.

"Then I shall be happy—"

She stayed him with a gently raised hand, glanced past his shoulder and tipped her chin in the direction of the opposite wall. "Your footman awaits your orders. I believe all is ready."

He turned, glanced at the servants now standing perfectly still next to the sideboard, and felt a jolt of frustration. He disliked the interruption immensely, since he could not help but feel he was making significant progress. Returning to once more gaze into her eyes, he said, "I suppose we must eat, but for the life of me I wish we might instead remain forever speaking thus." He searched her eyes and watched them grow pensive, even concerned. He offered his arm and added hastily, "However, I am also quite famished, as, I am certain, are Laurence and Charles. I will soon be in the basket if I keep them from their victuals much longer."

She took his arm and he watched her expression relax. "Then by all means let this summer feast commence."

Harriet took up her place at the table, wondering what had just transpired between herself and Connought. The only thing she knew for absolute certain was that had she not been in need of both his whip and his emerald in order to win her wager, she would not have permitted such an intimate conversation to have occurred between them. Since her breach with Connought so very long ago, she had taken great pains to keep him at a proper distance.

Today, however, because of her wager with Margaret and Jane, she had lowered her guard significantly. She had forgotten how adept he was at commanding her interest. She knew quite well that if she was not very careful, she stood in some danger of her losing her heart to him all over again. Flirtation, indeed!

Connought bid everyone to pile their plates as high as they wished, with good cause. The innkeeper, having ascertained that the Earl of Connought and a party of friends was to dine that afternoon, had prepared a sumptuous menu fit for the Prince Regent himself. The dishes included a succulent boiled chicken, roast sirloin of beef, several pigeons browned nicely, fillets of turbot covered in what Charles declared was a very fine Italian sauce, spinach, broiled mushrooms, cauliflower, broccoli, and a salad.

There was a camaraderie among the six guests which Harriet knew to be the result of several of their number having grown up together since childhood. Margaret and Laurence never ceased squabbling amiably from the moment a first glass of claret had been lifted in praise of Connought's excellent meal. Connought, for his part, teased Jane about having had to rescue her no less than three times over the course of their acquaintance, from the time she had gotten stuck in a cherry tree at Shalham to the more frustrating predicament of having found herself in a boat without an oar in the middle of Mr. Douglas's lake! Charles, in his turn, regaled them all with reminiscences of a ball at Michaelmas when Laurence had been completely foxed and waltzed Lady Eaves into a large pot of ferns.

The wine continued to flow, and the conversation never once seemed to languish. Harriet laughed at times until her sides ached, for Laurence had a remarkable ability to parody any of their acquaintance to such perfection and with such amusing anecdotes as rendered her nearly breathless. If, more than once, she found Connought regarding her warmly, she quickly turned away from him. She was no schoolgirl to have her head turned by a compliment or two whispered to her in the darkened corner of an inn parlor.

After a platter of fruit and cheese, along with a delicious apple pie and a dessert Madeira had been consumed, Harriet suggested that the gentlemen escort the ladies to Shalham Park, since the distance was less than two miles. She was not surprised in the least when all three men agreed to the plan readily.

Once beyond Kenningford, Harriet allowed Connought to slow his pace and, with one hand holding the reins of his horse, to cause her to fall behind the rest of the party. Not for the first time since she had begun this ridiculous wager with Margaret and Jane did she become aware that Connought could easily misconstrue her willingness to be engaged by him in conversation and even to be drawn apart from the rest of the company.

She felt fretful suddenly and glanced at him warily. Her only alternative, however, was to forfeit the wager—in which case, worse would follow and she would be required to wed Connought . . . were he willing to have her, of course. Her thoughts turned to Arabella and her glowing green eyes. Was it possible Connought was still in love with her?

"You have grown very quiet of a sudden," he announced, casting her a smile that set her heart a-flutter.

"Have I?" she parried. "Perhaps it is the strong sunshine and the afternoon hour which always beckons one's thoughts to the delights of, say, reclining beneath a shady tree and resting for a time."

"You could sleep, then?"

Harriet thought she was as far from sleep as the sun was from night in this moment. "Perhaps not to sleep, although I could enjoy reading an excellent book."

"You always were a great reader."

Harriet smiled, but her gaze was drawn to the riding crop which he carried in the same hand that held the reins of his horse. His white horse snorted as though able to read her mind, and she wondered if the fine gelding sensed her wicked purposes and intended to warn Connought of her mischief—an odd, ridiculous thought which caused her to chuckle inwardly. Only how to get that riding crop? she wondered.

"Do you ever mean to forgive me?" he asked.

Harriet glanced sharply at him. "For what?" Of course she comprehended his meaning completely, but somehow the question slipped from her lips anyway.

"For having kissed Margaret."

"I have already told you that I have."

He stopped abruptly and with his free hand took hold of her arm, meeting her gaze fiercely. "That is a whisker, I fear," he said. "Had you forgiven me I believe we would have been man and wife long since."

Harriet was not certain which had set her pulse to racing, the feel of his hand on her arm or the way his blue eyes seemed to pierce her very soul. "Connought," she whispered, but no words followed. Everything seemed to begin swirling about her in that moment, everything save his face, which was in perfect focus. His gaze drifted from her eyes and made a slow, deliberate progress to her lips. She blinked, wondering if he meant to kiss her. They were certainly some distance from the village, and a bend in the hedge-lined lane separated them from the rest of their party.

"Why the devil did you have to be so beautiful?" he began, but a scowl deepened over his features. Just as quickly as the moment had begun, it ended as he released her arm and turned back to the road. Once more he began to ride.

For her, the first step seemed to be of enormous difficulty. He had stunned her completely merely by holding her arm and looking at her. What a dangerous man he was after all!

Finally, she moved and caught up with him, but she could not speak. Her senses were still whirling, and she remained in some wonder that Connought was the only gentleman who had ever afflicted her thus. Tears bit her eyes. Here again was the true reason she had grown into an ape-leader. She refused to marry any man unless he could make the earth spin all about her merely with a touch or a glance. Wretched man!

"You will never forgive me," he stated harshly.

"Indeed, you are mistaken. I have forgiven you completely, but that does not mean that I can trust you."

He whirled on her once more. "Harriet, have I not proven myself to you a hundred times over in the ensuing years? Do you not see or comprehend how much my having met you and tumbled in love with you changed my life, my very existence? I was something of a ridiculous nodcock when you met me. I lived a debauched life, I will not deny it. I squandered my quarterly allowances, and at one point was in debt to the cent-percenters, but that has all changed these seven years. You know it has."

She stared at him, knowing that what he said was true. Everyone spoke of how greatly he had become subdued the year of his courtship, and yet . . . "I do believe you. Indeed, your present reputation supports your claims, but it was the kiss."

"Always that deuced kiss!" he cried bitterly. "It meant nothing. It was . . ." For a long moment, she could see that he was struggling within himself. "It was heedless and ill-conceived. Why will you not believe me?"

She shook her head. "I do not know," she countered truthfully. "But I have always thought there was something about it that was dreadfully wrong, even secretive and vile in origin, that to this day causes me to tremble when I think on it." She had never spoken with him so openly of that horrible event before. "Can you deny as much?"

Again, he was silent. Finally, he said, "No, I will not deny it. There was something evil in it, but I made a promise to myself that it would be the last folly of my youth."

Harriet could hardly credit that he had admitted as

much. She could not recall that he had ever agreed with her on this point. She paused in her steps. "Connought," she called to him, forcing him once more to bring his horse to a halt. "Then tell me the truth."

"There is no truth beyond what you have just said," he responded.

"But why did you do it?"

He looked away from her and shrugged. "I was a rogue, sunk in my ways, and too used to responding to every passing whim in a thoughtless manner to do anything else. Perhaps you have been right to hold my crimes against me." He then laughed, bitterly.

"Why do you laugh?"

"Because I have just remembered that if today is any measure of my life, I will very soon become betrothed to Arabella."

"Then it is true!" she cried entirely without thinking. She caught up to him and searched his face.

"You disapprove?" he queried.

"How could I not? She has but one motivation—to get a handle to her name. Or do you believe she loves you?"

He shrugged anew. "Perhaps she fancies herself in love with me, but the fact is that she is well bred, has a handsome dowry, and I could do a great deal worse than Arabella Orlestone. Even you must admit as much. Besides," he added, warming to his theme, "I must marry, and she has much to recommend her, in particular her beauty. I should not object to seeing her every morning over my eggs and toast."

Harriet was too stunned to speak for a very long time. She still could not credit that what had been merely a rumor the day before had suddenly become a terrible truth. "I beg you will not be hasty," she said at last. "I . . . I am convinced Arabella cannot make you happy."

Once more he shrugged, which caused her to think

he had resigned himself. "Again, I care little for happiness. *You* could have made me happy. Anyone else will fulfill a function, in which case it would be better if love was not involved on the lady's part. Indeed, the more I think on it, the more I begin to see that Arabella may be precisely the lady for whom I have been searching. Which puts me in mind of something I have wanted to ask you."

"And what might that be?" She was feeling so dazed that she could not imagine what he meant to ask her now.

"Do you intend to marry Frith?"

"What?" she cried.

He smiled ruefully. "Well, I have wondered time and again."

"I am surprised you would ask me such a question."

"Why? We have been friends for a very long time, and you did not hesitate to give me your opinion of Arabella's character. I felt my query to be within the context of our conversation, or am I mistaken?"

"Perhaps a little," she stated, lifting her chin a trifle. "I would not want anyone to fall prey to Arabella's ambition."

"I see," he murmured, then laughed. "But you have given me no answer. Pray, do you hope to wed Frith?"

"Why must you persist?" she asked.

"I have reason to."

"And what might that be?"

"To return the compliment of warning you once more against any such alliance. Frith is not all that I would wish for you in the married state."

She frowned slightly, but kept her gaze pinned to the dirt of the lane in front of her. She was quite uncomfortable discussing even the possibility of her matrimonial plans or intentions with Connought and did not know precisely what to say. "So you told me yesterday, but I have always found him to be gentlemanly, certainly in his conduct toward me."

"I have little doubt he has striven to appear so, but I beg you will believe me that he is not a man to be trusted."

At that, her gaze snapped to his. "And you are?" The words had been spoken before she thought how inappropriate they were. She saw at once that she had offended him, even if the context demanded that his own flaws be examined as well. "I beg your pardon," she said. "I should not have spoken thusly, particularly when we have already covered that aspect of our difficulties. Oh, dear, this is not at all what I would have wished for. I did not mean to begin brangling with you, not when the day is so very fine, and certainly not after such a delightful nuncheon."

For the barest moment, Harriet was put forcibly in mind of her parents and their brangling of the day before. She could not help but release a very deep sigh. No, this was not what she had hoped for in the least.

"Pray, do not worry your head over the matter. I am already fully acquainted with your opinion of me. You may at least *trust* me in that!"

Harriet released a sigh that became a chuckle. "I am sorry, Connought. Indeed, I am, but let us speak no more of such matters. Instead, I have just had a most intriguing notion. How would you care for a little contest just now, to be concluded by the time we reach the gates of Shalham?"

"You do intrigue me. What sort of contest?"

"A game of words. Choose a letter, any letter, and I shall choose one as well. Then we each must discover as many items in the surrounding flora and fauna that correspond with that letter. The one with the most, wins."

"And what does the winner receive?"

She pretended to think for a moment, hoping that she appeared to be contemplating the subject for the first time. "I do not know . . . unless . . . what do you say to relinquishing something of a personal nature? I could give up a lock of my hair, a ribbon, my bonnet if you wish, since I am not *particularly* attached to it, anything of your choosing."

"It is a very fetching bonnet," he said, shifting the subject slightly. "Was it not in the window of the milliner's? I am certain I saw it there but two days past."

She smiled. "Indeed it was, but how came you to notice it? Very odd in you, Connought."

"I remember thinking it would suit you to perfection."

"You did not!" she cried.

"Indeed, I did. I always favored you in blue, or have you forgotten?"

"I believe I did," she prevaricated. "Now, back to the contest."

"An article of my choosing. Is that what we were discussing?"

"The very thing."

"And you are certain this is what you wish for? I may request that you stake anything I desire?"

"Of course. I have said so. After all, it would only be fair."

"Very well, should I win this little game, I would desire . . ." Here he paused and narrowed his eyes. "Your kerchief."

Harriet gasped. She had forgotten about her kerchief. Her grandmama had embroidered the small square of cambric with her initials, HLG, along with an exquisite border of violets. She cherished the kerchief more than she could possibly say.

"Come, come!" he cried. "You will deliberate over a

piece of fabric whilst you, if I may remind you again, are presently in possession of my silver watch, which once belonged to my grandfather!"

"You are right, of course, but I wish you to know that I treasure my kerchief prodigiously."

His smile was crooked. "How well I know," he murmured.

The tenderness in his eyes was nearly her undoing. She had forgotten this about him, how completely understanding and kind he could be. She felt quite flustered. "Very well, I shall relinquish my kerchief. However, should I win, I think I would demand . . . your riding crop!"

"My crop!" he cried. "Whatever for?"

"Does it matter? As it happens, mine is old and tattered, and yours appears to be nicely worked and fairly new."

"It is," he stated harshly.

"Oh, come, come!" she cried. "You cannot mean to quibble over a piece of leather when you have already demanded of me a kerchief given to me by my grandmother, and embroidered by her hand, for my ninth birthday."

"Oh, very well," he returned.

"Excellent. And now that we have agreed on the stakes, which letter do you choose?"

"You are permitting me to go before you?" he asked.

"Of course," she returned grandly. "I am feeling quite generous today."

"Very well. *T,"* he stated confidently. "And you?"

Harriet glanced around and proclaimed, *"S."*

The ensuing competition was hardly noteworthy for two reasons: neither she nor Connought knew many scientific names, which would have helped them immensely, and the distance by that time to the gates of

Shalham was little more than a quarter mile. Harriet contrived, sycamore, shrub, stem, and slug, but Connought won the day with thrush, titmouse, tree, turnip, and trunk.

Harriet retrieved her kerchief, thinking she was the greatest simpleton in the world. "A very poor showing for both of us!" she cried. "I had thought to do a great deal better!" This was so very true, and so much was at stake, that her spirits threatened to become quite cast down.

However, when Connought took the kerchief, he caught up her fingers as well and gently kissed the back of her hand. The touch of his lips so stunned her that she no longer thought of how she had failed to get his riding crop but how such a kiss, so unexpected, had been worth her loss entirely. She could only wonder, as she passed through the gates of Shalham, just how long it would be before the back of her hand stopped tingling.

At the far end of the avenue lined on either side with well-cropped yew shrubs, Margaret appeared in the doorway. She waved with the full length of her arm, a certain sign she was excited about something. Harriet was not surprised when she began a hurried walk toward them.

"You will never guess!" she cried, once within earshot. "Jane's mama has invited all of us to a soiree this evening. Could anything be finer? I did not want our day's entertainment to end!"

"Nor I!" Harriet returned.

Lady Eaves, for all her lack of taste in matters of fashion, was an excellent hostess and because she had a very relaxed manner of entertaining her guests, a certain level of vivacity always accompanied her gatherings, which suited Harriet's temperament to perfection.

She glanced at Connought, who was smiling at

Margaret. She could not help but think that surely tonight she could contrive either the emerald stickpin, which the earl invariably wore with evening dress, or the promise of the crop. Surely!

Eleven

"So how did you fare with Harriet?" Laurence called out.

Connought walked his horse slowly across a stream just to the south of his estate, his friends trailing behind. "Well enough, I suppose. We quarreled but a trifle, so I daresay some would consider that progress."

"Hardly sufficient to get her to agree to wed you, though," Laurence said, easing his horse across the stream as well.

Connought glanced back at him. "Of course not," he answered firmly. "However, I do not despair, if that is what you are expecting me to do. I have barely begun my campaign."

"You have but five days!" Laurence cried.

"Nothing simpler than to win Harriet's heart anew," he said.

Charles snorted as his horse now picked its way across the stream. "As simple as shoeing a mare who's never known a shoe before."

At that, Laurence laughed heartily.

Connought knew there was a great deal of truth in what Charles had said, but he did not wish his friends to know even his smallest doubts. A happy thought occurred to him. "Charles," he said, feigning a sad tone. "I do believe you have the right of it, but if you do not take great care how you speak to me, I shall soon fall into a fit of the dismals!" He then withdrew Harriet's kerchief from the pocket of his coat and pretended to wipe at his eyes.

Laurence drew his horse abreast, staring at him. "What do you have there?" he cried. "I say, is that Harriet's handkerchief, the one her grandmother embroidered for her? She is forever prating about it. How the devil did you get it?"

Connought smiled. "A little contest . . . I won. So you see, Laurence, my situation is not completely hopeless."

As Charles's horse emerged from the water and he drew up on the other side of the earl, he reached for the kerchief. Connought snatched it out of harm's way.

"I cannot credit it!" he cried. "However did you get her to part with it?"

"A contest," Laurence said.

"Yes, I heard as much but *how* did you persuade her to set such an important article as her stake?"

Entering a rarely used lane which bordered one of his southerly pastures, Connought guided his mount in the direction of Kingsland, his friends following suit. He then related the particulars of the contest and watched as Charles frowned slightly.

"What are you thinking?" Connought asked.

Charles shook his head. "You lost your watch to her during the archery contest. What was it you staked in this contest?"

"Nothing to signify. Only my riding crop. But what are you thinking? I can see that something is troubling you."

"I am not quite certain, except that Harriet has been behaving quite peculiarly toward you of late, almost kindly. What do you make of that?"

Connought shrugged. "I haven't the faintest notion, nor

do I care particularly. I have only one interest here, to win this wager. If she happens to be disposed to treat me in an unusually gentle manner, I shan't complain. Or is it that you ascribe some sinister meaning to her conduct?"

"I cannot say," he returned. "But I intend to watch her more carefully. Something about this feels havey-cavey, if you ask me."

Connought watched the road ahead of him, his thoughts centering on Charles's suspicions. Was there a deeper meaning or intention to the contest she had just put forth? If so, he had no notion what it might be. However, Charles was very right in saying that she had been peculiarly agreeable to him, which made him wonder why, precisely.

Now that he considered the matter, she had been behaving oddly for the past two days. Was it possible the kiss he had taken from her in the cherry orchard on Thursday morning had had an effect? Was it possible her heart was, indeed, softening toward him? He could not say, yet he felt both encouraged and put on his guard at the same time.

The more pressing matter of the moment, however, was just how he was to go about gentling her heart further, if indeed her heart was being tamed at all.

"I say you give a ball," Charles called out suddenly, as though reading his mind. "Ladies always delight in a ball, and to my recollection more matches are made at such affairs than while partaking of a nuncheon at a local inn. What do you say to Monday night, Connought? Sunday would be far too soon to make all the arrangements, and Tuesday would not be sufficient time for you to accomplish your task. Yes, I think Monday night would be excellent."

He glanced at Charles. "So you mean to help me?"

Charles grinned as he gathered up the slack in his reins. "My dear fellow, you need all the help you can get!"

Connought rolled his eyes. "Regardless of your opinion," he retorted, "I could never saddle my housekeeper and butler with such a task. They would leave my employ on the instant. Have you not the faintest notion how much would be involved in giving a ball?"

"I suppose you are right," Charles responded.

"Not a ball, then," Laurence said, giving his horse a kick to keep up with the others. "A party, with dancing, thirty guests at the most. Although it might be a trial for the ordinary household, we are not speaking of a manor house with a small staff like Ruckings, but of Kingsland! Doing it up too brown to say you haven't the resources or sufficient servants to manage a little party, even if it is late notice."

Connought thought this over and knew quite well that a fete of limited proportions was something his excellent housekeeper could manage quite nicely. He also knew that Charles was right. Nothing held so much charm as a ball in the eyes of the ladies, and there could be no better occasion upon which to complete the task of winning Harriet's heart, particularly with the soiree this evening and whatever mischief he could manage on Sunday.

"Very well, my friends, I am persuaded two days' time would not throw my staff into complete confusion. A ball it shall be."

Once more he set to woolgathering as thoughts of Harriet again took possession of his mind. He recalled just how she had looked at the inn, standing with the sunlight beaming in the window and glancing in a shower of golden rays off her hair. She had grown even more beautiful over the past seven years and would probably do so until she was well into her dotage. He had felt that powerful sensation, so familiar to him, while speaking with her, as though a great volume of water was building behind a dam that threatened to burst at any moment. Laurence may have challenged him to win her heart anew, but he was beginning to accept the truly wretched fact that he was in danger of losing his own all over again instead.

The whole business was so deuced prickly, he thought. After today's conversation, he understood even better than before the depths of her distrust of him, so how was he to go about breaking down that particular reserve, nonetheless so quickly? Something about the challenge of it really brought joy to his heart. He had felt for a long time that someone ought to bring Harriet to her senses about how ridiculous her stubbornness was about the kiss he had taken from Margaret. Who better to do so than himself?

"Laurence," he said. "Did you suggest to Lady Eaves, oh, let us say at the picnic yesterday, that a soiree this evening would be just the thing?"

"Naturally," he said, grinning. "I find it beyond pleasurable watching you make a cake of yourself."

"And Lady Eaves was not in the least hesitant?"

Laurence shrugged.

Connought turned the other direction. "I daresay you said nothing to Lady Eaves about our wager."

"Good God, what do you take me for? A bleater like Laurence?"

The two men turned to stare at Laurence, who had taken to looking at the blue sky overhead and whistling rather loudly.

"The devil take it, Laurence, have you not an ounce of discretion? The wonder of it is that you kept that deuced wager with Frith a secret for so many years!"

At that, Laurence stopped whistling. "The stakes were wretched, dear boy," he returned. "I would not have breathed a word for the world. As for this wager, well, as it happens, you are quite mistaken. I did not tell Lady Eaves at all."

"But you did tell your father, of course! What a simpleton you are! Did you think he would fail to tell your mother and she, Lady Eaves? By now I expect the entire neighborhood knows of this folly."

"As to that, I would hazard a guess you may be right."

Connought shook his head. "I vow, Laurence, you are worse than the old women who sit in the back pew of the church, always gabblemongering about everything and everyone."

He grinned. "I shan't be in the least affected by you coming the crab over such a trifle. Besides, both my mother and Lady Eaves always thought Harriet the right female for you. Mama also vowed she had not seen anyone do the pretty so charmingly as you did yesterday at the picnic!"

"Good God! Was I that obvious?" he cried, startled.

"Cow-handed by half!" Charles cried.

"How would you know?" Connought retorted, "when you were half foxed by three?"

Charles scowled slightly. "By God, I was, wasn't I? Well, never mind that. Only tell us what you mean to do next in your attempt to win Harriet back—request her garter in the next contest between you?"

Connought laughed aloud, thinking Harriet would strike him hard across the face should he dare to suggest anything so improper to her. Or would she? he wondered suddenly. She was, as even his friends had noted, behaving quite differently of late. Perhaps she would not be so offended as he thought. Well, there was one way of ascertaining the truth—when he met her next this evening at Lady Eaves's home. He might not suggest her garter, but there were other things equally as wonderful.

* * *

That evening, as Harriet entered Lady Eaves's drawing room, she was struck yet again by the odd circumstance that whatever her ladyship might have lacked in fashion expertise, her home was meticulous in its furnishings, perhaps in great part because she allowed the castle, such as it was, to dictate the decor. The stone floor in the drawing room had been overlaid with a finely woven carpet, which she explained she had unearthed from trunks in the dungeon some ten years past. The furniture was quite ancient, darkened from centuries of use, with each piece appearing to have been carved from solid blocks of wood. A large settle flanked the massive fireplace, an effect which might have been severe save for the work of a skilled upholsterer, who had softened the bench with a fine cushion of heavy needlepoint. A kingly chair sat opposite, now occupied by Sir Edgar, who rose upon their entrance and offered a polite bow, along with Jane.

"He seems bored already," Margaret whispered over her shoulder.

"Hush," Harriet warned as Lady Eaves welcomed them to Ashworth Castle.

Turning to greet Sir Edgar as well, Harriet could not help but agree that the master of the house wished himself anywhere but in a formal receiving room. Lady Eaves then directed them to a table nearby, which had been covered in a tapestry and around which several stools had been placed, ostensibly for the younger set. Jane rounded the table, after which Harriet and Margaret followed suit.

Harriet gathered her skirts and sat down carefully on the Gothic oak stool. Again a cushion softened what otherwise would have been a quite uncomfortable seat. Once arranged, she glanced toward the high, beamed ceiling, noting with some awe the wrought iron chandelier in the very center of the chamber, which supported a dozen enormous candles.

"Do you think we shall have a visit from our ghost this evening, Miss Godwyne?" Lady Eaves asked, a prim smile on her lips.

"I cannot say, ma'am, though I rather doubt with so much excellent light, your ghost would be much capable of frightening anyone!"

Lady Eaves swelled her bosom and glanced around. "You are right of course. I have always believed a chamber ought to be well lit if it can. When I wed Sir Edgar, I told him how it was to be, that the chandler would know us as well as anybody. 'Light,' I said to my husband, 'I must have light,' and so I have."

"Yes, you certainly do," Harriet agreed, smiling. Glancing at her hostess, she bit her lip and averted her gaze. Poor Lady Eaves was arrayed this evening in a gown of red silk trimmed with large ruffles of sheer white tulle. She dared not think how Laurence might describe her, given the opportunity.

Margaret, seeing she was ready to laugh quite inappropriately, intervened. "I have often wondered, ma'am, if more than one ghost resides here."

Lady Eaves smiled her prim smile again. "As to that, I cannot say, although Jane insists she has seen a young maiden walking at the end of the garden near the turret, just below the dovecote. Though why she would walk beneath a dovecote I cannot imagine. Quite nonsensical, given the birds flying in and out all day. The ground is always marred with droppings."

"That may be so, Mama," Jane said, "but you are forgetting that a spirit would not be affected by such things. For myself, I am come to believe she was betrothed at one time and met an untimely death just there, beneath the dovecote."

"Have you been reading novels from the circulating library again?" Sir Edgar asked, narrowing his eyes.

"Of course, Papa," she cried, not in the least afraid of the severe expression on his face. "You know it is of all things my favorite pastime."

Sir Edgar smiled, some of his boredom vanishing. "Minx," he murmured, to Jane's obvious delight. He then glanced at the empty doorway. "Miss Godwyne, I had thought your mother and father would be attending you this evening."

"My father was still not well enough to leave the house. Unfortunately, the pain in his toe has not diminished sufficiently to allow him to leave Shalham for the present. My mother chose to remain behind and keep him company."

He nodded as though in approval. "She was always very attentive to your father, as I recall."

"Indeed, sir, I believe you may be right." She wondered about this for a moment and could only conclude he had the right of it. For all her mother's complaining and occasional throwing of pillows, she did seem to delight in assuring her husband's comfort. Tonight, she could have easily left him for a few hours to enjoy the soiree. Instead she had insisted—and not bitterly—upon attending him, proof, she supposed, of her aunt's assertions that a little brangling formed part of every marriage.

"And where are your parents, Miss Weaver? And your sisters?"

"We found it necessary to employ two carriages, since Mama hates to be crushed in a conveyance if she can help it. In addition, she had a charitable errand to fulfill. Do you know Mrs. Jenkyns, who resides in the hamlet of Alding Lees? The poor woman has been quite ill of late, and I believe Mama meant to deliver a basket of food before coming here. My sister Elizabeth had plucked several roses for her as well. They will undoubtedly be along directly."

"Mrs. Weaver has always been so kind to the poor."

Harriet watched as a warm expression entered Margaret's eye. "Indeed, sir, I do believe my mother is the very best of women."

A sweep of cool air from the direction of the hall, the sudden booming of masculine voices, and swell of feminine laughter bespoke the arrival of a great number of the expected party. A moment later, as Harriet rose to greet the newly arrived guests, nearly the remainder of those anticipated swelled into the chamber. Her aunt and uncle, along with Elizabeth and Mary, who was just fifteen; Lord Connought; Charles Badlesmere; Mr. and Mrs. Douglas, Laurence, his brother Evan, and his sisters Horatia and Nancy, who were of an age with her cousin Elizabeth; Arabella Orlestone; and finally Lord Frith. The latter joined Harriet immediately and began engaging her in conversation.

The younger girls gathered together near the pianoforte, giggling and sorting through music and determining who was to play first, since it was understood they were to take every opportunity of performing in order to prepare for any number of forthcoming London Seasons.

"That is a very bright dress Lady Eaves is wearing," Lord Frith murmured.

Harriet could only smile and pretend to look anywhere but at her hostess. "She does seem partial to vivid colors, I will say that much."

"Very diplomatic of you. Ah, she is summoning her servants!" He smiled and continued speaking in a low voice, "Whatever anyone's opinion of her choice of gown, there is scarcely a person here who can have the smallest complaint of her hospitality."

"The Madeira, as well, is especially delightful."

"Indeed, you are right, and here is a stream of servants bearing glasses and gleaming bottles from the buttery."

From that moment, Lady Eaves was in constant motion. She made certain that an array of refreshments was presented before her guests, and for the next hour saw to it that no one was without either a libation of some sort or a sampling of her victuals, which ranged from cold chicken to pickled beets to delectable sweetmeats.

Good food and excellent wine soon created a very merry soiree indeed. Only rarely did Harriet remain in one place for very long. She moved about the chamber, drawn by calls from one group to the next in steady succession. Conversations ebbed and flowed and at times bounced in a lively manner about the stone walls and, as promised, the younger ladies took turns showing their prowess on the ivory keys of Lady Eaves's very fine Broadwood square piano of rosewood and ebony.

While chatting with Margaret and tasting the pickled beets, Harriet chanced to observe Connought rendering a service to Mrs. Douglas. He had been conversing with her for some time and rose at last—not, however, to leave her side, but rather to fetch her a footstool.

She was close enough to overhear Mrs. Douglas say, "How kind of you, Connought. You must have noticed that I was shifting my feet about. I have a rheumatic complaint in my knee this year—most troublesome and unwelcome, for I have not been able to tend to my gardens as I would have wished this spring—and a footstool was just what I needed! Thank you."

"You are most welcome. May I bring you a glass of wine? The champagne is particularly fine—rather sweet, which is much to my taste."

"And mine," the lady exclaimed. "Yes, I will have a glass."

Margaret drew close to Harriet. "I see you are staring at your prey," she murmured.

"What?" Harried cried, turning to her friend.

"Imagining just how you were to get him to relinquish the emerald, no doubt?"

"Is he wearing it?" she queried, suddenly aware that so agreeably had she been entertained thus far that she had forgotten all about the wager.

"Indeed, he is."

Harriet's gaze immediately went to Connought's neckcloth. She scrutinized the exquisite arrangement of the fine linen and saw the pin tucked subtly within the folds. "Oh, yes, I see it now," she said, her heart suddenly beginning to thrum with excitement.

"You seem very composed this evening. Have you forgotten five days remain only? Actually, four if you consider that midnight is but three hours from now."

Harriet glanced at Margaret and laughed. "You do enjoy tormenting me, do you not?"

"Of course!"

Margaret's sister Mary completed the playing of a Clementi sonatina and rose to take her bow. She was all smiles as the chamber erupted into an enthusiastic round of applause. After a moment, Lady Eaves suggested that the young people might want to dance a few country dances. This recommendation was greeted with a general murmuring of delight, and several of the party began immediately to make up a proper number of couples. Evan Douglas was quick to ask Alison Eaves to dance, while her brother Harry approached Elizabeth. Charles asked Jane for the first set, and because Harriet had been looking away from Connought, she was surprised when he was suddenly at her elbow, begging her to go down the dance with him.

"With pleasure!" she cried, thinking that fate was

being remarkably kind to her. She only hoped that she would have her wits about her sufficiently to find a way to come into possession of his emerald before the night ended. As he led her to the far side of the room near the pianoforte where the parallel lines were forming, she asked, "Is your pin an heirloom, perchance?" Her breath caught. How could she ever persuade him to part with it were it of ancient or sentimental origin?

"No, not by half, but I have a great fondness for it. My mother purchased it for my birthday ten years past."

"Oh, I see," she murmured, taking up her place opposite him. Her spirits fell. Though she would certainly return the pin to him once the wager had been concluded, she could not imagine any circumstance under which he would willingly part with a mother's gift.

The country dance commenced, as well as a great deal of flirting up and down the line. A wonderful gaiety continued to permeate the soiree, which could not help but encourage Harriet. She saw that Connought, far from intending to set up her back as was his usual custom, had made her enjoyment of the dance his object. He kept an amusing conversation flowing throughout the various figures, and when once she missed her steps, he merely squeezed her fingers and smiled the next time they came together. She recalled quite abruptly that this was how it had been when he had courted her so many years ago. Always her comfort had been his first concern.

When at last the dance concluded, she declined going down another. When a sparkle of candlelight glanced off the emerald, inspiration struck. But would he rise to the bait? She leaned close to him and confessed into his ear that she had grown decidedly warm after such an exertion. Would he escort her outside to partake of a little cooling fresh air?

She waited as he met her gaze, the faintest of frowns

between his brows. Inwardly, she begged for him to say yes. Then she might be able to bamboozle him into another contest, with the emerald the prize. She held her breath and smiled in what she hoped was an innocent manner.

"What are you about, Harriet Godwyne?" he murmured, a crooked smile forming in his lips.

When she opened her mouth to offer an innocuous reply, he was before her. "Never mind," he said, laughing. "Far be it from me to question the motives of any lady who desires to be drawn outdoors on a fine summer evening."

With that, he directed her to the doors leading to the moat.

Twelve

As Harriet moved beside Connought along a path beside the moated walls of the ancient castle, the sounds of frogs croaking made her smile. "I always think of them as having heard a melody with which they are striving to keep pace."

"How very fanciful, to be sure," he said, smiling in turn.

"You are making fun."

"Only a very little," he responded.

When he offered his arm, she did not hesitate to take it. Once again she was reminded that the wager involving Connought had put her in dangerous proximity to the man. Never in the past seven years had she permitted such a nocturnal stroll, entirely unchaperoned, as this.

Walking along the stone path, the music grew fainter until finally, when they reached the low, charming turret, it could scarcely be heard. The remains of a once serviceable moat, replete with black swans and water lilies, was still in use along the eastern portion of the dwelling. Moss covered the gray stone in an uneven manner, and over the years sufficient soil had built up in dozens of crevices to sprout an odd variety of greenery in dappled clumps. The twilight of the summer evening, which lasted late into the night, cast everything in deep, misty shadows. A sprawling clematis bearing blue flowers had wended its way over much of the wall, creating so charming an effect that when gazing into the waters, Harriet expected a water fairy to suddenly burst from the blackness below. So strangely magical was the feel to the evening that she had to remind herself again and again that she had a particular purpose in permitting Connought to lead her so far away from Lady Eaves's guests.

She glanced up at him, at the faint smile on his lips, and wondered just what he was thinking.

For his part, Connought had led her to a distant place on the stone walk, as far away from the dancers and music as he could manage. He wanted Harriet to himself, something he had been desiring from the moment he had entered the drawing room, not because he had a wager to win but because Harriet was so deucedly beautiful.

Upon entering the drawing room earlier that evening, his gaze had been drawn immediately to her, for she was gowned in an elegant beaded apricot muslin confection which, against her light brown hair, dark eyes, and creamy complexion, made her appear almost as lovely as a heavenly apparition. She was standing nearly in the center of the room, and the stone walls and Gothic wrought iron had given him the impression that she belonged to another age entirely, an age of chivalry and romance of which the present age seemed sadly lacking.

Her hair was drawn up into a lovely knot of curls atop her head, with several long tendrils cascading behind. He realized she was, as always, dressed to perfection, from the gold band arranged against her curls at the crown of her head to the pearl eardrops dressing her gently curved earlobes to the amber cross gracing her swan's neck. She was elegant, exquisite, a diamond of the first stare.

He felt curiously inclined to speak poetry to her in whispers, after which he most certainly meant to steal a kiss or two, but what of Harriet? What was her desire?

She was the one who had suggested a nocturnal stroll, nor had she protested even a mite the farther he had drawn her away from the dancing. Ought he to be encouraged to attempt what it was in his heart to do?

He watched her now as her gaze tracked the progress of two black swans swimming near a stand of tall reeds and making their way to what was a nest of half-grown cygnets. Was the lady willing? She turned and regarded him in what he saw was her most speculative manner.

"Do I meet with your approval tonight, Miss Godwyne?"

"So formal?" she queried, a smiling teasing her lips.

His gaze dropped to her lips and a strong bolt of desire shot through him. Harriet had always affected him thus. How he longed to take her into his arms. "I suppose I was merely teasing you a little. You and I are not on formal terms, are we?"

"No, *my lord,* most decidedly we are not!"

He laughed.

"Which do you think will reach the nest first, the male or the female?" she asked.

Connought turned to watch the couple advance steadily through the waters. "The female. He will give way to her."

"Never!" she cried. "He will take charge of the nest before she does."

"Care to wager?" he queried.

She turned startled eyes to him. "A wager?"

He could not understand precisely why such a suggestion would surprise her, but of the moment he did not care. "Yes, indeed. Earlier today you had requested me to stake my riding crop. I shall do so again, if you like. My riding crop should you win . . . your kiss, should the female reach the nest first. You must answer quickly, however, for they are almost arrived."

He watched an excited glitter enter her eyes. "A kiss, you say?" She glanced at the swans, which seemed to be moving more swiftly still. "Not for the riding crop. Something else, perhaps. Your emerald, for instance?" Again she looked at him—only this time, there was a decided challenge in her eyes.

"My emerald against your kiss?" he asked, stunned by the suggestion and yet oddly intrigued.

"Yes," she returned breathlessly. "Unless you think such a kiss unworthy of an emerald."

In this moment, he thought quite the opposite. "Done," he whispered.

"You would risk your emerald?"

He nodded. "Most certainly."

"Connought, I do not know what to say. You have surprised me, but . . ."

What she might have said was lost as he stunned her by gathering her swiftly in his arms.

She planted her hands against his chest. "Whatever are you doing? Release me. You have not—"

"Won the wager?" he inquired. "Oh, but I have." He jerked his head in the direction of the nest. She turned to observe what he had already seen. The female was settling herself comfortably on the nest while the male stood politely by and waited for her. "She is completing her nightly toilette, I daresay."

"Oh," she said, her hands relaxing against his chest. "And I so wanted your emerald."

"And I so wanted this." He smiled faintly, searching her eyes intently. "Too beautiful for words."

He settled his lips on hers, savoring the feel of her in his arms and of this unexpected boon—a willing kiss.

Harriet received his kiss, the payment for a wager lost, feeling desperate of a sudden. She should not be kissing Connought. She knew her weakness where he was concerned, that his touch was enough to cause her to feel that the world began and ended with him. Kissing him made promises from the soul, promises not likely to be kept, so that the soul would continue to long for something never to be fulfilled. How would she bear it?

And yet, as she slipped into the magical place of the giving and receiving of a kiss, the music began, a song from so deep in her heart, sung with the volume swelling moment by moment, that very soon she could no longer hear the warnings of her mind or her soul. She could only feel how extraordinary it was to be kissed by a rogue.

The past was forgotten, the future so far distant as to be immeasurable. There was no longer a battle between soul and conscience, merely the giving and taking, the feel of his lips pressed to hers, of his tongue begging entrance, of her lips parting to receive what was so very forbidden.

Did Connought know the delight he was bringing to her? Did he fathom, even in part, the joy she always experienced when he kissed her? Even the theft of the kiss in the cherry orchard had deprived her of the feel of her feet for a very long time. She slid her arms about his shoulders and held him close. She tilted her head, and he drew her tightly against him. He shifted his arm so that he could encircle her more fully, and what had begun as a tender kiss became a sudden, passionate embrace.

Harriet lost all sense of time and place. She was in the world of the gods, dining on ambrosia, and with the smallest thought moving swiftly through the stars. She knew a sudden deep, profound desire to never let him go.

After a very long moment, he drew back and searched her eyes. "I know you are not indifferent to me, even after all these years."

Harriet looked deeply into his eyes. "No, I am not indifferent," she responded. "How could I be?"

She let him gather her more tightly to him. He took her chin with his hand. He looked fiercely into her eyes until once more she could no longer feel her feet. "My God, do you know how beautiful you are?"

She blinked, trying to recall just why it was she should repulse his advances. She shook her head.

The language he began to speak was in delicate searches across her lips until she was hearing the beats of his heart and the thoughts of his mind. Her arm slid about his neck, and he drew her yet more closely to him until she could scarcely breathe. Yet she hardly needed air to sustain life, merely the sensation of Connought embracing her and kissing her and speaking with the drift of his lips over hers.

He drew back again. "I have never won a wager so happily before. Harriet, what would you say if I asked you again to become my bride?"

She felt an odd tension in him, something that disturbed her. She shook her head. "No," she whispered. "You know very well I . . . I cannot marry you."

He released a breath he had been holding and relaxed his arms. "Then why do you kiss me as you do?"

Bit by bit, she drew out of the warmth of his embrace, until she was standing before him, cold and alone in the late evening chill. She did not know how to answer him. If she spoke of her cousin, she felt certain she would not be expressing all that was in her heart. But they had discussed the subject so many times, and always without a happy resolution, that she found herself entirely unwilling to answer him now. She merely looked at him.

"Because of Margaret?" he queried. She nodded, then watched as, even in the dusky twilight, a cloud passed over his face. "Harriet, cannot you see that we belong together?"

"No," she returned sadly, unwilling to meet his gaze any longer. "I must go."

"Before you do," he said, taking an unexpected possession of her hands. "I wish to know something."

"What is that?" she asked, afraid suddenly.

"Do you think I enjoyed kissing your cousin?"

"What?" she cried, appalled. She tried to withdraw her hands, but he would not allow it. "How could you even ask me something so . . . so cruel! Do you not comprehend how painful it has been for me to know that you kissed her at all, nonetheless to attempt to imagine the level of enjoyment you procured from the event?"

"Tell me anyway," he retorted sharply. "For, damme, you must have thought I believed myself in heaven while holding her in my arms, else I cannot explain this ridiculous stubbornness on your part. I have begged forgiveness a dozen times, and you will not relent. I have even forsaken all those pastimes that were my bread and meat for so long. Yet you will not relent, you will not see what is truly in your heart and marry me. Why, I wonder? Is it possible Harriet Godwyne has no heart?"

She felt he could not have wounded her more deeply. "I have no wish to discuss any of this with you. And I must say I think you have gone quite beyond the pale!" With that, she jerked her hands free from his and stormed away from him. She now understood there was more than one reason why she had refused to forgive Connought. He was a veritable brute of a man!

Connought remained staring at the darkening moat for at least a half hour after Harriet left him. He could not credit that he had made such a mull of things, and yet he could not quite blame himself entirely. He felt he had endured Harriet's stubbornness long enough and for several minutes contemplated the delight of seeing the expression on her face when she learned he fully intended, come Thursday morning, to offer for Arabella. That would certainly leave Harriet Godwyne gapped, if he did not mistake the matter. Whatever her protests, no matter how often she refused to acknowledge her truest feelings, he knew the truth, that she was still in love with him. No woman became so enthralled by a kiss without being in love.

When he finally returned to the drawing room, several couples were going down a lively reel, including Lord Frith, who was partnering Harriet. He scanned the remaining dancers and caught Arabella's eye. He smiled and bowed to her, which brought a decided glow to her lovely porcelain features. He knew one quite potent means of assuaging his ire, and meant to ask the beauty to dance the moment the reel ended.

Laurence approached him. "Have you noticed Lady Eaves's gown this evening? I vow she appears just like a tomato stuffed with clotted cream!"

Connought glanced at the red silk gown and the tulle ruffles about the neckline. "I suppose she does," he responded indifferently.

"In the mopes?" he queried, chortling. "As well you ought to be, if Harriet's countenance when she first returned to the drawing room was any indication of the nature of your, er, discussion with her."

Connought shook his head. "We quarreled."

"What the devil did you say to her?" he asked on a harsh whisper. "I have never seen her in such high dudgeon before."

Connought sighed heavily. "If you must know, I conducted myself like a complete simpleton. I do not know what came over me, but I became angry again that she would be so stubborn. I asked her if she thought I enjoyed kissing Margaret."

"Good God!" he returned. "The work of a mere whipster!"

"Ham-handed, by half!" Connaught agreed.

"The good news is, however, that I shall escape having to ask Margaret to marry me, in which case I am not at all overset that you've been such a cawker." The music ended and Arabella began making her way to the earl. On a low murmur, Laurence said, "Ah, I do believe *your bride* approaches even now!"

Connought frowned at him, but did not have sufficient time to give him the dressing down he so richly deserved. Instead, he turned to greet Arabella, caught up her hand in his, and kissed her fingers. Leading her out for the quadrille, he chanced to see Harriet flirting in a lively manner with Evan Douglas. For a profound moment he knew the strongest desire to plant Evan a facer.

Harriet awoke on the following morning with a dull throbbing at her temples. Her mind and heart were instantly at war as she recalled the truly wretched quarrel she had endured with Connought the night before. She still could not credit he had said so many vile things to her. And yet she could not entirely dismiss that there might have been some justice in all that he had said.

Yet how very provoking! Had he enjoyed kissing Margaret, indeed!

She sat up in bed, her head aching a little more. She tried not to become angry and disgusted all over again, but rather forced herself to recall the expression on his face when he had posed the question. She realized he had been angry, as he always was whenever they discussed that particular portion of their history. However, she had always felt it to be the outside of enough that he would feel he had a right to be angry on any score. She was, after all, the injured party. It would seem he would never have a proper amount of remorse for his conduct.

Her heart again took up a sword as she recalled the kiss she had lost to him last night and how for those few minutes in which she had been locked in his arms, she had wished there had been no past between them and no lonely future without him, only that present in which she could bask in the delight of his love for her.

She blinked quite strongly. *His love for her.* How these words began to torment her. Did Connought love her, truly love her? He had not spoken these words last night, but in every other way, he had made his sentiments known, even going so far as to ask her if she would marry him were he to ask. He had told her she was beautiful, he had kissed her so passionately, but did he truly love her, truly wish to marry her? It would seem he did.

She leaned back on her pillows as sudden, surprising tears seeped from the corner of her eyes. He loved her. He truly loved her. A great sadness swelled over her like a sail filling with air. She felt she might be driven to distraction by so much grief. Why had she entered this stupid wager with Margaret and Jane in the first place? After all, had the pressure of the wager not compelled her to attempt to get the emerald from him, she would never have allowed herself to be led into the shadows of the castle alone with him. Stupid, stupid wager. Had anyone in the world ever entered into a more wretched, foolish wager?

Harriet, cannot you see that we belong together?

His words haunted her. Did she belong with Connought? Should she marry him and share his bed, regardless of the past? She pondered the bed in which she was presently lying. She had been alone for a very long time, having left her parents' home to reside with Mrs. Farthingloe in London several years ago.

Forgetting the harsh nature of Connought's truly odious question concerning the kiss he gave Margaret, she thought that never had she felt so lonely as in this moment. The bed she was in was not even her own bed. But were she to marry, she would share her bed with her husband. She would begin a family, have babes of her own, hear the laughter of children in various rooms of the house and their squabbles down the halls.

She had even thought she would be wed by now. Not to Connought, of course, but wed nonetheless. She had had any number of eligible offers. Even Lord Frith had asked her no less than six times—seven, including the offer on Friday. She wondered suddenly why it was she kept Frith dangling as she did. Was it possible she kept him attached to her should one day she have need of him? After all, should she never fall in love again, she could always marry him.

She shuddered at the thought of it knowing it was true, that over the course of the past several years she had been making use of his *tendre* for her so that she might not have to worry about dwindling into an ape-leader. She covered her face with her hands, a powerful remorse deepening within her. How could she have used Frith so ill? He, too, should have long since been married, instead of traipsing after her like a faithful hound. How was it possible she had never seen herself before—which made her wonder if anything she believed about herself was true.

She leaped from her bed quite suddenly. She would drive herself mad thinking about so many hopeless things at once. She moved to the window overlooking her aunt's yew maze and watched as Edward approached

Mary and Elizabeth stealthily from behind. He removed something from his pocket, ran up behind Mary, and shoved what appeared to be a small animal down the back of her gown.

Mary began squealing and running in circles. Edward fell down in whoops, while Elizabeth stood over him, berating him. Harriet watched as one of Edward's pet mice emerged at the hem of Mary's dress and raced for cover in the maze.

How wicked Edward could be! Young boys could be so very trying. So could grown gentlemen. She remembered Margaret saying something similar yesterday, something about what monsters boys were, adding, 'and to think we grow up only to tumble in love with some gentleman, glowing with a little Town Bronze, who undoubtedly spent much of his childhood in just the same manner of mischief!'

But they did grow up to be more than mischief-makers . . . even Connought. She recalled just how kind Connought had been to Mrs. Douglas last night in fetching her not just a footstool when he could see she was in some discomfort, but a glass of champagne as well. He had been all attentiveness in that moment, kind and considerate, qualities she cherished very much. What was more, she knew that he had not performed these services in the hopes of impressing anyone. Connought did nothing with an eye to seeking the approval of others.

His character, therefore, was not wholly lacking, she decided, but did this in any way justify his exceedingly roguish kissing of Margaret seven years past and everything such conduct suggested for the future? As she watched Edward race into the maze after his pet and the younger Miss Weavers continue their progress in the direction of the duck pond, she realized that she was no longer so certain she was entirely correct in her judgment of him.

Turning away from the window, she crossed the room to ring for her maid. Whatever arguments Connought might employ, however, in his attempts to dissuade her from her opinions of his character, his words would always be matched against the incontrovertible truth that he had kissed Margaret.

As for today, she had a wager to win, which meant two items to acquire from Connought—his riding crop and the emerald stickpin. In order to be at ease again, therefore, she knew exactly what she must do. She must get these things as soon as possible, after which she began to think it would be a very wise thing if she left Kent earlier than she had planned. She could go to Brighton and spend the remainder of the summer there on the Steyne, where she had a great many friends. Happily, Connought was rather indifferent to the place. Yes, she would go to Brighton, where Connought would not be present to brangle with her.

But first, the crop and pin. Only how to go about the business? An idea struck her, something quite unexpected and not particularly in the usual order of things. In truth, quite wicked. But, yes, it would serve her well, indeed!

An hour later, she was mounted astride her favorite mare and riding in the direction of Connought's estate.

Thirteen

Harriet felt completely dwarfed by Kingsland the closer she drew to the Jacobean mansion. The present structure, four stories in height and all of a beautiful but formal red brick, was rather overpowering. Several bay windows served to soften the aspect, but not sufficiently to relieve her of the sense that she was storming a citadel.

"Good day, Mollash!" she called cheerfully to Connought's butler as he opened the door to her. Whatever her trepidations upon approaching Connought's home without an invitation, she felt a bold face would be serve her best.

"Good morning, Miss Godwyne."

"I have come to call upon Lord Connought."

"Very good, miss," he returned, directing a footman to take charge of her horse.

She entered Kingsland in a quick manner, which helped to reduce some of the dread she felt. However, given her rather wicked purpose this morning, she did not think a decided show of nerves would in any manner benefit her.

"Would you be so good as to inform his lordship that I have a matter of some urgency to discuss with him and would he be so kind as to wait upon me at his convenience?"

Harriet knew Mollash quite well, and though she had

little doubt she was offending his sense of propriety by arriving unexpectedly while his master was perhaps preparing to attend church services, she had at some point in her long history with the earl won his butler's respect. He did not hesitate, but was all politeness as he responded, "Very good, miss. Would you prefer to wait in the grand salon?"

She smiled. "On no account! The entrance hall will do well enough, even if I am to endure so many of his lordship's predecessors staring down upon me."

A faint twitch beside the butler's lips indicated his reaction to her remark, but his sense of decorum allowed him only another brief bow before he quit the black and white tiled chamber.

Left alone, Harriet turned in a slow circle and yet again gazed upon one of the most magnificent entrance halls she had ever seen. The chamber had been constructed in the round and rose by a winding staircase to a high domed ceiling. Light from an array of windows above lit the vestibule in a glow. She felt dizzy and yet inspired in a manner that made no particular sense to her. On the walls of the curved stairwell hung portrait after portrait, a long succession of the earls of Connought.

She moved closer to better see them, the first being of the present master himself, which had been captured when he was a younger man, some five years past. His countenance was careless, almost roguish, for his smile was crooked and somehow the artist had achieved a twinkle in his eye. There was something so oddly innocent in his expression that she found herself caught by old feelings, and a strange lump formed in her throat. Once upon a time, she had loved him so very much.

When Mollash returned with word that Connought would receive her, she felt very subdued and strove to remind herself just why she had presented herself unannounced, uninvited, and at so early an hour at Kingsland. Straightening her shoulders, she marched behind the proper butler. She could only wonder what Connought would think of her this morning.

Entering the chamber, she watched as Lord Connought, who had just taken a sip of coffee, returned the cup abruptly to its saucer. He rose politely, and Mollash announced her. She saw that the earl appeared both pleased and suspicious.

"Harriet . . . Miss Godwyne," he murmured, his lips twitching. "I bid you good morning."

"And a most excellent morning to you," she returned brightly.

"Thank you, Mollash. That will be all."

As the butler quit the chamber on his stately tread, Harriet surveyed the expansive, well-appointed morning room. Though there was a large table commanding attention and fitted with twelve simple but elegant mahogany chairs, she noted that Connought had chosen to partake of his meal at a small table situated in one of the bay windows. A newspaper was scattered about the floor at the base of his chair and a pot of coffee settled within easy reach of his cup. Through the window, she could see a well-kept garden, a line of sycamores in which magpie nests resided, and the rolling weald hills beyond.

"What a charming view," she commented moving toward him. "Do you know, of the numerous times I have been to Kingsland, I do not think I have ever been in the morning room."

"That would be, I daresay, because you have never been here in the morning. I do not open this room during our evening entertainments."

She glanced at him. "I trust I have not disturbed you?" He was dressed simply in a blue coat, buff breeches, and shoes with but the smallest of buckles.

His smile was suddenly crooked. "You always disturb me," he returned, chuckling.

This was not in the least what she had been expecting to hear. Her lashes fluttered and her gaze swooped around the chamber to light upon anything except the unexpected expression in his blue eyes. "What an odd thing to say, to be sure," she said, attempting for a light note. "As it happens, I was hoping I might persuade you to ride out with me this morning, by way of apology for having flown into the boughs last night."

"Is that what you did, then?" he queried.

Her gaze shot back to his face. "Oh, I can see that you are quizzing me! Well, what do you say, Connought? The morning is very fine and the hour early enough to permit both a pleasant ride as well as attendance at services later."

She watched a speculative light enter his eye, and she knew that he was trying to determine why precisely she had come to his home. Seeing that his suspicions were deepening, she added quickly, "You seem quite surprised to see me, and I suppose you ought to be, particularly since I did not even bring a groom or one of my cousins to attend me. However, I did so hope for a little private conversation with you. You cannot know how much our quarrel of last night has distressed me. I was hoping we might discuss it at greater length, particularly since you seemed to think it would be of some use to do so."

He frowned slightly. "If that is what you truly wish, then yes, of course, I shall be happy to ride out with you." He glanced down at the table. "Do you care for a little coffee or tea? Breakfast, if you like."

"As it happens," she replied amicably, "I have little appetite, but I would favor a cup of coffee."

"Then coffee you shall have." He gestured to the seat

opposite him. "I was just finishing when you arrived, but if we are to ride out with time to spare for church afterward, I ought to change into riding gear directly."

During the entire conversation with Harriet, Connought had felt oddly disjointed. He fetched her a cup and saucer from the sideboard as she gathered up the long train of her riding habit and sat down. He watched her pour herself some coffee, completely at ease.

When he remained looking down at her, curious as to why the deuce she had really come, she glanced up at him. "Was there something else?" she asked.

"No," he drawled. "I suppose not. You will excuse me?"

"Of course."

He left the chamber, wondering what forces were at work that had actually brought Harriet to Kingsland. He could not for the life of him comprehend why precisely she had come. She had said she wished to speak of their brangling of the night before, but he fully believed that was all a hum. There had been nothing in her expression to evince real concern about the subject. So why, then, was she here?

He sensed some mischief afoot, which only served to make him smile. He realized he did not give a fig why Harriet had come to him, only that she had come. He had awakened this morning with memories of the kiss they had shared last night dominating his mind. Yes, there had been a quarrel as well over the usual nonsense, but the kiss was what had lingered.

He wanted Harriet Godwyne as he had wanted no lady before. In some manner that was entirely inexplicable, he felt she belonged to him, and if either of them made the monumentally foolish error of wedding another, it still would not eradicate what he felt was a fixed bond between them. Only how to get Harriet to see the truth of it?

Perhaps today he would find a way to begin that process, which was all well and good, he thought as he changed into buckskin breeches and black leather boots. However, if he did not convince her by Wednesday midnight, he would be obligated by every honorable code to marry Arabella.

Twenty minutes later, Harriet strolled beside her prey, the train of her riding habit looped over her elbow. She was painfully aware that he had not brought his riding crop with him. She could only hope that he did not keep his crop in his bedchamber, but rather in the stables.

"So," he began. "You wished to have a discussion about last night?"

"Last night?" she queried, her thoughts rambling ahead to the stables and wondering precisely where the tack room was and whether or not his crop would be there, or if he kept it in a different place entirely.

"Harriet," he drawled. "Have your wits suddenly gone a-begging? You told me earlier that you wished to discuss our squabbling of last night. For myself, I had much rather examine at length the kiss we shared."

She glanced up at him, her breath catching in her throat. "How wicked of you, Connought!" she cried. However, she was still only half attending to what he was saying. Perhaps he kept the crop by his favorite saddle. She had been in his stables only once before, but that had been many years prior, and she could not quite recall the general arrangement of the stalls, feed, and tack, let alone which rooms belonged to the head groom or others of the staff.

"As it happens," he said, "I was hoping to see you today. I feel I must apologize for pressing you as I did last night. It was very wrong of me."

"Handsomely said," she returned. The estate had a small smithy. With so many horses to be shod every six weeks, at least one of the stableboys was trained in the arts of bending a shoe to fit. She was fairly certain, if memory served, that the smithy was located behind the stables.

"And I have also grown hair on the bottom of my feet."

"I see," she said. So if the smithy was outside the stables, she would not have to look for the crop there.

"Laurence has sprouted two curved horns atop his head. I told him last night he looked like the devil, and I meant it! What do you say to that?"

"Hmm? Well . . . I think you ought not to curse in my presence." She was fairly certain the tack room was just beyond the head groom's office, which made sense, since he would likely wish to keep a close watch on the condition of all the saddles, bridles, reins, and the like. Goodness, if the crop was within the tack room, as large as she remembered it to be, she would likely spend the entire morning searching for it.

When Connought burst out laughing, Harriet stopped in her tracks and turned to him. She sought about in her mind as to why he might have been so vastly amused, and then realized what he had just said to her. "Did you just say Laurence has sprouted horns?"

"Harriet, I have never known you to be so distracted. Are you certain you wish to ride?"

"Of course." Inspiration struck and as they neared the stables, she mentioned that it was surprising how it hot it was today. She then placed the back of her hand to her head and sighed quite loudly.

Connought looked up into the sky, which was nicely streaked with high, cooling clouds, and lifted a brow. She did not wait for him to comment on the weather, but instead passed quickly into the stables. In doing so, she also passed her horse, which was stationed at the mounting block, beside which was Connought's horse, saddled and ready. If her conduct would be considered rather odd, she did not care. Let the earl think what he might. She had a wager to win!

Connought followed behind her but said nothing.

She smiled perfunctorily at the head groom and three of the stableboys, who were mucking stalls at various points down the length of the red brick building. The office was the first chamber to her right followed by a narrow staircase to the loft above where she knew some of the servants slept. The tack room came next.

"My goodness," she cried as though utterly fascinated. "You do have a great many saddles!" She glanced frantically about the room and finally saw what she was seeking. On a peg nearby—in fact, wonderfully within reach—was Connought's riding crop. She felt her cheeks prickle with sudden heat and excitement.

"Which is your favorite saddle?" she inquired moving briskly within.

"The one already on my horse," he responded baldly. He had taken her place at the threshold and gestured in the direction of the yard.

Harriet once more placed the back of her hand to her forehead, only this time she added a fluttering of her lashes for effect.

At that, he started. "What is it, Harriet? For I vow you have grown quite flushed!"

"I do not know how it is, but I . . . you must forgive me, but I am not feeling at all the thing. Sudden headache. I believe I must forgo our ride altogether. If you would just lead me to my horse . . ."

"If you wish for it, but I must say if you are so very ill, I promise you I am quite willing to drive you back to Shalham Park. We can tie your horse on behind."

"You are very kind," she said. "But I had as lief ride

back alone. I shall cross your southern pasture, with your permission. From there, as you know, Shalham is but two miles distant."

"Of course, if you are very certain."

"Indeed, I am."

"Very well." He then held his arm out to her. "Come. I shall at the very least escort you to the block."

"No, no, I am not so invalidish as that." She smiled and strolled toward the door. Just as she reached the doorway, however, she pretended to trip, all the while listing to the right. In a swift movement, she slid the crop from off the peg. Righting herself, she whirled around and quickly concealed the crop within the deep pocket of her riding habit.

He caught her elbow and supported her. "Now I am persuaded you are not well! Harriet, perhaps you should retire to my house. I shall summon the doctor."

"No! No!" she cried. "I beg you will not! I am only suffering a trifling dizziness, but I believe I ought to be going right away."

"As you wish." By now, he was frowning heavily.

He escorted her to the block, supporting her as she gathered up the train of her habit and mounted her favorite mare.

Taking up the reins, she was just preparing to give her horse a tap with her heel when he stayed her with his hand on her arm. "Are you certain you would not much rather that I drive you? It would be no difficulty. As you can see, I have an excellent staff who will have my curricle harnessed upon the instant."

"You are very kind, but I thank you, no." If only he would release her. "I should be going."

"But Harriet, indeed, you are not—"

When he broke off his appeal so swiftly, she turned toward him. "Yes?"

He had an odd expression on his face, as though he had just sucked on a sour lemon. "Nothing," he murmured. "I can see that you are determined. Very well. Good-bye."

She wondered what was the matter with him, but since she was anxious to go, she merely responded in kind, offered him a proper nod of her head, and gave her horse the long-awaited kick. Her mare, too, seemed ready to run, and within a few seconds she was trotting nicely in the direction of the gate which led to the southern pastures of the estate.

She could hardly wait to reach the open field, for the elation she felt at having succeeded in stealing his riding crop was beyond description. A fine, hard gallop at the moment would suit her to perfection. For the present, she walked her horse sedately, not wishing to make the earl more suspicious than he already was. Oh, but how happy she was, for her wager was now two-thirds won and Connought was none the wiser. If he somehow determined that she was the culprit who had taken his riding crop, well, once the wager was fulfilled she would of course return it to him with a complete explanation of the reason for her thievery. She wondered suddenly at the tremendous joy she was experiencing of the moment, all because she had *stolen* something. Goodness, if she was not careful, she could easily become addicted to such wicked deeds!

Connought watched Harriet leave, and only as she passed through the gates to the lanes beyond did he give relief to the amusement that had twisted his face into what he was certain had been a rather quizzical grimace. He laughed outright for several minutes, wondering how he had held himself in check for so long.

Before she had slapped the reins and prodded her horse, he had noticed his riding crop protruding from the pocket of her habit. He had broken off his sentence and bit his lip hard, for nothing seemed more ridiculous to him in that moment than the knowledge she had arranged the entire encounter merely to steal his crop—from having pretended to call on him in order to talk over their argument of the night before to feigning her illness to stumbling in the tack room so that she might lift the crop off the peg. He had watched her leave, still holding back his amusement with great difficulty, for though she sat her horse beautifully—indeed, she was an excellent horsewoman—the crop stuck out at a very pronounced angle and appeared as a conductor's baton with each step her horse took, shifting back and forth, back and forth.

He could only hope it would not work itself out of the pocket entirely and be lost somewhere between Kingsland and Shalham. But what the deuce did Harriet Godwyne want with his riding crop? For that matter, what did she want with his grandfather's watch, or, as he recalled their wager of the night before, his emerald stickpin? Strange doings, he thought.

As he reentered the house, he heard voices in the distance coming from the direction of the entrance hall and realized Laurence had come to call. Before Mollash could send him away, he hurried to inform both that he had not gone out riding after all.

Laurence looked him up and down. "Excellent!" he cried. "For I had hoped for a cup of coffee or two before services. Who were you to ride out with?"

Connought addressed his butler first. "Coffee, Mollash! Another pot, I believe!"

"Very good, m'lord. The morning room?"

"Yes, thank you."

After the butler had disappeared down the hall, Laurence shook his head as though quite confused. "I am here, but not in riding gear, and Charles detests riding out at so early an hour. So I must ask again, with whom were you to ride out?"

"Harriet!" he exclaimed, gesturing for Laurence to follow him to the morning room. "Yes, well you may stare. She was here and left but ten minutes past by the south lane, which is why you did not meet her."

"Harriet rode over from Shalham to ride out with you?" he cried, clearly stunned.

"Not precisely. It would seem riding out was only a ruse. She actually came to steal something from me."

"You're gammoning me!" he exclaimed. "Our staid little Harriet coming to Kingsland to commit a hanging offense?"

Connought laughed. Entering the morning room, he crossed the room to the bay window once more, where his newspaper had been gathered up from the floor, reassembled, and once more settled tidily on the table. He sat down and told Laurence to do the same. He then regaled him of Harriet's extremely odd visit, which had involved her false headaches and dizziness and culminated in a description of her walking her horse out of the stableyard with the crop bouncing from side to side from the depths of her pocket.

Laurence was in tears he was laughing so hard. "And . . . and did she really pretend to swoon?"

Connought nodded. "Her performance was quite convincing," he said. "I believed her completely, for she had the prettiest flush on her cheeks while in the tack room—although now that I think on it, I am persuaded it was because she was so delighted with her success!—and only realized I had been tricked when I saw the crop."

Laurence chuckled for some time afterward, wiping his eyes with his kerchief. "She was always the devil of a girl—or at least she was until you kissed Margaret. Then she became a saint. You know, I am convinced the trouble with her is that she does not see herself for who she really is. She conducts herself with elegance and grace, but beneath her beautiful and very polished exterior is this extremely playful, even at times hoydenish, young miss begging to be released."

"Is that how you see her?"

"Indeed, I do, which was one of the reasons I always felt you were so well suited."

Connought smiled faintly. "In truth, I share a similar opinion. However, I fear Harriet does not. Only tell me, why have you come to call this morning? You are not wont to do so before services."

"Mama wished for it. She has decided to serve a large dinner for the younger set on the island this evening and hopes you will join us. She said you were so kind to her last night that she insisted I offer the invitation as quickly as possible. What did you do, if I might ask?"

Connought shrugged. "I do not recall, unless she was referring to my having brought her a footstool."

"Ah, she would have thought that a great service. She does not complain, but she suffers greatly."

"I am happy to have helped her. You may tell her I am most grateful for the invitation. The hour?"

"Five."

"Five it is."

Fourteen

Harriet stared at the several small rowboats lined up on either side of the narrow dock on Mrs. Douglas's lake. She could not help but smile and wondered just how many of her friends gathered this evening at Laurence's home for dinner on the island opposite had begun to think her a simpleton, for she could not seem to stop smiling.

Ever since her experience that morning in concocting a scheme to steal Connought's riding crop, then executing it to perfection with a little tomfoolery toward the end of her visit in pretending to be ill, she had known a sense of exhilaration that simply would not desert her. The committing of her small and quite temporary crime had changed her—indeed, had caused her to experience certain quite peculiar emotions and sensations which she had not felt in a very long time. In truth, she felt very much alive, every sense alert, in a manner she wondered if she had ever before experienced.

She was the first, therefore, into a boat, stepping aboard confidently with her skirts caught up in her hand to keep from tripping on them. If the boat rocked a trifle, she only laughed. She did not think she cared even if she should take a tumble into the lake and ruin what was one of her favorite green silk gowns. "Come,

Charles," she cried, taking up a seat. "You, Nancy, as well!"

Charles did not hesitate, but led Nancy Douglas to the boat and assisted her in stepping into the swaying craft. Harriet extended her hand, which further stabilized her movements. A moment more, and Nancy was seated next to her.

"Take the oars, Charles, and be quick about it!" Harriet cried. "Let us see if we can be first to the island."

"Excellent notion!" Charles returned.

"Not if I can help it!" Connought cried.

Harriet glanced at the adjacent rowboat on the other side of the dock and saw that Connought, too, had taken up the oars. In his boat, Arabella sat opposite him, along with Alison Eaves.

"Hurry, Charles!" she exclaimed.

"Never fear!" Charles called out in response. He set his oars in the water in a confident, masterly manner, and before long the little boat was carving a path across the lake in strong leaps.

"Row faster, Charles! Row!" Harriet cried. She was quickly joined by Nancy, the pair of them keeping up a chant of, "Row, row, row, row," that made Charles settle his shoulders grimly into the task.

Harriet glanced to her right and watched as Connought as well began to pull hard toward the shore of the island. Both Arabella and Alison supported their captain as fully as she and Nancy. So it was Harriet squealed, cajoled, and pleaded, but just as they were drawing near the docks, Charles's hand slipped a trifle on one of the oars, his momentum flagged, and the earl's boat flew past them to the first of the island's two short docks.

Harriet and Nancy both groaned. However, she did not care overly much. The race had been fun in its way, but was not of the smallest import and certainly held nothing attached to it—say, a wager for an emerald, for instance—which could cause her the smallest concern. She had little difficulty, therefore, in offering her congratulations to the winners, after which she praised Charles to the skies for having given Connought an excellent race. Nancy followed suit, but soon after drew Alison aside as together the younger ladies moved to the adjacent dock, waiting for the next boat to arrive, which carried their particular friend Elizabeth, Harriet's cousin. All the while, Arabella fussed and carried on about Connought's prowess until Harriet finally whispered to Charles, "If you do not lead me away from her this instant, I vow I shall box her ears!"

Charles barked his laughter, wrapped her arm about his own, and led her in the direction of the tables where dinner was to be served. "I do not see Frith this evening," he commented.

"Mrs. Douglas said he declined her invitation. Apparently, he had an engagement in Tonbridge Wells and would not return until tomorrow."

"How fortunate!" he cried.

"What a dreadful thing to say!" she retorted.

"I cannot help it, Harriet! He is quite prosy and, in truth, I never did like the fellow. He used Connought quite ill once. I daresay I have never forgiven him for that."

"In what way?" she queried, her curiosity aroused.

He cleared his throat. "As to that, I should not have mentioned it. A matter between gentlemen, best forgotten!"

She sighed. Once any man spoke of something being a 'matter between gentlemen,' she knew she would learn nothing more of it no matter how hard she pressed.

The island, though not large, was draped with five beautiful weeping willows, beneath one of which three musicians were already plying their instruments to welcome the guests. The repast was laid out on a long table, the aromas having been beckoning them since their small craft landed at dockside.

When everyone had arrived, Charles relinquished her arm to Laurence, and she soon found herself seated with him at the end of one of the scattered linen-covered tables and enjoying the fine meal. She was situated at just such an angle that the Douglas home was in full view, and her gaze was drawn to the house again and again. The ancient house was a fine Tudor mansion which contained several formal gardens and a pretty wilderness attached to the most easterly rose garden. There, Connought had kissed her, just beyond the rose arbor that led to the wilderness. Her mind flew back to those unexpected, halcyon days. Had she ever been so young, so free of spirit and heart? Love had bit her hard and she had succumbed willingly, even if several of her friends, including both Margaret and Jane, had warned her about Connought's roguish reputation.

Connought had been her first love. Indeed, as time had proved, her only love. She glanced at him now. He was seated beside Arabella and listening intently to something she was saying. It would seem they were destined. Certainly nothing in his conduct refuted the rumors they would soon be engaged. If her nerves prickled at the very thought of it, she ignored such sensations. After all, she had given Connought up many years ago.

Beside her, Laurence chewed vigorously on a leg of cold chicken while she nibbled in silence on a slice of cucumber. She drew in a deep breath, letting her gaze drift to the opposite shore yet again. She was finding it very hard to have kind thoughts where Arabella Orlestone was concerned.

"What are you thinking?" Laurence inquired, licking his fingers, then taking a sip of champagne. "For you have a strange light in your eye."

"I was remembering," she said, her gaze still fixed in the direction of the estate where she knew the rose garden to be situated.

Laurence cast his gaze along the line of hers. "He still loves you, you know," he murmured.

"And I him," she answered boldly, admitting the truth to herself. Yes, tonight she was a different creature. Nothing like theft to change things.

Laurence glanced at her, stunned. "I had not believed it possible. Why the deuce do you not tell him?"

"He knows."

Laurence turned toward her quite abruptly, toppling over his glass of champagne. Righting it quickly, he spoke in an urgent undertone. "The pair of you are the queerest couple I have ever before witnessed. You still do not mean to hold that kiss against him? It was a fool's errand, that."

"A fool's errand?" she queried stiffly. "A rogue's errand, more like!"

"But you don't understand!" he began. A quick flush burned his cheeks and he said nothing more.

"What is it I have not understood?" she retorted in a hushed voice. She lifted her chin, then added, "He dotes on the attentions of women. It is as simple as that."

"You must be right," he responded somewhat coldly. When his color had receded, he glanced at the sky above the manor house. "Pretty time of day."

She looked at him, frowning. She thought there was something odd about the way he had become disconcerted and now affronted. She had the strongest sensation that he was concealing something.

"Why did you never marry?" she asked suddenly.

"You are of an age with Connought. Indeed, how is it possible none of you have wed?"

"I cannot answer for anyone but myself. I will say only this: the lady I love has loved another since time out of mind and for some reason no one else will do for either her or me."

She waited for him to elucidate his response, to give a name or even the smallest hint, but he remained silent. Though it seemed possible by the nature of his remark that he could be referring to herself, she knew this not to be true. Laurence had never evinced even the smallest interest in her, never a look, a smile, an attentiveness that might indicate he was to any degree attached to her.

She searched about in her head, viewing him in her mind's eye, Season upon Season in London. She tried to ponder to which lady he might be referring, but no one came to mind upon whom he had ever gazed with a sense that his love was unrequited. Besides, in considering all the ladies of their mutual acquaintance, there was not one who had been in the grips of a hopeless *tendre* for several years—only her own ridiculous self.

When the small group of musicians began playing a Scottish reel, Evan Douglas caught up Sophia Eaves's hand and begged Charles to get a partner and go down the dance with them. Charles sought out Arabella very quickly and soon to follow were Harry Eaves and Elizabeth, all taking up places opposite one another. Connought quite kindly asked her cousin Mary, who was but fifteen, to stand up with him.

"Would you care to dance, Harriet?" Laurence asked.

"I should like nothing better!" She rose to her feet and took up her place opposite him on the grassy sward.

The dance, though beginning politely enough, soon became a romp, for the ground was uneven, and more than once someone tripped and collided with another dancer. No one seemed to mind overly much, however, and the longer the dance continued, the greater the laughing and shouting. Harriet was perspiring by the time the reel was concluded and with some relief resumed her place at her table, once more nibbling on cucumber.

The evening progressed with more of Mrs. Douglas's champagne, a great deal of riotous dancing and shouting, and more and more hilarity. Harriet danced as much as she did not, as did all the ladies present, since there were ten ladies and only five gentlemen to go around. After two hours, the poor gentlemen finally called a halt. Since a stiff evening breeze had arisen, the island party drew to a close.

Harriet then set about inquiring of Charles if he would wish for a second race with Connought. Charles agreed readily, expressing his belief that he could best him if given another opportunity. "Excellent!" she cried. "For I could not help but notice that had not your oar slipped, you would have won the race."

"Precisely so," Charles returned.

"Then allow me to arrange things," she said.

"With pleasure," he returned.

After a few minutes, she sidled up to Connought. "Would you care for a wager?" she asked, her voice little more than a whisper.

He turned to her, startled. "Another wager, Harriet? You begin to shock me exceedingly."

"I daresay nothing shocks you," she countered.

"That is not true. I am shocked, for one thing, that after having been taken so ill this morning, you should be so well recovered as to dance several quite vigorous dances this evening, though only one of them with me."

She could not keep from grinning. To be reminded of her secret triumph this morning only served to brighten her spirits even more. "I have a wonderfully healthy constitution and found that by the time I had returned to Shalham I was fully recovered. We could therefore have enjoyed our ride after all. If only I had known the little spell I endured at your stables would pass so quickly!"

"Indeed. Quite unfortunate." He narrowed his eyes, but his lips twitched.

She wondered if he had grown suspicious of her. Regardless, she had an emerald to acquire. "So what do you say, my lord? A wager?"

"The stakes?" He touched his emerald pin.

Her gaze fell to his hand and she laughed. "Precisely."

"You are determined to have it, then?"

"If I am able."

"Very well, but there is only one thing I want of you tonight and it is *not* another of your kerchiefs." A wicked smile touched the corner of his mouth.

At that, she met his gaze and smiled, believing she understood him. "Done," she responded promptly.

He took her elbow, drawing her away from the crowd. "You will agree to another kiss, and that so readily?" he whispered. "Harriet, now you shock me truly!"

Harriet looked into his eyes and took in a deep breath. How was it that she had but to feel the smallest pressure of his hand on her elbow or experience the sweep of his whispered breath against her cheek and she was fairly trembling? For a moment, she could not answer him. She was entirely at a loss for words.

"Harriet, do you wish for your shawl?" Jane called to her from several feet away, bringing her back to earth.

Harriet glanced at her friend, who was presently holding the elegant length of silk in her arms. How grateful she was for the unexpected distraction. Perhaps now she could think. "No, I thank you," she returned. "I am quite warm. Wear it if you wish." Jane immediately wrapped herself in the ivory silk fringed confection.

Harriet reverted her gaze to Connought, her cheeks feeling decidedly warm. Now, however, she knew she could speak. "I have agreed to your terms because I am persuaded we cannot lose!"

"*Who* cannot lose?"

"Charles and myself. The wager involves a return race to the docks, Charles and I against you and a lady of your choosing."

"Charles agreed to this when I trounced him earlier?" he asked.

Harriet nodded. "Most enthusiastically! He is certain he can beat you this time, and I am of a similar mind!"

Connought laughed aloud. "Let him try. Very well, a wager it is!" He leaned forward and breathed against her cheek, "But you will soon owe me another kiss!"

Before she could protest, he left her side, immediately seeking out Mary Weaver again, delighting the young lady anew with his attentions. Harriet, however, frowned at his choice, and doubt suddenly rippled through her mind. Mary was exceedingly petite, indeed! She was herself of more queenly proportions and knew that Connought's boat would be far more easily propelled across the lake than Charles's. She had thought, most stupidly, that Connought would choose Arabella who, though small, was not nearly so diminutive as Mary.

"Oh, the devil take it!" she muttered in a most unladylike fashion. Fortunately, no one was nearby to hear her.

Before long, Harriet was seated opposite Charles and shouting for him to go faster and faster. She directed him toward the reeds just past the docks which had been designated as the finish line for the race. She guided him carefully, since he of course could not see where he was headed. For a long time, the boats raced with even bows. Halfway across the lake, however, Charles began pulling ahead and Harriet's heart soared. The emerald would soon be hers, she would win her wager, and then she would leave for Brighton!

"Fly like the wind, Charles!" she shouted.

Young Mary Weaver, however, having entered into the spirit of the race, urged her partner on as well with an almost frantic, "Go, my lord! More quickly still! The terrible pirates are about to make land!" Mary was a wonderfully fanciful girl.

Harriet heard Connought laugh, and perhaps it was his delight in Mary's absurdity or perhaps Connought had always had more strength than Charles, but he began to close on their boat. Harriet watched Charles strain with all his might and knew that he was putting forth a monumental effort. The reeds drew close. The boats flew through the water. How much she wanted the emerald!

In the last few seconds, however, Connought pulled ahead, flying past the reeds, clearly having bested Charles for the second time.

Harriet had lost the emerald for a second time. But what was worse, she had wagered another kiss!

However, she could not be sad, not for a moment, especially since Charles had given a very fine accounting of himself and was huffing and puffing as he turned the boat and began rowing to the docks. The race had been exhilarating and the remainder of the party, lined up on the dock as they were, greeted them all with wild cheering. Harriet felt as though fairy dust had been sprinkled all over her skin. The race and the wager combined had brought a warm flush to her cheeks, and now she must kiss Connought . . . again!

He said nothing to her, but the look in his eye and the extremely contented smile on his lips spoke his every thought. Knowing quite well that a rogue of Connought's stamp would hardly wait very long to receive his reward, she allowed the party to pass by her as the entire group, anxious to be out of the mounting wind, began walking up the slight incline to the gardens and the house beyond.

"I suppose you will be wanting your kiss now," she said, accepting his arm by way of escort. "I am most willing to accommodate you,since I believe the moment to be sufficiently propitious. Besides, in such cases, I would rather fulfill my obligation immediately rather than tarry, although I only hope you do not mean to linger at the task."

Connought chuckled. "How very romantic of you, Harriet," he said facetiously. "And to think for a moment I thought you might not be desirous of kissing me. But here you are, so evidently anxious to find yourself in my arms . . ."

"I intend only to keep my promise!" she responded severely, hoping that she appeared more confident than she felt.

"All for an emerald stickpin—"

"And I mean to keep my promise!"

"Just as I knew you would."

She was about to pass beneath the stone archway that led to the back of the house, but he caught her hand and pulled her back, drawing her close to the yew hedge and taking her in his arms. "We cannot be seen from here," he whispered. "However, since I have won this kiss, staked against something I cherish quite dearly, I *intend* to linger *at the task* as long as it pleases me to do so!"

Harriet could hardly breathe. She still felt flushed with the excitement of having engaged in a race, and now he was holding her fast. "What a beast you are," she whispered unconvincingly. "I beg you will kiss me and be done with it."

"First you must tell me why you desire my stickpin. This is the second occasion you have asked that the emerald be held in a wager."

"I suppose it is because I am particularly fond of emeralds."

He laughed outright. "What a whisker. What are you up to, Harriet? You are not generally so kind to me, nor so attentive, as you have been during the past several days. In any other lady, I would have supposed you to be flirting with me."

Harriet knew that by the terms of her wager with Margaret and Jane she could not allow him to guess at the nature of her interest in possessing his emerald, so she said, "Perhaps I am. Perhaps I wish to serve you with your own sauce. Perhaps I mean to engage your heart and, once having professed my love, then, oh, let us say, kiss Laurence for good measure!"

He scowled, but a smile quickly curled his lips. "I should like to see that. I daresay I should grow so very jealous that I would call Laurence out! We are both excellent shots, and we would both undoubtedly perish on the dueling field. Would you weep for me, I wonder?"

"I could never weep for anyone so foolish!"

"Yes, you would. You would cry day and night into your pillow for having lost me. Admit it is so!" He stroked the curls at her hairline near her left temple.

She shivered. "Oh, do kiss me, Connought, and be done with it!"

"I am in no hurry. You will have to accustom yourself to hearing me do the pretty. Have I told you how much I love the color of your hair?"

"Yes." She stated baldly, her pulse racing madly. "Yesterday, at the Bell Inn."

He kissed her temple.

"There, we are done!" she cried.

"Nonsense! That was hardly a kiss, and well you know it."

"Oh, very well. Only why do you delight in tormenting me?"

"Because I know you are not indifferent to me and that you desire this kiss nearly as much as I do. I can see how quickly your heart is racing."

"You cannot!" she cried, frustrated at having been found out.

"Yes, I can. There, at the base of your throat." First his gaze followed and then his lips.

He had never kissed her thus before, at her throat, forcing her head back. She was so overcome with sudden passion that she nearly fainted and truly could not catch her breath. Nor did he cease kissing her throat for a very long time.

When he had ceased, he caught her at the nape of her neck and, feeling her knees buckle, gathered her tightly about her waist. His lips then found hers in a searing kiss that stole the final bit of breath from her.

How long the kiss lasted she was never quite certain, nor was she certain she had refrained from swooning during part of it. That she felt as though she had been transported to a world which existed only in dreams was her only real thought. She had been aware that somewhere in the middle she had begun to breathe again, but only in small gasps that sounded like a dove's coo. Otherwise, when he had taken the last of her lips, she had blinked unsteadily at him and said, "Are you finished at last?" How hoarse her voice had sounded, as though she had been screaming against a strong wind for hours.

He thumbed her lips and her cheek. "For now. Can you walk?"

She shook her head. "You have crippled me."

"I take that as a compliment. Now I must ask you a

very simple question. If you delight so very much in a mere kiss or two, just how much do you think you would take pleasure in our marriage bed?"

She blinked a little more. "I believe I would perish," she said.

He laughed heartily at this. "Oh, my dear Harriet, you charmed me from the first. I beg you, marry me. Say you will marry me!"

Finally, sensation returned to her limbs and she could once more feel her slippers on the lawn beneath. Her trusted mind, as always, asserted itself. "No," she whispered. "Do not you see? I . . . I could never really trust you. Never."

"You could never trust yourself," he countered.

"What do you mean by that?" By now, his arms had grown slack about her so that she could have moved away from him, but the question stopped her.

"Only that when you finally give of yourself, you lose all sense of being able to control yourself or your destiny. Confess it, Harriet. Loving me frightens you out of your wits."

Harriet stared at him, unwilling to believe what he was saying to her. She was struck again by the strangeness of her own conduct over the course of the past several days. Even her willingness to enter into a wager with Margaret and Jane that was so wholly improper increased her sense of bewilderment. Was it possible that she did not know herself?

A memory tugged at her, something from many years ago, an event which had occurred long before she ever became acquainted with Connought, something she had forgotten until this moment. The month was August and quite hot, but the stream at the southern end of Paddlesworth ran cool. She had been sixteen at the time and had made her way to the stream, removed her stockings, and waded up and down the mossy rocks with her skirts caught up about her waist. She had delighted in what had been a rather scandalous thing to do, even though she had been quite alone at the time. She remembered thinking, *What would life be like lived so freely, without restraint, without so much fretting over propriety?*

The reverie slipped away, and Connought was before her once more. Her mind was jumbled so very strangely. Suddenly, she grabbed Connought by the lapels of his coat, pressed her lips firmly against his, and kissed him for a very long moment.

She drew back equally as swiftly and cried, "I should not have done that!"

Before he could respond, or perhaps kiss her in return, she slipped sideways and disappeared on a run around the arched entry into the formal garden.

"Harriet!" he called to her.

But like a child, she covered her ears.

Connought watched her go. He was stunned by her odd but wholly exciting conduct. She had kissed him so suddenly, so brazenly that he could only stand gaping at her retreating figure as she finally disappeared into the house. What had she meant by it?

He turned away, unwilling to follow after her just yet. He marched in the direction of the lake, shaking his head.

She had kissed him.

Harriet Godwyne had kissed him!

She had taken his coat in hand, pulled him toward her, then boldly and with some strength pressed her lips to his. He could still feel the imprint of her kiss, and his senses felt on fire suddenly. He had never been kissed like that before and could only wonder at her audacity. Was she perhaps hoping he might relinquish his emerald because she had kissed him?

He shook his head anew. No, Harriet was many things, stubborn and willful and perhaps manipulative at times, but in this moment, he sensed she had simply wanted to kiss him. And he had loved it!

If his mind immediately told him to beware, to be careful of unwittingly entrusting his heart to her, he was not as yet able to do so. Perhaps later. Perhaps tomorrow. He sighed heavily. Perhaps never!

Fifteen

When Harriet returned to Shalham Park that night, she went in search of her parents to see how her father fared. The housekeeper thought they might be found in the small parlor which opened onto the billiard room, but she could not say for certain. Earlier, she had brought Mrs. Godwyne a pot of tea, but that had been two hours past, at least.

Harriet made her way slowly toward the far end of the sprawling manor house. She felt uneasy, as though she had done something very wrong, but for the life of her could not recall just what that was. She was tired, however, which may have been the cause of her restlessness. So much dancing on uneven sod, besides the race with Charles against Connought, not to mention so much unwanted kissing—well! A young lady would have to be made of steel not to feel a trifle fatigued, let alone unsettled.

As she drew near the billiard room which preceded the small parlor, she heard a faint giggling and recognized her mother's laughter. How her heart warmed at the sound. That was something her father had always been able to do, to make her mother laugh. When his chortling followed, she realized the very same thing was true in the reverse.

Were they properly paired? she asked herself again.

From the time they had arrived brangling about her papa's gout, she had been doubting the wisdom of their union. Yet so much seemed to have happened in between which had set her to thinking that she had been a little too nice in her opinions of just what constituted a happy marriage. More laughter followed as she reached the door, which was ajar. She pushed it open and would have entered, but her mother was kissing her father. Her mother was seated on her husband's lap, well away from the offended toe, her arms clasped about his neck.

The sight was so shocking that she gasped and immediately backed out of the room, but her mother stayed her. "Harriet, wait! Do come in!"

Harriet returned, but she knew a blush was climbing her cheeks.

"What did you think, that I never kissed your papa before? But how nonsensical! Do come in, though, and tell us if your evening prospered." At the same time, she slid from her husband's lap and took up a seat in a nearby wing chair. The chamber was small and cosy and the tea things were still settled on a table within reach of her mother's chair. "Was the food to your liking? Were all your friends there?"

"Indeed, yes, on both accounts, with the exception of Lord Frith, who had gone to Tonbridge Wells. He is expected to return tomorrow."

"In time, then, for Connought's ball."

"Yes, I suppose so."

"How very nice." She glanced at the window. "A rather strong breeze came up earlier in the evening. We thought it might have affected your party."

Harriet sat down near her mother. "Indeed, it did. We took to our boats shortly after, for we could no longer dance and most of the ladies were distressed about the effect upon our coiffures. However, we once again took up dancing in the drawing room."

Her mother smiled. "Do you say, then, that you danced on the grass?"

Harriet laughed and told her how uproarious it all was, that there were so many stumblings and collisions that Laurence at one point had said that they had invented a new country dance called the island reel.

"How very droll! And not a sprained ankle among you?"

"Not one, although I do believe we were fortunate."

The conversation continued in this manner for nearly half an hour. Even her father was laughing at some of her anecdotes. Finally, when she had told them everything—well, nearly everything—she addressed her father. "And how is your foot tonight, Papa? Are you feeling much improved?"

"A little. I might be able to walk about with a crutch tomorrow. But, oh, how I miss my wine!"

"You will miss it a little more before much longer," her mother said firmly.

This brought a martial light to her father's eye and an answering one to her mother's. Harriet decided the moment was propitious to retire. "For I must say," she said, rising to her feet, "I have been wanting my bed this past hour and more!"

"Of course you have, dearest," her mother said. "Particularly since you went riding to Kingsland so early in the morning."

At that, she turned toward her. "You knew of it, then?" she asked, surprised.

"My dear, you know what small country neighborhoods are. You cannot tie your garter without the world knowing of it!"

"Oh, dear," Harriet murmured, laughing anew. She

could not believe her mother would say such a scandalous thing!

"You do mean to have him, though, do you not, my dear?" her father asked.

Harriet turned to stare at him. She was quite taken aback that he had broached the matter, since he so rarely offered his opinion about anything having to do with the course of her life. "I . . . that is no, of course not!"

He grimaced. "Still smarting after seven years because he kissed Margaret?"

"I believe it is a little more serious than that."

He beckoned her forward and took hold of her hand. "Now listen, puss. I've known you for a very long time, and I've known Connought as many years as well. He'll do, trust me, he'll do. He's enough bottom for an entire brigade. Always thought he should have purchased a pair of colors along with his brothers. Good lads, to the man! At any rate, I will give you my opinion just this once, wanted or not. Marry the man. He's right for you. Frith couldn't pound his way out of muslin bag, but Connought will meet you toe to toe, see if he won't. There, I've said it. Now off to bed with you!"

Again, she was stunned and, after kissing both parents on the cheek, turned and walked from the room.

Once having climbed between the sheets, Harriet found she could not sleep. Her parents' odd, affectionate conduct mingled with their brangling and accompanied by her father's opinion that she should wed Connought had given her a great deal to ponder. Since all of these thoughts were further complicated by the recent kisses she had shared with Connought, it was many hours before she finally fell into her slumbers.

Once awakening in the morning, however, her need to win her wager with Margaret and Jane soon took precedence. After all, there would be time enough to sort out all her complex feelings where love, marriage, and Connought were concerned. For the present, she must concentrate on somehow getting his emerald stickpin.

So it was that evening that she stood at the perimeter of Connought's ballroom and frowned slightly. Though she had not yet been bereft of a partner, having danced with Lord Frith, Charles, Evan Douglas, and Mr. Eaves, she had yet to enjoy either a dance or even a snippet of conversation with Lord Connought.

Having arrived at his home three hours past, she had barely been able to exchange but a handful of words with him. Of course, he was performing his duties as host to their small neighborhood, but she sensed something else was at work, for even when she approached him—and that at least three times—he had made quick work of being rid of her as fast as he was able.

The first time, he begged her to speak at once with Lady Eaves, for she had been ignored, even if unwittingly, by everyone present for the past fifteen minutes. On the second occasion, he had fobbed her off to dance with Harry Eaves, who trod on her slippers twice during the course of the cotillion. The last time she had approached Connought, she had joined the small group among whom he was numbered only to watch him almost equally as swiftly bow and move away.

Why was he ignoring her so steadfastly?

Worse still was the wretched panicky feeling she had been experiencing from the time she had awakened that morning until the present moment all because of the odious wager she had made with her cousin and Jane. Yes, she had Connought's watch as well as his riding crop, but for the life her she thought it a complete impossibility that he would ever part with his emerald. And as for suggesting another wager, somehow she doubted she could ever win another one against him. In short, she had less than three days now to accomplish the impossible!

As she perused the ballroom floor, where a waltz was in progress, she watched Connought guiding her cousin Mary about the floor. Harriet could not help but smile, despite her own frustrations. Mary was so small and Connought of such fine athletic proportions that it almost seemed as though he was dancing with but a child. Mary, only fifteen, was quite inexperienced, yet she smiled up into his face in the sweetest way, the top of her head not even meeting his chin. Her obvious ease with her partner she knew was due solely to Connought's considerable abilities. In this, he was truly a gentleman, and nothing could have been kinder nor more beneficial to Mary than to have had his tutelage during her fifteenth summer. When she one day enjoyed her first London Season, she would know herself equal to anything, for when she was so young, and so lacking in experience, she had waltzed with the Earl of Connought!

As Harriet once more surveyed the ballroom and all the dancers swirling about the floor, she found her agitation diminishing appreciably. She even found herself appreciating anew Connought's home. She had always thought the ballroom at Kingsland to be one of the most sensible chambers ever designed. The long, elegant room had been fitted on adjacent walls with rows of leaded glass windows, each of which could be opened to allow a flow of air when needed as the ball progressed. Connought's most exemplary housekeeper had additionally taken pains to lessen the exceeding grandeur of the ballroom by bringing a host of plants and flowers from the succession houses, which presently formed a dense wall of green at the northernmost portion of the room. The effect, in Harriet's opinion, was decidedly charming. Since the party was so small, the same group of friends and family was present this evening as had been at the lake on the evening before.

"It is lovely, is it not, Miss Godwyne?"

Harriet turned to find herself addressed by Arabella Orlestone, who regarded her from large green eyes wholly speculative in expression. She was struck again by how lovely Arabella was, a raven-haired beauty with exquisite green eyes, a delicate complexion, and lips perfectly bow shaped. She would have perhaps been accounted the most beautiful lady ever before seen, but there was a sharpness to her eyes, an expression of ambition, which Harriet had never been able to warm to.

"Most certainly!" Harriet responded. "Mrs. Billings is an exceptional creature, always an eye to balance in her arrangements, her object to make everyone comfortable."

"Oh, yes, I suppose the plants are a pleasant addition. I was referring to the architecture. Kingsland has no equal."

Harriet thought there were many equals to Connought's estate and any number of great houses which exceeded the obvious beauty of Kingsland. "His lordship's home is very fine, indeed," she countered with a smile.

Miss Orlestone laughed. "Perhaps I do make too much of it."

Harriet was surprised. Almost in this moment, she liked her. But since Miss Orlestone excused herself, making a beeline to Mary's side since the waltz had just concluded and Mary was still conversing with Connought, she merely shook her head. Laurence approached her at that moment and begged her to go down the next set. "Sophy has so badly trampled my feet that I am in great need of a partner who knows her steps. And you, Harriet, I daresay have never missed a step in your life!"

"Flattering me, Laurence? To what purpose, I wonder?" The opening refrain of the country dance began. Laurence lifted his arm and she placed hers atop his.

"No purpose!" he cried. "If you could but see the bruises on my feet—and I believe I have a tear in my slippers!"

"What a sham!"

He lifted his foot and, indeed, she could now see that he had not been telling whiskers. She could only laugh. "Poor Sophy! She practices her steps every day, but she seems to have none of Jane's grace and not one whit of Alison's skill."

The music commenced, and what conversation could be had was enjoyed in sometimes amusing fits and starts. What struck Harriet the most, however, was that at one point, she caught Laurence staring in the direction of the far corner of the chamber where Margaret stood in conversation with Lord Frith.

"Margaret appears rather fetching tonight in her gown of blue silk, does she not?" she asked.

Laurence snapped his gaze to her face, as he lifted her hand high in the manner of the dance. "Why, yes . . . I . . . er, suppose she does," he stammered.

"And I particularly like the manner in which she is wearing a host of blue flowers in her hair to match. They are from the garden at Shalham, I believe."

The dance separated them, but Laurence lost no time in directing his attention to the far corner yet again. Coming together, he said, "She must have stripped a bush completely bare!" he cried, scowling.

Harriet's suspicions jumped to the forefront of her head. She remembered what Laurence had told her only the night before, that he had been in love with a young woman for ages who had loved another and who had therefore remained inaccessible to him. "You love her," she whispered, knowing instinctively it was true.

She heard his gasp. The steps of the dance drew them apart, and when they came together again, she saw at once that his color was much heightened. His smile, however, was rueful. "If you have guessed at the truth," he whispered in return, "I hope that you will be discreet."

"Perhaps I will, perhaps not," she murmured tormentingly. The dance drew them apart once more. When he approached her this time, his brow was a trifle thunderous.

"You would not dare say anything to Margaret!" he cried, appearing somewhat panic stricken.

"For a price, I might keep silent."

He moved away, performing his duty to the nearest lady, and drew back. "What price?"

"Something very simple. I must have a waltz tonight with Connought, only I believe him to be avoiding me."

"Indeed?" he queried, frowning slightly. "That seems rather odd, unless . . ."

"Unless what?" The steps separated them and when they drew back together, Laurence insisted he had not the faintest notion what was amiss, if anything.

"Will you help me, then?" she asked.

"What? Oh, that! Yes, I suppose I will have to." There was a smile in his eyes, however, which led her to think he would not mind overly much if Margaret did learn of his interest.

When the dance ended, she watched him march up to Connought. She would have given anything to have heard what he was saying to him.

Connought, for his part, had turned to find Laurence at his most intense and could not help but laugh at him. "What the deuce is wrong now?" he cried.

Laurence however, appeared rather fierce, as he drew him aside. "Do not tell me you have decided to wed Miss Orlestone!" he whispered harshly. "She will not do!"

"What the devil are you talking about?"

"Only that I know you have already danced with Arabella, but Harriet tells me you have been avoiding *her.*"

"Indeed?" Connought said, taking his snuffbox from the pocket of his coat and taking a pinch. "She said as much?"

"Precisely so. Have you been avoiding her to a purpose?"

He shrugged faintly. "I suppose I have," he murmured, snapping the enameled box closed and slipping it back into his pocket.

"Why the devil would you do that, then, unless you have reconciled yourself to wedding Miss Orlestone?"

"I have my reasons."

"Are you wishing the wager undone?"

"Yes," he stated, feeling weary of a sudden. "Tell me, why do you think Harriet wishes to dance with me?"

"I really cannot say, old boy, but I thought it quite hopeful. She wished a waltz with you."

"A waltz, is it?" he queried, his suspicions deepening.

"Aye, that is what she said."

"And she sent you to do her bidding?"

"Yes, but it was a form of blackmail. She learned something about me that I do not care to have bandied about. Said she would tell if I did not secure a waltz with you. Sounds to me like you have but to make a push and she will be falling into your arms again."

He searched Laurence's eyes. "I am not so certain," he said. "I am convinced she has some game of her own afoot."

"Even if she does, it seems to have worked quite well in your favor."

He nodded. "I suppose it has. However, I do not like it and mean to press her a little. So what has she learned that she is using against you?"

Laurence's eyes drifted in the direction of Margaret, who was still engaged in conversation with Lord Frith. "That I am in love with her cousin, but it hardly signifies. I just don't care to have Margaret aware of it for the present, so if you would oblige me, I beg you will ask Harriet for the waltz, the sooner the better."

"Very well," he murmured. He couldn't ignore her the entire evening. Besides, he was not entirely content with the notion of wedding Arabella, however pretty she was!

Harriet watched in some relief as Connought left Laurence's side abruptly and fairly marched across the ballroom floor to beg her hand for the waltz. She was a little stunned, but accepted him politely. Whatever Laurence had said to him had worked with quick magic.

"So it would seem I have been neglecting you," he began, eyeing her with a crooked smile on his lips.

"Only a very little, but I have been wondering if perchance I have offended you in some manner."

"No, not in the least, I assure you."

They took up their places and assumed the proper pose, arms elevated, her hand on his shoulder, his on her waist. The music began and with no small degree of skill, the same he had employed with Mary, he guided her into the marked rhythm of the music and began moving her up and back, round and round.

Harriet felt an excited knot take shape in her stomach. "Oh, I do so like this dance!" she cried. "And you perform it so wonderfully!"

At that, he frowned upon her. "Harriet, I vow you trouble me deeply these days. If I did not know your words to be utterly ingenuous, I would say you were attempting to flatter me. But there is nothing in your present manner to indicate you are insincere, nor was there last night while we, er, *chatted* beside the yew hedge."

Harriet sighed inwardly. Though she had had every intention of limiting her remarks to subjects of unexceptionable merit or interest until she was ready to address the matter of the emerald stickpin, she realized that before she had made even a single turn about the ballroom floor, she was already being plunged into the extremely difficult topic of her relationship with Connought. His honest remark forced her to be drawn back quite suddenly to events of last night, while, after having been kissed quite unmercifully by Connought she had, for no reason she could as yet comprehend, kissed him in return. She could hardly tell him that her horrid wager with Margaret and Jane had forced her to engage his society anew, nor did she wish to elaborate on the truly frustrating theme that she enjoyed his companionship beyond bearing, nor could she possibly explain why she had kissed him as she had.

She chose, therefore, to apologize. "I went ridiculously beyond the pale yesterday," she said, the swirling motion of the dance beginning to make her dizzy. "I should not have kissed you."

"But you did. Why?"

"It was an impulse, best forgotten."

"You are still intent on repulsing me."

"Of course," she responded. "Has anything changed?"

He scowled and the arm about her waist tightened. Up and back, round and round.

"I would hazard a guess that if I have been avoiding you, Harriet, this is why. You might have kissed me and you might have been bowled over by the first kiss we shared after the race, but I knew how it would be. Right now, I feel so angry with you that if we were not dancing I vow I would throw your across my knees and flog your derriere very hard indeed!"

She was stunned by this speech and merely stared at him, wondering first how she was able to keep dancing without missing her steps, and secondly just how she was to go about closing her mouth, which had fallen agape.

"Yes, well you may stare, my dear," he continued, warming to his theme, albeit in a more subdued tone, "but you have been leading me a merry dance these past several days, and I am grown sick to death of it, blowing hot one moment, then cold as ice the next! Do you think I am made of stone that you may behave however you choose and I am to remain unmoved? No, Harriet. Whatever your game, I am not playing anymore. There is only one thing I wish to hear fall from your lips from this moment on, that you desire to become my wife. Anything beyond that I shall consider an absurdity!"

Harriet felt dizzy, strange, and a little ill. If Connought truly meant what he said, and she had no reason to believe he was dissembling, then she would be forced by the nature of her wager with Margaret to marry him after all.

She shook her head in some disbelief, unable to credit that as of this moment, she had all but lost her wager and yet in doing so would give Connought the very thing he demanded of her—her hand in marriage. How great an irony!

However, she would not despair and thought that there was a very, very simple solution to her situation, which could be resolved, but not until the dance was concluded. Betwixt times, she said, "I have used you ill and for that I am sorry. Could we for the moment, until the dance is concluded, forget our unhappy differences and enjoy the remainder of the waltz? Perhaps then we might converse, for there is something I must ask you."

He regarded her for a long moment. Up and back, round and round. "Of course," he murmured at last. And in keeping with the man she knew him to be, propritious and honorable, though a rogue, he began speaking of indifferent things like the pleasant state of the weather, a cut his horse had sustained when he had ridden out this morning, and just how soon she meant to remove to Brighton. "For I know you always go there after your summer sojourn with Margaret."

"Within the next sennight," she said, forgetting for the moment that she had told no one of her plans.

His gaze shot to her face at that, and something in his expression, disappointment perhaps, quite wrung her heart. Only then did she truly begin to comprehend the great disservice she had done him by all her actions since having agreed to Margaret and Jane's wager five days ago.

"I see," he murmured, frowning.

Conversation faltered, and nothing more was said until the dance was concluded.

Once he took her hand to escort her from the floor, he suggested they retire to the billiard room, where they might converse with a little privacy. She agreed readily. There were far more dangerous places in Connought's home or on his estate than a room taken up by a large table—the garden, for instance, or even onto the terrace, or, worse, the deep shadows of the home wood.

She sorted her thoughts the entire distance to the billiard room, which, given the enormity of Kingsland, must have been at least an eighth of a mile. By the time they reached the chamber, which was devoid of guests, fortunately, Harriet knew what she wished to say. "I have done something very foolish, Connought, for which I have neither explanation nor excuse. But I beg you will give me your emerald and then I shall leave you in peace."

He leaned against the table his arms folded over his chest. "Somehow in this moment, I am reluctant to give you anything. You already have my watch, *my grandfather's watch.* Why on earth would you need my emerald? You know my mother gave it to me."

She could see he meant to be stubborn. She chose to prevaricate. "I want your emerald as . . . as a memento of our . . . our love. I find I cannot seem to embrace the future as much as I would like, and I have been told that mementos of these kind help to place the affection as well as the discord outside of the heart, freeing one from the enslavement of such otherwise completely hopeless and useless feelings."

"Hopeless, perhaps," he said sarcastically, "but not useless. For if nothing more, they remind you, Miss Godwyne, that you do have a heart, even if you choose not to make use of it."

"That is not fair, not when it was you . . ."

He flung his hand up as though her words needed to be warded off with a physical blow. "Enough! I kissed Margaret and I am unworthy of you! Well, let me tell you something, Harriet, you are not worthy of me. When I first met you, I thought I had found a young woman whose spirit spoke to mine, whose heart was open to all manner of adventure and sensation. That first time you kissed me—and I knew it was a first kiss—the entire experience revealed precisely who you were. Previously, I had been enamored of you, but at that moment I was completely captured by your obvious passion not just for love but for living."

"What happened to you, Harriet? Why did my kissing Margaret that night completely quell all the liveliness and daring, the courage and trust in life that you so fully possessed? For I cannot believe a mere kiss could have such power. Indeed, I will never believe such a thing possible. You have told me, of course, that the kiss ruined your trust in me, but why did you allow it to quench who you were, who I believe you still are? My only delight has been that this week, in your pursuit of my watch, my riding crop—which, of course, you have not asked for again—and my emerald, have I seen something of the young woman with whom I fell so blindly and madly in love. I begin to think I have loved a ghost."

Harriet remained stunned for a very long moment. She stared at him, her thoughts an uneasy mass. She had not precisely organized them when she blurted out, "But it was you who inspired me. I was not . . . that is, oh, I cannot explain it! I . . . I was so frightened . . ." She got no further. The hallway was filling with the sounds of masculine laughter and shouting.

Harriet stood away from the door and was not surprised when Sir Edgar, Mr. Douglas, and her uncle appeared in the doorway.

"Hallo! What's this? Do we intrude?" Mr. Douglas cried.

Harriet relaxed her countenance. "Of course not. Lord Connought and I were quarreling, as we usually do, but I believe we are near enough to being finished that we might relinquish the billiard room to you."

"If you are certain!" Mr. Weaver cried, frowning slightly. There was, however, a dancing light in his eye.

"Without question," Connought reiterated. He drew close to Harriet and offered his arm. "And now, shall I return you to the ballroom?"

"If you please, I should be most obliged."

Harriet found herself utterly relieved when Connought relinquished her at last to Lord Frith, who kindly took her down the next country dance and afterward in to supper. As they entered the room, Laurence weaved past them.

"Laurence!" She called out. "Foxed again?"

He turned and offered her a crooked, droopy smile. "Half, perhaps, but not completely." Then he hiccuped.

"He never could drink but a glass or two without feeling the effect of even the weakest of wines," Frith observed.

Harriet could only smile, but not for long. Her thoughts were too caught up in remembering all that Connought had said to her in the billiard room. She took up a seat next to Frith, but scarcely touched the excellent victuals placed before her.

As she sat listening to him, or perhaps not listening to him, she came to an abrupt realization of just how much Connought meant to her. Suddenly she hoped she would never get the emerald from him, that fate would decide for her that she should wed him. She did love him. That had never changed. Oh, how dearly she loved him. She recalled her father's sweet, surprising words to her. *He's right for you. Frith couldn't pound his way out of muslin bag, but Connought will meet you toe to toe, see if he won't.*

The truly horrible thought then struck her that given all Connought had just told her, particularly in having said he believed he loved a ghost, that even if she now wished to marry him, there was an excellent possibility he would in the end reject her completely for all the trouble she had been.

"So what do you say, Harriet, my darling?"

She suddenly found that Frith was taking her hand and squeezing her fingers gently. "Oh, dear!" she whispered, withdrawing her hand at once.

A look of chagrin stole over his features. "Do not tell me you were not listening *again?"*

"I do beg your pardon, my lord. Indeed, I most earnestly beg you will forgive me, but my thoughts were engaged elsewhere." Her attention was caught by the sight of Connought entering the large dining hall at the far end of the room. He was escorting Margaret, who was clearly entertaining him quite well with some anecdote or other, for he was grinning delightedly.

Jealousy erupted in her so profoundly that even though Margaret was a most beloved cousin, she would take delight in tugging every last strand of red hair from her head.

She averted her gaze.

"So that is how it is," Lord Frith murmured.

"What? Oh, no! If you are thinking of Connought—no, you are greatly mistaken!" She did not know why she had begun rattling off a string of whiskers. "I am so sorry, Frith, but I am inexpressibly distracted this mor—this evening! Perhaps you could call on me tomorrow?"

"Yes, I would like that." He had leaned forward and spoken in so intimate a manner that she realized he still had not relinquished his hope of winning her. Well, she would tell him the truth tomorrow, that she could never be his wife.

Arabella drew near them both. "Your cousin certainly seems to know how to entertain Lord Connought," she said.

"Indeed, Margaret is a most amusing companion," Harriet said, surprised that Arabella would approach her for the apparent purpose of discussing the subject with her. She was further dumbfounded when she begged Lord Frith to excuse them, saying that she had something of vital importance to tell Miss Godwyne. There was nothing for it. Lord Frith rose, bowed, and moved away from the table.

"You have astonished me," Harriet said, unable to imagine what it was that Arabella might have to tell her.

"I would not have presumed upon interrupting what appeared to be a comfortable cose with Lord Frith," she said, her voice little more than a whisper, "but some startling news has just come to me by way of Laurence Douglas, who is quite in his cups, which I felt obligated to impart to you. Though ordinarily I would never presume to interfere, I felt as your friend that this was something of which you should be apprised,and that with the greatest possible haste."

Harriet turned more fully toward Arabella, utterly astonished. "And what would that be?" she queried.

"Only that you have been the brunt of a wager amongst Connought and his friends. To wit, he made a wager with Laurence and Charles involving you."

Harriet felt heartsick. She had, of course, suspected something like this, but knowing it was true, and that perhaps even some of Connought's conduct toward her had been because of the wager, distressed her greatly. "A wager?" she inquired on a murmur.

"Indeed, that Connought was to make pretty love to you until you were fairly swooning to marry him. Once you had agreed to marry him, the wager was won and the loser of the wager, Laurence Douglas, would in that moment be required to offer for your cousin, Margaret Weaver!"

Harriet digested this latest revelation. So Connought's purpose had been to get her to agree to marry him? This did not make sense.

"If I agreed to marry him, was I then expected to wed him?"

She shook her head. "It is quite despicable, but no, he

would not have then been required to marry you. The wager involved only the proof that he had won your heart."

"I see," she whispered, trying to make sense of it all. She knew intuitively that whatever Connought's interest in the wager, whatever his purposed in winning the contest with his friends, he was sincere in his sentiments toward her, however odious the nature of the wager. Connought was many things, but he had never once wavered in his love for her. And yet she knew she had provoked him badly enough to have given him a disgust of her. No, she thought she understood all of it quite perfectly and therefore if Arabella expected her to be shocked, she had missed her mark.

She felt Arabella's hand on her arm and turned to see her pitying countenance. "Are you well, Miss Godwyne? Have I erred in informing you?"

Harriet drew in a deep breath. She also felt she understood quite clearly Arabella's motivation in informing her in the first place. If Harriet were to take a pet and either ignore Connought completely or, better yet, leave Shalham for the summer, Arabella would find herself without the smallest competition for Connought's attention.

"There is nothing so pleasing as a friend who is quick to reveal every scandalous occurrence. This is not the first time you have been just such a friend to me. And now, if you will excuse me, I see Margaret waving to me."

"Of course," Arabella responded, her eyes wide with shock. There was just such a conscious expression on her pretty face that Harriet had little doubt she had taken her meaning completely.

She rose to her feet, anxious to speak with Margaret, but before she could reach her, Charles had commandeered her for the quadrille, which was just as well. The conversation she wished to have with her cousin ought to wait for a more private moment. Given all she had learned of Laurence's interest in Margaret, she was suddenly anxious to know what, if any, her cousin's interest might be in Laurence!

Sixteen

Later that night, Harriet rapped on her cousin's bedchamber door and entered when she heard Margaret call out to her. She then told her all that Arabella had said to her of the wager involving Connought, Laurence, and Charles, as well as their own part in the stakes.

"What do you think of that?" Harriet cried, settling herself with a flop on the end of Margaret's bed.

Margaret sat before her dressing table, staring wide-eyed at nothing in particular, all the while brushing her thick red hair ever so slowly.

"Margaret?" Harriet queried, when her cousin did not respond.

The brushing stopped, but still Margaret did not speak. Harriet watched her carefully and was stunned when tears began to trickle down her cheeks until she finally collapsed on her dressing table and began to sob.

Harriet went to her and attempted to comfort her, patting her shoulders and speaking in soothing tones. In truth, however, she was not at all certain why Margaret was so upset. Finally, Harriet rounded the side of the table and dropped to her knees so that she could look into her cousin's eyes should she choose to lift her head from her arms.

"Margaret, what is the matter?" she asked gently.

Margaret rose up slightly and met her gaze. "He does

not love me, you see. He never will. Was any young woman more foolish than I?"

Harriet squeezed her arm, finally understanding the source, however surprising, of her cousin's distress. Though she could not break her promise to Laurence and speak openly of his feelings, she felt she could at least give Margaret a hint. "I am come to believe that Laurence is not entirely indifferent to you. In fact, I believe he holds you in some affection."

At that, Margaret sat up, frowning severely. "What are you saying? You believe Laurence to be in love with me?"

Harriet was happy to be able to reassure her. "Yes, I believe he is . . ." She might have said more but it finally occurred to her that Laurence had told her only last night that the lady he loved happened to be most unfortuitously in love with another. She looked at Margaret and blinked several times. "Oh dear God," she murmured, the shock of the actual truth of the situation hitting her like a charging bull. "You were not speaking of Laurence just now, were you?"

Margaret sat very still, and more tears trickled down her cheeks as she shook her head.

"Connought?" Harriet asked on little more than a whisper.

Margaret nodded.

"How . . . how long?"

Teardrops fell onto the bodice of Margaret's nightgown. She did not answer for a full minute. Harriet remained silent, her knees and legs now aching from having remained in a cramped position.

Finally, Margaret drew in a deep breath. "Since ever I could remember. There has never been anyone else. I am such a fool!"

Harriet rose to her feet so greatly stunned that she felt as though she was moving through a dream. She made her way back to the bed and sat down. "Then," she murmured. "That day that he kissed you . . . Margaret, you must have wanted him to."

"I did. It was so very wicked of me when I knew that he was in love with you and you with him. He had said the kiss was meant to be in celebration of the betrothal, and though I thought it a little odd, I permitted it. However, from the first, I knew he meant only to touch my lips in an innocent manner. The moment he did so, I threw my arms about his neck and would not let him go. I wanted that kiss so very badly. You can have no notion. Afterward, when you broke off the engagement, the guilt I felt was beyond bearing, yet at the same time I knew such an elation that Connought was now free, that he might be able to love me instead." At that she turned fully to Harriet, "I have not been a friend to you! All these years, I have treated you far worse than Connought ever did. I . . . oh, Harriet, you will despise me when you know all!"

"There is more?" Harriet cried. She could not imagine what else Margaret meant to reveal to her. When her cousin remained white-faced, rather wild-eyed and silent, she pressed her. "Margaret, what did you do?"

"I . . . oh, it is too horrible, too vile. I have known you all my life, I know how you are, and had I just encouraged you instead of agreeing with all your stupid opinions about love and marriage, you would have long since wed Connought. But I thought, *If she does not soften her heart, then there will be a chance that in time . . . he will be mine!*"

Harriet looked down at the floor, trying to comprehend her cousin's confession. "Then . . . then you do not think I was right in refusing him all these years?"

She shook her head. "Everyone saw how devoted he was to you, and that kiss, at least where he was concerned, was wholly innocent."

Harriet stared at her in utter disbelief. "You would tell me this now, after all the times you abused his character?"

"There can be no excuse for my conduct," she said quietly.

Harriet slipped off the bed and crossed slowly to the door. When she had come to her cousin's bedchamber to talk over the news of Connought's wager, the last thing she would have expected was to hear Margaret confess to so despicable a thing. She could not respond when Margaret called out softly, "Harriet, please forgive me. Please!"

Entering the hall, Harriet closed the door with a snap behind her and began making a blind progress to her own room.

Harriet sat in a chair in her bedchamber near the windows and sipped a cup of hot chocolate. She had awakened on this Tuesday morning with her heart heavy beyond words. Scarcely six days had passed since the inception of the wager. So much had happened, so many words exchanged of an unhappy nature with both Margaret and Connought, that she felt at this moment as though she carried the burdens of the world on her shoulders. Margaret's betrayal of their friendship weighed heavily upon her heart nearly as much as certain of Connought's words, which kept returning to her. *You have told me that the kiss ruined your trust in me, but why did you allow it to quench who you were, who I believe you still are?*

She began to wonder if all this time she had been caught in a wholly unconscious manner between Margaret's love for Connought and her own inexplicable resistance to the man with whom she had tumbled in love. These were mysterious matters that hardly made the least sense to her. The first question which arose, however, was whether she had actually known of Margaret's love for Connought but had somehow chosen not to see it. Yet as she reviewed Margaret's behavior from times past, she could recall nothing of a particular nature which would have revealed the truth of her sentiments. Margaret was in that sense a very private person, but so she had always been.

The only real clue she had was that Margaret had allowed Connought to kiss her as he had seven years past, yet this she had dismissed as the act of a rogue who knew how to beguile any young lady, even a young lady of quality. As she pondered the circumstance now, she realized for the first time just how wicked her cousin had been regardless of Connought's skill as a rake. Whatever his fault, Margaret had been fully apprised of her betrothal to Connought, indeed of how violently she was in love with him, so the fact she had permitted Connought to kiss her could only be construed as an act of monumental betrayal. Only why had she never thought of it in those terms until now?

She took another sip of chocolate, then settled her cup on the table at her elbow. Why had she never seen it before? How obtuse was she? She could only conclude that for some reason, she had never *wished* to know the truth and so had ignored whatever signs were present.

The second matter which troubled her deeply was that Margaret had continued her betrayal by supporting her in those opinions of marriage and love which had kept her separated from Connought all these years. Yet as she contemplated this truth, she felt it ran along the same vein as the original betrayal, that whatever Margaret's duplicity, Harriet had purposely been refusing to see what was before her eyes. But why?

These were hard, painful subjects, to be sure. She had

so prided herself in her opinions, even justifying her stubbornness by calling it a virtue of principle, that she had never questioned them, not once in seven years, until now, until she was so full of unhappiness that she had no recourse but to examine her heart and her professed principles.

What if . . . oh, how her heart trembled at the notion . . . what if she had been hiding all these years behind her principles? How great a character flaw was that?

She turned to the final prickly matter—Connought's opinion that she had changed, that she had for all these years forsaken something of great value within her own spirit.

How much of what he had said to her last night was true? What had happened to her, she wondered, to that young miss who had walked with her skirts up about her hips the length of the stream at Paddlesworth? What happened to the young woman who had kissed Connought with such abandon, who had given her heart to so reckless a rogue so easily? He had upbraided her about these very things, and now she must ask herself if there was indeed merit to his opinions.

As she looked back on the past, in particular that first season of courtship when he had pursued her so relentlessly and she had followed suit with an equal degree of enthusiasm, she saw in herself someone she scarcely recognized. For those delirious weeks of his courtship, she had followed his lead not only mindlessly but with complete abandon and adoration. She had loved every moment of it, the stolen kisses, his touch which played at the edges of all that was improper, how he made her spirits soar with his heedless disregard for propriety.

Now, however, as she looked back with a clearer eye, she also recalled other occasions when, after a particularly impassioned embrace or a daring defiance of society's rules by forming secret assignations just to see him and to be with him, she would in the late hours of the night, while in her bedchamber, find herself trembling with fright at all she had done. She recalled that more than once she had been prepared to end the courtship because she felt anxious about his reputation and her worries that she would go beyond the pale and embarrass her family. Once in his presence, however, she would lose all sense of herself, her fears would disappear, and she relegated her anxious thoughts to the deepest parts of her mind.

She began to understand that his conduct in kissing Margaret had given her an excuse by which she could break off the engagement.

Crossing her arms very tightly over her chest, she allowed the conclusions of all her ruminations to rush over her, the force of it as powerful as a hurricane. She now recalled the very moment Arabella had come to her with the news that Connought had kissed Margaret. Yes, there had been a part of her that had been devastated, but there had also been a part that had felt the most profound relief. She no longer had to be afraid, though of what she was still not certain.

Margaret's face had been white with grief and embarrassment over the incident, but Harriet had assured her cousin that she did not blame her in the least, that she had known all along what Connought was, and that he had behaved just as she would have expected a rogue to behave. She then spent a great deal of time marching indignantly about the room, expostulating about his odious character, and building a very fine wall about herself.

From that moment, her conduct had become entirely withdrawn and unyielding. When Connought called on her, no amount of protestations, of abject apologies, of pleadings had softened her heart toward him. He had apologized for the kiss, begging forgiveness, but she had set her heart against him in that moment, for now and for always. Last night, when Arabella had told her of the present wager in which she played a significant role, the news certainly should have given her the ease she was presently seeking. After all, her ill opinion of his character had been once more vindicated. If she desired, she could preen herself on her remarkable perception and could go about thinking as badly of him as she liked.

Except . . . she had never been more miserable in her entire existence. What might have served when she was a young miss of eighteen did not settle so well on her more experienced mind and heart of five and twenty.

She spent the next several hours dissecting all that had happened and laying open as far as she was able the truth of her heart, her mind, and her spirit. Her fears she examined at length and was surprised to find that with all her outward boldness, she was a far less courageous creature than she had heretofore thought.

In the midst of her cogitations, she summoned her maid and dressed for the day. Once ready, she found she was not yet prepared to quit her deliberations. She therefore carried a book about with her from room to room in the manor itself and from garden to garden once out-of-doors. As soon as someone would appear, she would open her book and pretend to be engrossed, thereby fobbing off any of her dear family who would intrude into her reveries. She was able, then, to continue reviewing her life, her strengths, her failings, lost in a state of quiet if agitated reflection.

Of Margaret, she saw nothing and learned that she was laid down upon her bed with a sick headache. Poor Margaret—and yet how could Margaret have betrayed her so completely? Worse, why had Harriet never seen her betrayal for what it was? Worse yet, why had she made singular use of Margaret's actions to hide behind her own shortcomings?

She had just entered the rose garden for the third time when a gentleman appeared at the far end. For the barest moment, she thought Connought had arrived, and how her heart leaped! More than anything she wished to speak with him, to lay her difficult thoughts before him and see if he might be able to untangle the unhappy threads of her life. Instead, however, she recognized the tall figure of Lord Frith, who smiled as he doffed his hat in making his approach.

"Do I disturb fair Aphrodite?"

"You are too kind. No, you do not disturb me in the least. Do you care to take a turn about the garden?"

"Of course. I should like nothing better."

She could be at ease with Lord Frith, she realized. She was always comfortable in his society, and though she knew she had a labor to perform today in coming to understand herself, she found she was grateful for the much-needed pause in her intense musings. "So what brings you to Shalham today?"

"I should be telling a Banbury tale if I gave you any other reason than your own dear self, Harriet, to which purpose I would add that I had cause for concern last night. I could not help but notice that after your conversation with Miss Orlestone, you became rather distraught. Indeed, your complexion remained quite high the remainder of the evening."

"Did it, indeed?" she cried. "And you took notice of it? I must say, my lord, you have proven an excellent friend to me time and again."

"Then will you tell me what is amiss? Even now you seem distressed."

Only with the most strenuous of efforts did Harriet

withhold the sigh which threatened to escape her throat. "I fear I am in the most ridiculous coil, from which I have no certain knowledge at present just how to escape."

He was silent a moment, then finally queried, "And will you tell me the nature of the coil? Perhaps I might be able to advise you."

"As much as I value, even cherish our friendship, my lord, I fear I cannot. I am searching my deepest thoughts, you see, and only I can succeed at the task."

"This sounds quite serious, but I have often found that even in such moments, the careful, considered listening of a good friend will often cast new light on a difficult subject."

"You are very kind, but I fear it would avail nothing."

"You do me an injustice," he said quietly.

She glanced up at him. "In what way?"

"In not trusting me sufficiently to tell me your troubles. I have always wished to be your confidant. Indeed, I have always felt that were you to trust me a little, you might be surprised in the ways I could add to your comfort, even your happiness."

She stopped and turned toward him. "You have been the greatest friend I have ever had. You have always been at my side in my most dire moments, and in this moment I truly do not wish to cause you either offense or grief, which I feel certain that were I to relate the particulars of my woes, you would be both. I . . . I am not always the most virtuous, well-bred young lady I should like to be, or even at times you think me."

"Now you do yourself an injustice," he cried. He possessed himself quite suddenly of her hands, giving them a tender squeeze. "I know that you have a very lively, a very playful disposition, which you reveal so sweetly to those closest to you in your most unguarded moments. I have only one wish at present, that you might be mine, to love, to cherish, to see sitting across from me when I look up from my morning paper. Harriet, will you marry me?"

Harriet blinked several times. She saw the earnestness in his face, and certainly his speech could not have been prettier or more pleasing. She wished more than life itself that her heart was inclined toward him. She wondered . . .

"If you would but kiss me," she began, intending to say more, but an instant light suffused his face and he interrupted her.

"My dear Harriet!" he cried, releasing her hands and catching her up in his arms. He kissed her quite abruptly. All the while, her right arm was trapped across her stomach.

She would have bid him cease at once, but then she understood what she had wanted in the first place, to know how she truly felt about him, if she could ever truly love him. She waited and wondered when the magic would begin. She opened her eyes and looked at the sky beyond his face. Where was the odd tingling that should accompany so impassioned a kiss? Why could she still feel her feet, and how could there yet be so much strength in her knees?

At long last, the kiss ended. Though the duration could not have been much above fifteen seconds, it seemed to have lasted an eternity—but not in the happier sense. He drew back, his features wreathed in smiles. "You have made me the happiest of men!" he exclaimed.

"I have?" she queried, uncertain how this was possible.

He took her arm, hooking it about his own, and began, "When we are married . . ."

Enlightenment dawned so swiftly that she jerked her arm away from his more rudely than she intended. "My lord!" she cried. "You have misunderstood me entirely.

I realize it is my fault, but you were so hasty, so precipitous that I was unable to complete my thought. I had meant to say a moment ago, 'If you would but kiss me, perhaps then I could better judge my sentiments.' I realize now that I should not have put my emotions to the test in such a manner, particularly since you misconstrued my intention, but I beg you to believe me that I must give you my answer now. Lord Frith, I fear I cannot marry you, for in truth, I do not love you. I do not believe I ever shall!"

His face drained of color and became perfectly white against lips that remained strangely red. "I do not understand."

"I feel I must apologize for having kept you dangling for seven years. That is how long it has been, has it not? Oh, dear Lord Frith, what have I done? I should have spurned your advances so many years ago, but until this moment, until this sennight, I do not think I ever truly understood myself. Indeed, in this moment I am still horribly confused—"

"Then you should not be so hasty if you are confused. Wait for a day or two—"

"You mistake me. I am confused about many things, but not about my sentiments where you are concerned. Lord Frith, I can never be your wife. Never, do you understand? I do not love you as a wife should love her husband, and I do beg you will forgive me."

"Forgive you?" he uttered bitterly. "Good God, Harriet! Do you know what you are saying? What you are rejecting? You must be very confused, indeed! I have twelve thousand a year! Even Connought does not have so much!"

Harriet took the smallest step backward. She had never seen Lord Frith angered before. He had always showed her a most amiable and quiet countenance. "I . . . I am sorry, my lord." She searched his eyes and watched as a film of red overcame them. She took another step backward.

"All this time, I have been waiting, hoping, believing that you would get past this ridiculous *tendre* for Connought. That is why you cannot love me or any other man, is it not, Harriet?"

She knew it was far more serious than a mere *tendre*. She looked away from him, unable to give him answer. She shook her head and tears started to her eyes.

"Answer me!" he commanded. "I deserve to know at least that much!"

"I beg you will not press me," she responded quietly.

"Not press you!" he snapped. "I have danced attendance upon you for seven years, as you have said, always with the hope that my kindness to you, my persistence would one day reap the reward I feel I deserve. Instead, you tell me now you do not love me, that you can never marry me! I do not hesitate to say that I feel very badly used."

"But not purposefully!" she cried. "Not intentionally! I simply did not know my mind or my heart. I suppose I kept hoping that my sentiments would change, and indeed there were times . . . but that no longer matters. I know now I cannot be your wife."

His eyes blazed with indignation and rage. His entire being grew stiff as he glared at her. She wondered if he meant to strike her. His countenance then altered strangely and his demeanor softened. "You are an innocent," he murmured. "You always were." He bowed suddenly and turned on his heel, but she heard him mutter, "Damme if I do not know precisely at whose door to lay this mischief."

She watched him go, knowing full well he felt Connought was to blame and not her own dear self. How wrong, how terribly wrong he was in that. She had led him a merry dance, however much done in ignorance, all so that she might not feel as frightened as she truly was.

She knew an impulse to call him back and to explain the truth to him, but given that she had overset him by at last refusing him, she thought it might be best to wait to speak with him at another time

She moved slowly about the rose garden once more, her thoughts drawn back to Connought. She looked down the years, reviewing her memories of her time with him. How very much she had adored him. Yet she understood so very clearly now that fear had been her overriding flaw, something she could scarcely credit, for she had always seen herself as full of pluck. Perhaps that was true when riding out on her favorite mare or learning to handle the ribbons at the age of fourteen, and even in the more demanding environment of the drawing room at the pianoforte. In these surroundings, she had always excelled and met each challenge with great courage and fortitude. However, it seemed in the less well-defined aspects of life that she did not rise to the occasion so well as she might. Connought had been one of those occasions.

What joy Connought had brought to her, yet what wretched fear. She had never been so afraid in her entire existence as when she would return from an assignation to a crowded assembly room or drawing room. As she pondered these truths, however, she realized that her fears had had nothing to do with being found out, but rather from the growing depths of her feelings for a rogue who could not be managed so easily as, say, Lord Frith.

Understanding as brilliant as the July sunshine poured over her in heavy, repetitive waves. She felt dizzy and euphoric all at the same time. She had feared him because he had loved her as a man loves a woman, without the smallest reservation. She had been too young to properly receive that love in the deepest parts of her heart. She had felt sunk completely, as one being drawn into the deepest parts of a lake without the smallest possibility of ever rising to the surface again. At the same time, she had not known how to give expression to these sentiments, certainly not without seeming like a schoolroom chit. At the time, such a notion had been utterly reprehensible. What would Connought have thought of her? So it was she had taken a different course, one of silence, separation, and a loneliness so intense that there had been times she wondered if she would ever be happy again.

When Connought had kissed Margaret, she had used his disloyalty like a drowning child clinging to a floating bit of debris until the tide should carry her safely to shore. Only what was to be done now?

Seventeen

Connought leaned on his pool stick and watched Laurence turn his back on Charles. The latter, seeing his opportunity, moved a ball an inch to the right.

"Put it back," Laurence stated coolly, shifting around to glare at him.

"How the devil did you know?" Charles cried.

"From the corner of my eye, I watched you bend at the waist."

"Given such a position, how did you know I was not just lining up my shot?"

Laurence stared at him in disbelief. "Do you take me for a flat?"

Charles laughed, lined up his shot properly, and sank the ball. He was an excellent player, so there was no accounting for why he attempted to cheat at billiards, and that only with Laurence. Connought chuckled, but he felt far from jolly himself. This latest quarrel with Harriet had worn on his mind like a steady stream of water working away the jagged edges of a rock.

Mingled with his unhappy thoughts were all the more recent memories, beginning with his assault on her in the cherry orchard nearly a sennight past, of holding her in his arms and kissing her several times since, and finally quarreling with her quite strongly last night in this very room. He felt a change within him, of fatigue born out of despair. In a way he could not explain, he did not care if he ever saw Harriet Godwyne again.

The billiard balls clattered again, drawing Connought's attention back to the game. Despite Charles's attempt to cheat, he still won the game honorably, a circumstance which piqued Laurence to no end. He had just begun animadverting on Charles's lack of character when a commotion was heard in the hall.

Connought straightened up and listened to what increasingly sounded like Mollash brangling with an unwelcome visitor.

"What the deuce!" he cried, stepping forward. When he reached the doorway and glanced up the hall, he saw Mollash barring the hallway at the far end. To his utter astonishment, Lord Frith towered over his loyal retainer, his countenance much heightened as he threatened to plant the butler a facer if he did not step out of the way.

Connought frowned. "Let him pass, Mollash!" he cried. "Frith, what the devil are you doing insulting my butler?"

Frith moved rapidly toward him. He was in high dudgeon, but just why was entirely unclear.

"Of all the scoundrels, the blackguards, you are the worst!" he cried.

Connought lifted a brow. "Indeed? And when did you draw such a conclusion?"

"You have cheated me out of the only prize I have ever coveted and, by God, you shall answer for it!" With that, Frith ran the last few steps and threw a wild punch.

Connought feinted easily and, at the same time, slapped Frith across the side of his face, sending him hard to the floor. Frith lay on the carpet in the hallway, glaring up at him, his eyes blazing. "Bastard!" he cried out.

Connought stared at him, unable to comprehend what could have happened to have brought Frith to Kingsland in a towering passion.

"Should not have said that," Laurence said from behind him.

"Badly done, Frith!" Charles agreed.

"Well, have you nothing to say?" Frith yelled.

Connought glared at him. "Have you gone completely mad to come to my house in such a manner?"

Frith's eyes narrowed as he slowly rose to his feet, his mouth turned down bitterly. "I always knew you were a coward. I can see it in your eyes even now. A coward, a blackguard, and a bastard!"

Connought's temper shot through his head. He lifted his arms, only to find them pinned as quickly by Laurence and Charles. He shook them off, then responded in a controlled manner, "Name your seconds, Frith! You have desired to face me across a green for any number of years, so let us be done with it this time. Douglas and Badlesmere will act for me. Swords or pistols?"

"Pistols. I shall send word to your seconds before nightfall with the names of my seconds and location." With that, he quit Kingsland.

"A duel?" Harriet cried. "Between Connought and Frith? Impossible!" Yet, even as she looked into Jane's pale face, she understood what had happened. Frith had left Shalham in a dreadful state and had gone directly to Kingsland. She recalled now that he had said he knew who was responsible and realized he had meant Connought. "Swords or pistols?" she asked, her heart hammering in her chest.

"Pistols," Jane responded quietly.

"Oh, dear God." It was well known that Frith was one of the finest shots in England, holding numerous records at Manton's Shooting Gallery in London. Connought's abilities were less well known. He was an avid sportsman, as were many gentlemen, but a love of shooting cock pheasants and wood pigeons was hardly an indication of skill with a duelling pistol.

Harriet shuddered.

"What are we to do?" Jane asked, taking up a seat beside her on the sofa nearest the fireplace. The drawing room was empty at present, the rest of the family having taken a walk in the home wood. Margaret was still closeted in her bedchamber.

"I am not certain in the least what can be contrived. You know how the gentlemen are about codes of honor. No amount of reasoning will bring them back from that cliff, I fear."

"Do you know why Frith forced a duel? It is my understanding that he stormed into Kingsland, attempted to plant Connought a facer, then called him every manner of horrible name. Charles could not repeat them all, so bad were they!"

Harriet thought back to her distressing interview with Frith and nodded. "When he left me earlier today, he was as mad as hops."

"Whyever for?"

Harriet looked at Jane. "Because I finally refused him. I mean, I finally came to understand that I could never love him, and so I made my sentiments clear."

"And after all this time," Jane murmured. "He must have been expecting you to relent at some point. How shocked he must have been."

"Indeed, I believe he was, and quite angry as well. I have behaved so very badly toward him, but never once did I truly comprehend that I was keeping him dangling after me. Truly I did not! Which is most lowering, for I have always thought I was an intelligent creature!"

Jane patted her hand. "And so you are, just not where

Connought and Frith are concerned." She paused for a moment, then cried out, "Goodness, Harriet! A duel!"

"There is something else I think you should know," she said. "Perhaps it is not so bad as a duel, but quite unsettling." She then told her about Margaret's earlier revelations.

Jane listened in stunned silence. "She has loved him all this time?" she asked, incredulously.

"So it would seem," Harriet murmured.

"And she confessed to having used arts in an attempt to keep you apart from him?"

Harriet nodded. "But I do not blame her, Jane, for I have come to see, to truly understand, that I kept myself blind to my own fears." She spent the next several minutes discussing at length the recurring panic and frights she had experienced throughout the course of Connought's courtship. Finally, she reiterated, "You must see now that I am equally to blame with Margaret. What she did was wrong, but it would have had no significance in my life whatsoever had I not already determined to steel my heart against Connought. Do you understand?"

"No," Jane retorted, smiling faintly. "Not in the least, but I will choose to believe you. Only, where is Margaret now?"

"She has been weeping into her pillow for hours, or so her maid told me."

"Do you think I should go to her?"

Harriet squeezed her arm gratefully. "I was hoping you would do so. Convince her I am not in the least upset. She has asked for my forgiveness, but I have not had a chance to speak with her and to make it clear that I hold no grievances against her."

"I shall be happy to do whatever I can," she said, rising to her feet. Before departing the drawing room, however, she turned back, "Harriet, what are we to do about the duel? We cannot permit Lord Connought to be killed!"

At that, Harriet rose to her feet as well. "I do not know," she stated. "However, I mean to do all that I can to put a stop to it!"

"But how?"

Harriet laughed. "I have not the faintest notion, but mark my words, I shall contrive something!"

Once Jane quit the drawing room, Harriet paced the long chamber for several minutes, attempting to concoct some means by which she might effectively end the duel. No immediate remedy came to mind, however, and it was not many minutes later that she suddenly stopped in her steps, awareness of a different kind striking her hard.

She stood rooted before the sofa, her thoughts centered upon Connought. There had remained from her earlier reflections one kernel of truth that snagged her now and held her hostage, a truth which could not be denied—she loved him. She loved him, she would always love him, and he would always be the ideal against which the rest of mankind would suffer comparison. The difference of seven years' time, however, was simple—she was no longer afraid. Indeed, she knew in this moment that she would risk everything—her reputation, her fortune, even her life—to prove herself worthy of Connought's love. Only how to prove it to him?

She shuddered. Was it possible, though, that it was now too late? Would he ever be able to understand or to forgive her?

There arose within her the strongest need to speak with Connought, the sooner the better.

Just as she turned to quit the chamber, however, Margaret appeared in the doorway, alone. Her face was extremely pale and her lovely blue eyes were swollen and red-rimmed.

"My dear cousin," Harriet said.

"Jane sent me to you," she said. "Oh, Harriet, how you must despise me!"

Harriet ran to her and caught her up in a tight embrace. "It is no such thing, I assure you," she cried. She felt a sob shake Margaret's shoulders, and she held her more tightly still.

"I am so sorry, Harriet. You can have no notion. I do not deserve to be forgiven, and yet Jane tells me you somehow think you are to blame, but I do not see how that is at all possible."

Harriet chuckled softly. "After you hear what it is I have to tell you, I wonder if it is you who will despise me."

Margaret's attention caught, she drew back and wiped her face with an already drenched kerchief. "That would be impossible!" she cried. "You were completely innocent, the virtuous one amongst us—you and Frith, of course. Perhaps you are suited after all."

At that, Harriet began to laugh and could not seem to stop. "Oh, if you only . . . knew!" she exclaimed between chortles.

Margaret regarded her quizzically. "Have you been in the sun too long? I begin to think you have developed a brain fever."

When at last Harriet had caught her breath, she once more hooked her cousin's arm. "Come. Let us share a cup of tea in the conservatory where we may be private, and I will tell you all."

Sometime later, with a cup and saucer balanced on her lap, Margaret shook her head in disbelief. "And these are the conclusions you have drawn? But I fear I do not understand. Your reasoning is not sound."

"My reasoning is quite sound," Harriet said, strolling before a large fern and letting the frond tickle the tips of her fingers. She sighed heavily. "I was afraid of my love for Connought, so terribly much. Every action from the moment of learning that he had kissed you—or that you had kissed him, whichever is the case—was dominated by these fears."

"Are you afraid now? Of him?"

She shook her head. "Not in the least. It is the most amazing thing. I believe I needed these years to grow out of my girlhood. Now that I am arrived, however, I begin to think I might be too late."

"Connought will forgive you."

Harriet shook her head. "I do not know that for certain. Besides, at the moment I wish to know if you will be able to forgive me."

"For what?" she asked, clearly stunned. "Particularly since the shoe is so completely on the other foot."

"Only in the most superficial sense. Don't you see? In hiding behind my supposed virtue, I allowed you to continue in your guilt."

"We are both at fault then." She drew in a deep breath and sipped her tea. A smile trembled brightly on her lips. "Well, since you mean to take such a generous view of my scurrilous conduct, there is only one thing to be done." She set aside her cup and saucer and rose to her feet. A moment more and Harriet was embraced fully in her arms. "I forgive you, my dear, dear Harriet."

Harriet held her tightly. "My dearest and best of friends."

After a time, Margaret drew back and resumed her seat near her easel. "What do you intend to do about the duel?"

"I do not know yet, but I shall contrive something!" She then addressed the original subject of last night concerning the wager between Connought and his friends, which involved Margaret so nearly.

"Margaret, do you think you could ever love Laurence?"

She had expected her cousin to be surprised by her asking such a thing. Instead a troubled light entered her eye.

"I should not have pressed you," she said earnestly. "Pray, do not feel compelled to give me answer if you do not wish to do so."

"It is of little bother. Indeed, I am glad you asked, for I have been pondering the very same notion since last night." Margaret lifted her gaze to her. "I feel as though our conversation after the ball opened my eyes to everything. I think, given time, I could love him. For I can now recall with perfect clarity several times that I thought him remarkably handsome. Then my ridiculous *tendre* for Connought would rear its vile head." She laughed, "I suppose, however, that if you are able to obtain Connought's emerald stickpin, you will force me to accept of his hand anyway."

Harriet shook her head. "I believe I would happily get the stickpin for such a reason, but only if I believed it would truly secure your happiness. For the present, therefore, I shall not, since my losing our wager would allow me to have the prize I desire most. Only, will the prize want me?"

Margaret smiled. "There is only one way to find out. If I were you, I should do so at once!"

Harriet could not have agreed more, and instantly summoned her father's traveling coach to be brought round.

The ride to Kingsland was one of the longest in Harriet's existence. The five miles which separated the estates could easily have been fifty for all the anxiety she was experiencing. Her heart could not seem to settle into a dependable rhythm, and every bend in the road sent her heart racing anew. Now that she had come to understand her heart, she would have given her considerable dowry to have been able to grow wings in that moment in order to fly immediately to Connought's home.

Of course, she had but to consider the unfortunate truth that the earl might not be desirous or even mildly interested in what she had to tell him and she grew amazingly grateful for the plodding of the horses in the dry, dusty lane. Tears touched her eyes briefly. What if she had come to understand her heart at too late an hour? What if he no longer loved her? What if . . . oh, she could not bear her thoughts. If only the coachman would urge his horses faster!

At long last, the coach drew before Kingsland, one of Shalham's grooms opening the door and letting down the steps, the other setting the iron ring on the front door to sounding loudly. By the time Harriet had made her descent, Mollash appeared in the now open doorway. He bowed politely to her and answered her gentle inquiries as to his health. With trembling heart, she then inquired if his master was at home.

"Aye, miss. If you will but wait."

Harriet nodded and tried to draw in a breath, but she could not, or at least not very easily. In all the years of her acquaintance with his lordship, this was the first time she had ever been truly afraid of meeting him.

When Mollash returned to show her to the library, she followed after him, her hands clasped tightly about the strings of her reticule, fairly strangling the poor, beaded purse. After a march of what seemed like a mile or two, she found herself entering the tall chamber where the collecting efforts of several generations had seen books arranged floor to ceiling on every wall of the elegant room.

Connought stood by the window opposite, his hands clasped behind his back as he looked out into the garden. His expression was wholly grave.

He turned slightly toward her. "Why have you come, Harriet?"

This was not a propitious beginning. "There is something I would say to you, if you will allow it."

He stared at her, his blue eyes cold and unfeeling. "Yes, I will allow it, but I beg to inform you that I have an appointment with my bailiff in ten minutes."

Harriet's heart sank. "I shan't detain you long, my lord," she responded in kind. Since he made no move to surrender his position by the window, she crossed the room quickly and with as much confidence as she could summon. Once before him, she met his narrowed gaze and drew in a deep breath. "I have been utterly mistaken in myself and in you these past several years. Since our conversation of last night and . . . and Margaret's confession that she had deliberately encouraged me in my self-righteous conduct, I have come to understand that I have been something a hypocrite. I have come to beg your pardon."

A flash of something sparkled in his eyes, then died. "Indeed?" he responded.

"I loved you so very much that season of our courtship. You can have no notion."

"Not enough, it would seem."

"You have spoken truly. Not enough to overcome my fears. I was a coward that day. No, for all those many weeks when you courted me. I lived in the worst fear of being sunk in my feelings for you, frightened that I would one day awaken to find I no longer existed. I know this cannot be making even the smallest sense, but . . ." She paused, searching for the right words.

"Go on," he murmured.

"Every night after we had met secretly, I would lay in bed awake for hours, trembling, not with desire as any sensible miss would, but rather with such frights as you cannot imagine nor can I explain. You were an overpowering soul to me, and I . . . Connought, I was a child then, scarcely more than a babe, a chit just removed from the schoolroom. I loved you so desperately, but without even a jot of worldly experience or knowledge to be able to handle so much passion and true delight with the smallest equanimity. The kiss you gave Margaret became my excuse to let you slip from my life."

He was frowning. "Are you saying that all those weeks, months, of our courtship, these were the feelings which held you in thrall?"

"When away from you, yes. In your company, I was held captive by your love, so sweetly, so wonderfully. Then I would return to my bedchamber . . ."

"You never spoke a word, nor did I ever apprehend such a thing of you. How could I have known?"

Harriet felt a blush rise on her cheeks. "Because when we were together, I was no longer afraid."

He shook his head. "I do not understand."

"I am not certain I do, either. But all those fears are gone now. I . . . I told Lord Frith I could never marry him."

"Yes, that much I do know."

"And now you will fight a duel with him."

He lifted an imperious brow. "That, Harriet, is a subject I will not discuss with you."

She nodded her understanding. "Of course. It would not be gentlemanly."

"No, it would not."

She was silent apace and decided she would ask the hardest question of all. "Do you think you could love me again?"

Connought looked into tender, beseeching brown eyes. He knew Harriet to be utterly sincere, and he valued quite deeply her honesty today, but after their quarrel last night, something inside him had changed, utterly and irrevocably. "No," he stated flatly. He watched her blanch and weave on her feet. He caught her elbow. "I should not have spoken so abruptly, but I have given you the courtesy of a direct answer."

"Which I appreciate, truly," she responded, lifting her chin. She swallowed quite hard, and he saw the beginnings of tears in her eyes. He grew uncomfortable and turned back to the window.

"I grew tired of our brangling," he said. "I am finished with it all. I loved you for so many years, but you were so stubborn. How could we ever have made a good marriage with your obstinacy as our foundation? No, Harriet. I do not believe I love you anymore."

"Then I believe I must take my leave," she murmured. "But first I just wanted you to know that had you asked, I would have agreed to marry you."

At that, he glanced at her, wanting to understand her. "You were apprised of the wager?"

She nodded. "Arabella was so kind as to have informed me herself last night of the details involving not just myself but Margaret as well."

"I see. You understand that Arabella was also included in the wager?"

She frowned slightly. "No, that was not my understanding."

He shrugged. "Arabella would have been my bride had you never spoken the words you just did. I had made a promise, as a condition of the wager, to marry Arabella should I fail to win your heart."

"Then your marrying me was never the object. You never intended to ask me in earnest to wed you?"

He shook his head. "I engaged in that wager originally to punish you for all the hurt you caused me over the past seven years. My object was solely to win your heart back in order to break it. It would seem I succeeded."

She felt his words like a hard slap across her cheek. She drew in a quick breath. "I have never known you to be cruel. Why have you chosen this moment?"

"My intention is not cruelty," he responded. "I simply no longer find myself interested in protecting your feelings as I once did."

"I see." She fought back her tears and once more lifted her gaze to Connought. There seemed to be nothing left to say. "You must not keep your bailiff waiting. I shall bid you good day."

"Good-bye, Harriet."

At this, she turned on her heel and walked from the chamber. She held her head high, hoping desperately that he would not know that already tears were streaming down her cheeks. Once in the hallway, she hastily grabbed for her kerchief and strove to dry her eyes. She had no interest in meeting any of Connought's servants along the way with anything other than a composed countenance. Otherwise her visit to Kingsland would be bandied about from servant's tongue to servant's tongue until the entire valley knew of it. What she intended for no one to know, however, was just how desperately her heart was breaking.

Eighteen

Once within her coach, Harriet allowed one or two more tears to fall, then ordered her sensibilities to grow calmer. After all, whatever Connought's present sentiments, there was of the moment something a great deal more pressing than her sad heart with which to contend.

There was a duel.

Gentlemen were quite barbaric when it came to dueling. Nothing, no matter how rational or sensible, was permitted to interrupt the course of a dueling field battle other than death itself. This would not do, however. If she ever had any hope of winning Connought back, then it would be of no use were he to have been killed at the end of Frith's pistol. No, this was not the moment for hysterics or melancholy, but for action.

A glimmering of a smile worked at the edges of her lips. She was in that stream again at Paddlesworth on a hot summer day. She was marching to and fro with her skirts up about her hips quite scandalously. For the first time in years she felt free, really and truly free.

The lightness which swept over her being, of hope, of happiness, of joy, was very sudden and very intense. She felt as though she was floating, so happy did she become in the merest twinkling of an eye.

Here is that young lady, she thought, the one

Connought had referred to during their quarrel last night. *Here I am.*

Drawing a deep breath, she set her mind to solving the dilemma before her, and a great problem it was, since ladies were barred from the dueling process from beginning to end. How to effect an end to this one?

A very odd thought returned to her in this moment, something that Frith had said about his horse having been an investment that had not as yet paid off. She remembered Connought having acquired one of Frith's horses, a horse—though a thoroughbred—he had soon sold, never having exhibited an interest in it the entire time he owned it. She had assumed he had purchased the horse from Frith, but now she realized that could not have been the case. Connought had tried several times to buy the horse, but Frith had always refused. How curious! But why was she recalling these things now? How were they connected to the duel?

Since they seemed to have no relationship, she tried to cast them aside. However, they would not be denied a place in her thoughts. She remembered the night she had become betrothed to Connought, how romantic he had been, how ecstatic. She had retired to bed. The gentlemen had played at hazard until the early hours of the morning. The following day, he had kissed Margaret.

She recalled Laurence having said that Frith had once used Connought ill, but Laurence had fallen abruptly silent on the subject—perhaps held by an oath not to speak of it.

Her thoughts froze and her lips parted, a hiss of horror passing between them. She knew! She understood it all, including Frith's part—Frith, who had always wanted her. He . . . he had devised a means by which he could separate them.

Connought must have agreed to a wager, Frith's

horse as one stake and something Frith had held over Connought's head for seven years the other part of that stake. She knew Connought. As much as she had tried to convince herself over the years that he was lacking in honor, she knew that he would never have betrayed her wittingly. Surely he had been in his cups when he had entered so despicable a wager—if there was a wager.

She was absolutely persuaded now that there had been a wager that night, one that could only have been fulfilled by Connought kissing Margaret. Yet who would have demanded of him to do so, except someone who wanted the betrothal brought to a sudden end?

Only one name returned to her . . . Frith.

So Frith had been the author of that damnable kiss between Margaret and Connought! She was as certain of it as she was that the sun would rise and the moon set. Connought had tried to warn her against Frith's character, yet had been unwilling to elaborate on why he was not to be trusted. The older gentlemen's opinions of Frith also rose in her mind, of Mr. Douglas snorting his disgust and of her father saying that he could not pound his way out of muslin bag.

Her entire being relaxed. In understanding Frith's role, in comprehending that for all his pretense to goodness he was a corrupt man, she now knew precisely what needed to be done. Besides, she wanted absolute proof of her convictions before acting, and she had every confidence a brief conversation with Frith would confirm her beliefs. Calling to her coachman, she directed him to the Bell Inn at the village of Kenningford.

An hour later, she entered Frith's bedchamber at the inn, much to his utter shock.

"Harriet!" he cried. "Whatever has possessed you to have come here as you have? Do you not comprehend the nature of the scandal you have just initiated in doing so? This is so very much unlike you."

"I do not give a fig for that!" she cried, her earlier sense of utter freedom taking full rein. "As it happens, I have a matter of some import to discuss with you. Actually, it will not be a discussion, since that would require that you and I have an exchange of ideas."

"You are making no sense," he countered.

"Then I will attempt to express myself more plainly. I am to speak, and you are to do nothing but listen and acquiesce."

He chuckled in disbelief. "I believe you are gone mad. Why do you speak to me in that tone of voice? Surely you are not still disgruntled that I showed my temper a little at Shalham?"

"That? Oh, no. That is of little consequence. No, I'm referring to the wager over hazard some seven years past involving you, Connought, Margaret, and your horse."

He started. "The devil!" he cried. The very next moment he appeared quite smug. "How did you hear of it? Laurence? Connought himself? For I tell you now, part of the condition of that wager was the utmost secrecy. You forgot to mention the property in Lincolnshire, the hunting lodge which Connought's family has owned since time out of mind. It would appear it now belongs to me."

Harriet began drawing off her gloves and at the same time took up a chair by the fireplace. "That was the only piece of this rather tragic puzzle that I had been unable to place—just what it was you have been holding over Connought's head these many years and more. But you needn't look quite so self-satisfied, Frith, since *you* were the one who told me of the wager. I was merely casting my fly, and you rose to it quite nicely. So secrecy was a condition of the wager. Only tell me, was Connought in his cups at the time?"

He narrowed his eyes. "I never said a word to you of the wager. Who told you? I mean to have what is mine and, yes, secrecy was a condition."

"You have coveted his land just as much as you coveted me," she stated, a great sadness taking sudden hold of her.

"It would have added to my estate appreciably. So, yes, I suppose you could say I have coveted his land."

Harriet shook her head. "You hedged your bet, even when it involved my heart."

"If you choose to see it that way. I do not, of course. I loved you. I wanted you to be my wife and Connought, who was wholly unworthy of you, stood in the way. What I really want to know is who told you, for I vow, upon my honor, that you could not have surmised the whole because of something I said."

"Actually it was. We were discussing Lightning Velvet, and you made it clear you had not sold the horse to Connought, even though I knew he had made several offers for it. There are only two ways property can be exchanged without a bill of sale, through a trade or through a wager. Since Connought never spoke of having traded you for it, I surmised a wager. It was not a long walk to figure the rest—that Connought was in his cups and that you had tricked him into the wager, demanding he do the one thing you knew I would not forgive him for, kissing Margaret. Afterward, if you will recall, he took no pleasure in that horse, but sold him off within a year."

"I still do not believe you. Somehow, either Laurence or Charles told you of the wager and you just now tricked me into confessing to it before we began this conversation."

"No one told me, Frith, although at this juncture it no longer matters whether I was informed of it or not, since the result will be the same. You are to leave Kenningford at eleven o'clock tomorrow night, an hour before the duel is to take place. Yes, that much I do know, for Charles told Jane of it, apparently fearing the worst might happen, since you are known to be a very fine shot. She also told me that you used some quite *elegant* language to provoke the duel—how very unhandsome of you. However, that is of little consequence. For the present, I insist that you take your place at your writing table and pen an appropriate note, addressed to Connought, stating that the wager is at an end, the Lincolnshire property is safe from you forever, and apologizing for whatever it was that brought about this duel. You will then explain you have no intention of breaking the King's law by engaging in a forbidden confrontation."

He remained standing rooted in one place and laughed harshly. "I shall not leave Kenningford, and I shall write no such note."

"Then you risk, my lord, enduring a separation from all you love in London. That was the one thing you taught me, you know, how to travel in the first circles with grace and dignity, for which reason I am on the best of terms with every high stickler in Mayfair, as well you know. Given this great evil which you contrived on the evening of my betrothal, I would not hesitate to lay my grievances before each and every one of them. You, sir, would be banned from all polite society, at least in London. All I would be required to add is your having forced a duel upon Connought because I rejected your hand in marriage, and your fate would be sealed."

His eyes had widened. She watched his brain feverishly at work, trying to see some way out of his present scrape.

"There is nothing you can do," she said, stroking the soft leather of her gloves.

"Ah, but there is. I shall serve you with your own sauce and speak of all the assignations I was forced to observe seven years past."

Harriet chuckled. "You have mistaken an important element, I fear. Should I ever be given the cut direct, I should not care one whit. I could easily bid farewell to my London acquaintances. What I desire is here in Kent."

He stood staring at her for very long moment, the air tense with his anger and dismay. At last, having weighed all that she had said, he took up a seat before the writing table near the window, and began scratching out his apologies and intentions.

Harriet read his progress so far, then said, "There is one more thing I wish you to add."

He snorted his disgust, but completed the note per her request, sealed it, and presented it to her.

Harriet tucked it within her reticule. "Remember," she said, her gloves and reticule in hand, "you are not to say a word to any of the gentlemen about my visit or your intentions of departing at eleven. Should you do so, I shall follow through with my present threat." She smiled faintly. "And to think I was used to consider you one of the finest gentlemen of my acquaintance."

With that, she quit his bedchamber.

That night, Connought stared at Laurence. "Harriet was seen coming from Frith's rooms at the Bell?"

"So it would seem. I thought you should know, since it would appear all of Kenningford knows of it!"

"Good God! Has Harriet gone mad?"

Charles sipped his brandy. "Maybe she's accepted him after all."

"What the devil do you know?" Connought cried. "The chit's in love with me. I told you all about it!"

Charles nodded in what was meant to be a wise manner. "Yes, but since you no longer love her or wish to marry her, perhaps she felt desperate. Some females do. I had a cousin, Penelope—you remember her, quite platter-faced! Anyway, she married a complete idiot, a vicar in Devonshire. She was five and twenty, Harriet's age. Couldn't bear the thought of becoming an ape-leader. Looked like an ape, though." He shuddered. "Produced the ugliest brats you've ever seen!"

"Do stubble it!" Laurence cried. "Harriet has more sense than to marry Frith. At least, I think she does."

"She does, indeed!" Connought cried, tossing off his own snifter of brandy. "And you, Charles, may go to the devil! Now, what are you smiling about?"

"You still love her. You always will!"

At that, Connought took his glass and, rather than throw it at Charles's head, which was his fondest desire of the moment, he shattered it on the hearth. Afterward, he stormed from the chamber.

At eleven o'clock on the following evening, Harriet waited in a closed carriage across the street from the Bell Inn. She was dressed in a suit of gentleman's clothes which once had been worn by her uncle but which had been consigned to the attics at least five years past. She drew back the blind very slowly and through a small crack watched as a traveling coach emerged from the innyard of the Bell. She recognized Frith's profile, illuminated by the carriage lamps, as his coach bowled in the opposite direction of the appointed dueling field. She released a deep sigh of relief.

Leaning back against the squabs, she found that her heart was pounding furiously. If Frith had somehow disobeyed her instructions, she had not known what she would do. However, her doubts as to his intentions had always been minimal. After all, Frith valued his consequence above everything.

She looked at her companions seated opposite her, and though she was still trembling, could not help but smile. "Margaret, you make a dashing gentleman! I vow I am half in love with you myself."

Margaret chortled her glee. "I vow this is the most fun I have had in years!" she cried.

Both ladies turned to Jane, who rolled her eyes. "You have both gone witless!" their less adventurous friend cried. "We should not be dressed in this manner! Oh, Margaret, are you certain your coachman and grooms are reliable? If we are found out—"

"You always were hen hearted!" Margaret cried disparagingly.

"Well, yes, I always was! Oh, dear, my mother will fall into a decline when she learns of this scrape."

Harriet leaned over and patted her hand. "Well, if she does, at least you will no longer be obliged to wear that ugly brown dress of yours!"

Jane gasped, then burst out laughing, as did Margaret.

Harriet then drew in another deep breath. "Let us away," she cried. "For though I might have concocted this truly ridiculous scheme in what I am certain will prove a hopeless attempt to secure the heart of the man I love, I am presently in great danger of losing what little pluck remains to me."

Margaret called to the coachman instantly. "To the southern pasture at Kingsland! At once."

"Very good, miss."

The coach rolled forward, jerked, swayed, and was soon bowling in the opposite direction to Kingsland.

Once they arrived at a secluded low place in the pasture near a thick stand of trees and shrubs, a lantern guided Harriet, her cousin, and her friend across the field. At least she was no longer quite so frightened about the course of action she had laid out for herself.

She had concocted her scheme of facing Connought across a duelling field in Frith's place for the sole purpose of proving to first herself and then to Connought that she had not become completely lost in the last seven years, that there still resided within her a lady of some courage and daring.

Margaret tugged on her sleeve. "Let us speak with Laurence and Charles first," she whispered. "I believe that is what seconds do. They try one last time to see if a reconciliation is possible, then they check the weapons."

Harriet straightened her neckcloth and settled her uncle's tall beaver hat more squarely on her head. "But you know nothing of pistols," she murmured, a bubble of laughter catching in her throat.

"Nor do you," Margaret countered.

Harriet drew in a deep breath. She smiled at Margaret. "I suppose there is nothing for it. We must proceed."

"Do you think your plan will work?"

"I haven't the faintest notion, but I mean to try anyway."

She waited at some distance, not wanting to reveal her identity yet, and watched as Laurence and Charles approached her seconds. She could see that a fourth man was present, standing beside Connought on the far side of the lantern. Squinting through the darkness, she recognized the rather portly figure of good Dr. Steele of Kenningford. The realization that a physician was in attendance brought a chill to her heart. For all the silliness of she and her friends having dressed up in gentlemen's clothes to take the place of Frith and his seconds, she was now struck by the deadly nature of the situation. She had little doubt that had she not intervened, bloodshed would have occurred tonight.

When a burst of laughter erupted from first Charles, then Laurence, she knew that the identities of Margaret and Jane had become known. They returned to her forthwith.

"We are to inform you," Jane said, her face in dark shadow save for the sight of her teeth in the moonlight since she was grinning, "That Lord Connought will never relent, that his character was so badly savaged by *you*—that is, Lord Frith—as to make him utterly unwilling to relent."

Margaret's laughter caught in her throat. "Indeed, the duel must go on!"

Harriet nodded, but she could not laugh as her friends were. They were clearly in high gig, but her own fate rested in the tall figure now sauntering farther out from the shrubberies and trees and onto the duelling field. She must face him now as herself. This was the moment, then, that would speak for the rest of her life, whether or not she would be able to succeed in winning Connought back. With each step, her doubts mounted. How could he be won merely because she wore a man's hat, top boots in which her feet slid about dangerously, and breeches that sagged behind?

Onward she marched, however, straight toward him.

"What the deuce!" he cried when he reached her at last.

"Good evening, Connought!" she cried out with a great deal more confidence than she felt.

"Harriet! Good God!" He turned toward his seconds. "Is this why you were laughing?"

"Indeed," Laurence returned. They were grouped as one, Margaret and Jane, Laurence and Charles, and Dr. Steele. Their expressions were perfectly visible in the light of the lantern, and not a single smile was absent.

Connought drew closer. "What is this meaning of this? Where is Frith?"

Harriet removed Frith's letter from the pocket of her coat. "He will not be coming tonight and requested that I give you this."

In the lantern light slanting across his face, he narrowed his eyes. "You visited him in his rooms yesterday."

She nodded.

He broke the seal, but in the dim light was not able to make out the words sufficiently. He strolled in the direction of the lantern, the sheet of paper held out at a deep angle to better catch the light. When he had finished reading, he stood upright.

"What does it say?" Charles called out.

He raised a hand to silence Charles, then returned to Harriet.

"So you arranged this," he stated, drawing near again.

"Yes," she responded.

"What the deuce does this mean, that you are to take his place in the duel?"

"Precisely that. I am to face you at the end of your pistol in order to salve your honor." When she had demanded that Frith add this particular directive to his missive, he had looked up at her and sneered scornfully. She, of course, had no use for his opinion and so had ignored him.

"I do not understand. How did you possibly get Frith to agree to this? He is not the sort of man who would willingly walk away from a duel, particularly since he holds so many records at Manton's." She could see that he was amazed.

"It was simple, really. I told him that if he did not do as I bid him, he would find himself unwelcome in Mayfair."

"You cannot possibly wield such power."

"There you are mistaken, I fear. Over the past several years, I have formed very superior connections in London. I am approved by all the patronesses of Almack's, as well as any number of high sticklers. My rejection of your proposal so many years ago was received at the time with a great deal of enthusiasm. I had thought the reason was because you had a reputation as a rogue. It was only later that I realized their purposes were rather self-serving—I watched as one after the other introduced a hopeful relative to you. I was vastly amused. However, having obliged so many ladies by not marrying the Earl of Connought, I acquired any number of fast friendships. So, to answer your question, I could quite easily ruin Frith's position in the first circles."

"I begin to fear you myself."

She laughed. "You fear nothing. Not even death. I've always admired that about you."

"I learned a great deal from my brothers, who faced death quite often on the battlefields of Europe."

She smiled, her heart warming to him anew. She loved him so very much. Would tonight's antics serve to soften his heart, even a little?

"Be that as it may, however," he continued stiffly, "you still have no business here tonight."

"On the contrary, something had to be done—or did you believe yourself Frith's equal with a pistol?"

"Of course I am," he countered strongly. "But that is hardly the point. Even were I the worst shot in England, I would still be obligated by every dictum by which I live to accept of his challenge. Though I daresay a female could never comprehend the code of honor by which a gentleman must live."

She had certainly posed him the wrong question.

"As in kissing a lady to fulfill a wager in order to protect your estate?"

At this, he frowned heavily. "You have learned of it then?"

"I guessed at it and, quite unwittingly, Frith told me the rest."

He was silent and for a very long moment stared at the ground. "I was foxed," he said at last. "Wretchedly foxed. Frith took advantage."

"Yes," she agreed. "It was quite despicable of him—of you both, really."

"I have wished the deed undone a thousand times. You know that."

"Yes, I do," she responded softly. "However, I did not come here tonight to argue the point, but rather to fulfill Frith's part in the duel."

"This is absurd, Harriet," he said. "And hardly necessary."

"Whatever you think, I am quite determined to see it through. Besides, I can manage a pistol. Try me, if you like."

Even in the moonlight, she could see his lips twitch. "Very well. Charles! Bring me the box."

"You do not mean to continue!" Charles called to him from the group near the lantern, astonishment edging his voice.

"I suppose I must, as a point of honor. Harriet insists upon it!"

"You've both gone mad, then!" he cried. "Laurence, speak to them!"

Laurence shrugged. "Connought has always done as he pleased. Why would tonight be any different? Take him the pistols!"

"You are all mad, and I will have nothing to do with it!"

Laurence took the box from Charles rather abruptly, brought it to Connought, and returned to his former place.

Connought opened the lid and offered a pistol to Harriet. She stared at the finely carved handles, the gleaming barrels, and found that her heart had begun pounding in her chest again. Using her forefinger and thumb, she gingerly lifted the pistol from the box, letting it dangle in the air as though it was covered in something vile that must be kept at arm's length from her.

"I begin to be in awe of you," he said facetiously, his lips twitching anew.

Harriet answered in kind. "I beg you will not attempt to turn me up sweet, my lord! After all, I am still in the business of trying to kill you."

At that, he repressed a chuckle. "Harriet, you are being quite ridiculous."

"I am not such a bad shot," she proclaimed.

"Be that as it may, you will have no success at all if you do not take your pistol properly in hand. Also, you have no powder in your firing pan."

She frowned down at the pistol. "Where is the firing pan?"

He pointed to what appeared to be a very small metal dish near the handle of the weapon. "There. As you see, no powder."

She whirled about. "Laurence, would you be so kind as to prime my pistol for me? There is no powder." She tilted the barrel toward the earth, and the pistol ball rolled right out and struck Connought on the tips of his boots. With that, all four gentlemen present roared with laughter.

Harriet, however, cast Connought a scathing glance. "You may find this duel a form of amusement, but I promise you I am quite serious in taking Frith's place in a proper manner."

Connought checked his laughter, cleared his throat, and bid Laurence to come to Harriet's aid.

Laurence did just that. Within two minutes, the pistol was ready to be fired.

When he handed the pistol back to Harriet and withdrew, she lifted a challenging brow to Connought. "Are you ready, my lord?" she asked.

"Are you certain this is what you wish, Harriet?" he asked, his expression sober.

She nodded slowly.

He said, "You realize one or both of us could be injured or killed in the next few minutes."

"Precisely so," she responded, beginning to tremble in the boots she had borrowed from her uncle, whose feet were much larger than her own.

"Very well. Then it shall be as you say." He called to one of his seconds. "Charles, mark the paces at thirty. Harriet, your back, if you please!"

She turned around. A moment later, she felt him bump against her. "Are you ready, Harriet?" he asked, in what sounded a deadly serious voice.

"I am," she responded, equally as serious.

"Very well. Charles, you may begin!"

"As you say!" Charles called back. "One . . . two . . . three . . ."

With each number piercing the air, Harriet took a step. Her heart had begun to thrum against her ribs as she marched away from Connought. She tripped once on the sod beneath her feet and nearly tumbled as the loose boots slid beneath her feet. She caught herself, however, and continued the march.

When thirty paces had been called out, she turned to find Connought far away, indeed, which she felt was a very good thing.

"Ready!" Charles called. "Aim!"

Harriet leveled her weapon in Connought's direction, but shifted it a marked degree to the right, away from [illegible]

re!"

She pulled the trigger, and her pistol exploded with a burst of flame and smoke. She stumbled backward, unused to the recoil. Her hand felt very odd, as though it was now bruised. She wondered when the tingling would stop.

She looked up, blinked, and then realized that Connought was stumbling backward again and again. Finally, he fell hard to the earth. How was this possible, when she had taken such pains to divert her pistol away from him? Oh, dear God, she had killed the man she loved!

She ran in the sloppy boots, falling once and scraping her knees and hands. Connought's friends, however, must have been suffering from shock, for they had remained standing where they were, with Margaret and Jane and the doctor.

"Doctor, come quickly!" she cried. Finally, she reached Connought and immediately began speaking to him, all the while feeling his head, throat, chest, and limbs all in a quick sequence to discover the precise location of the wound.

"My darling! My darling! Oh, I beg you will speak to me! I did not mean to hurt you! Tell me you are not dead! Oh, my dearest, my most beloved Connought! Speak to me!"

His eyes fluttered, and before she knew what was happening, she found herself caught in his arms and dragged onto his lap, his lips on hers in a forceful kiss. She was so stunned and so relieved at the same time that she could barely respond. She pushed away from him.

"I did not kill you?" she asked.

He shook his head. "Not by half!"

"I did not even wound you?"

"No, my dear, you were well off the mark! I believe I shall be forced to give you shooting lessons. This will not do, not if you intend to take up dueling as a pastime."

She relaxed in his arms, his face but a collection of shadows in the dark field. "You are not dead," she whispered sweetly, stroking his face gently.

"No, my darling." He kissed her again, then drew back. He looked at her for a long moment, not seeing much of her features, just a decided glitter in her eyes. His heart began to swell, beating in an old, familiar manner that he had believed dead. This was the woman he had tumbled in love with, the playful, proud, vixenish creature who would don gentleman's clothing, which fit her very ill, indeed, and shoot at him across a dueling field. "Have you returned to me, my dear, Harriet?"

She understood him. "Indeed, I have."

"You are no longer afraid?"

She was thoughtful for a moment. "Only a very little, but I mean to do much better."

"If tonight's antics are any measure, you will do, Harriet Godwyne. You will do very well indeed!"

When he leaned down to kiss her again, she placed a hand on his chest, preventing him. "Am I forgiven? I mean, will you ever forgive me for having kept us apart for so long a time?"

"I am not entirely certain," he said, pushing a stray curl off her cheek. "But I fear you will have to work very hard to make it up to me."

"Would the rest of my life be sufficient to engage in such a task, do you think?"

"Perhaps," he murmured, his lips once more touching hers. The fire he had once known burned brighter than ever before. He loved her with all his heart and spent the next several minutes telling her so by word, touch, and the pressure of his lips on hers.

[illegible]riet responded in kind, aware of the incredible gift [illegible] been given, and determined this time to do a [illegible]l better, indeed!

* * *

"Why have you brought me here?" she asked as Connought led her into the cherry orchard. A sennight had passed, the betrothal had been announced, and her father's gout had finally mended sufficiently to allow him to walk about Shalham at will, albeit with a cane.

"Because this is where it all began, a fortnight past. Remember? I accosted you here and forced a kiss on you. I mean to take it back today."

"Oh, you do, do you? Rather sure of yourself, if I may say so."

"I am now," he said, looking down at her, his expression tender and loving.

Harriet thought she would never be so happy as she was in this moment, her arm entwined with Connought's, her heart full of joy and contentment. In the distance, Margaret and Laurence walked ahead of them.

"Is it a match?" Connought asked.

"Yes, I believe it is," she responded. "Margaret spoke only last night of something or other he had done, and there was quite a light in her eye and a softness in her expression I have never seen before."

"I am glad of it," he responded.

"I understand Arabella is leaving today for Bath," Harriet said, giving the subject a slight turn. "A rather sudden departure, I think, and I have been given to understand she has been pouting for an entire week."

Connought smiled faintly. "I daresay she will manage her disappointment."

"Do you think so?" she asked.

Connought grimaced. "You know deuced well she never loved me."

"I believe she tried *very hard* to love you."

At that, he laughed.

Harriet looked up at him. "But how do you know she was not in love with you? I mean, she was quite devoted to you and made you her first object."

"If I needed some proof to convince you of my opinion, though I am persuaded I do not, regardless, I would have to say that it is very simple—a woman truly in love would never make use of gossip to manipulate a situation to her advantage. Telling you of my wager with Laurence and Charles was as telling of her heart as it was unpardonable."

"Nearly as unpardonable as the wager itself!" she countered readily.

He whirled her into his arms. "Ordinarily I might agree with you," he said, taking her firmly in his arms. "However, I wish to remind you that you were involved in a rather odious wager as well."

She giggled. "So I was."

"By the way, I should like my watch back . . . oh, and my riding crop as well!"

She gasped faintly. "How did you know I had it?" she asked.

"Because I saw it sticking out of the pocket of your riding habit when you trotted from my stableyard the same morning you asked me to go riding and then feigned being ill."

She laughed outright. "How ridiculous I must have appeared."

"I laughed heartily for an hour afterward."

"I imagine you did."

Harriet was happy thus, exchanging banter with him while being held in his arms. "You still should not have engaged in so shameless a wager, risking my poor heart all the while!"

"I would remind you, my darling, that *that wager,* and the ridiculous one you shared with your cousin and Jane, had the wonderful effect of bringing us back together."

"You are very right," she said, smiling sweetly up into his face and touching his cheek with the back of her fingers. "I promise never to complain of either again."

He did not wait for a further invitation, but kissed her soundly. Harriet felt her knees grow very weak and finally buckle. His arms grew strong about her waist. She drifted into that familiar place of miracle and enchantment where there was no past and the future appeared as bright as the sun, moon, and stars together. How very much she loved Connought. She always would.